Albert R. Parsons, Henry M. Burt

Cornet Joseph Parsons one of the Founders of Springfield and Northampton, Massachusetts

Springfield, 1636 - Northampton, 1655. An historical sketch from original sources -

Vol. 1

Albert R. Parsons, Henry M. Burt

Cornet Joseph Parsons one of the Founders of Springfield and Northampton, Massachusetts
Springfield, 1636 - Northampton, 1655. An historical sketch from original sources - Vol. 1

ISBN/EAN: 9783337367770

Printed in Europe, USA, Canada, Australia, Japan

Cover: Foto ©Andreas Hilbeck / pixelio.de

More available books at **www.hansebooks.com**

PARSONS
OF OXFORD

PARSONS
OF HEREFORD
A.D. 1481

PARSONS
OF NORFOLK

PARSONS
OF HART HALL

PARSONS
VISCOUNT AND EARL OF ROSSE

PARSONS
OF RADNOR

QUID RETRIBUAM

PARSONS
OF DORSET

PARSONS
EARL OF ROSSE

PRO DEO ET REGE

PARSONS
OF GLOUCESTER

PARSONS
OF BUCKINGHAM

PARSONS
OF EPSOM

PARSONS
OF SUSSEX

PARSONS
(Place not Mentioned)

PARSONS
(Place not Mentioned)

CORNET JOSEPH PARSONS

ONE OF THE FOUNDERS OF

SPRINGFIELD AND NORTHAMPTON, MASSACHUSETTS

SPRINGFIELD, 1636
NORTHAMPTON, 1655

AN HISTORICAL SKETCH FROM ORIGINAL SOURCES, VIZ., TOWN, COUNTY, COURT, AND PRIVATE RECORDS

BY

HENRY M. BURT

WITH SUPPLEMENTARY CHAPTERS

" On Colonel Joseph Lemuel Chester's Alleged English Parsons Ancestry,"
" The ' Honorable Family of Parsons' in England and its Connection by
Marriage with Sir Edward Pynchon, Knt., Cousin of William
Pynchon, Founder of Springfield, Massachusetts,"
and " Parsons Genealogies "

BY

ALBERT ROSS PARSONS

PUBLISHED BY

ALBERT ROSS PARSONS
GARDEN CITY, LONG ISLAND, N. Y., U. S. A.

INTRODUCTORY.

By HENRY M. BURT.

This biographical sketch of one of the founders of Spring-

ERRATA and ADDENDA

facts concerning the life of one of the very earliest settlers of Springfield and Northampton are brought into that relation with what was transpiring and with those associated with him, which gives the true perspective to the more important events which were then crystallizing into enduring history. It has been the aim of the writer to give the every-day transactions and life of the subject of this sketch in such detail as to set forth the mode of life in a period which has been obscured by the lapse of time. Cornet Joseph Parsons was pre-eminently a man of business and, with perhaps a single exception, the most prosperous and successful of any of the settlers, at a time when this garden of New England had hardly reached the dignity of a hamlet. Two and a half centuries ago this valley

3

INTRODUCTORY.

By HENRY M. BURT.

This biographical sketch of one of the founders of Springfield and Northampton, Cornet Joseph Parsons, who for many years was a leading and influential spirit in the early settlement of the Massachusetts towns in the Connecticut Valley, was written at the request of General Lewis B. Parsons of Flora, Ill., President Albert Ross Parsons of New York, and Professor Charles L. Parsons of Durham, N. H., who for many years have taken great interest in that history of their ancestor and of the time and place of which he was a part. General Parsons has, during the last fifty years—he has recently passed his eightieth birthday—given the subject much study, although residing far remote from where his ancestor spent the greater part of his life.

This historical review is almost entirely from original sources—town, county, court, and private records, for the first time, having been carefully searched for this purpose. The facts concerning the life of one of the very earliest settlers of Springfield and Northampton are brought into that relation with what was transpiring and with those associated with him, which gives the true perspective to the more important events which were then crystallizing into enduring history. It has been the aim of the writer to give the every-day transactions and life of the subject of this sketch in such detail as to set forth the mode of life in a period which has been obscured by the lapse of time. Cornet Joseph Parsons was pre-eminently a man of business and, with perhaps a single exception, the most prosperous and successful of any of the settlers, at a time when this garden of New England had hardly reached the dignity of a hamlet. Two and a half centuries ago this valley

3

did not promise much to the majority of the incomers beyond a very scanty living, and the toilers in this field took their reward in a feeling of entire independence of the depressing religious and political influences which surrounded them in the English homes from which they had come. Freedom of thought and action and limitless extension of opportunity were sufficient in themselves to make the simplest life here attractive, and far more to their desire than the homes which they had left behind them.

Although there has been a long lapse of time since the aboriginal inhabitants of this land passed the titles to the soil of this valley to the people of Anglo-Saxon origin, our forefathers, the past. dim as it is, has not been obliterated, and there is more than ever a growing pride in what has been accomplished; and that which marked the early settlements in purpose is still retained, broadened and adapted to newer conditions. It is the spirit which came here at the beginning that has been preserved and which has made New England conspicuous among the great commonwealths of our country.

The autograph of Cornet Joseph Parsons can be seen in Volume II. of the Transactions of the town, in the Northampton town records, and in petitions sent to the General Court from Northampton, in the State archives at Boston, now in the custody of the Secretary of State.

SPRINGFIELD, MASS., May 6, 1897.

I.

CORNET JOSEPH PARSONS.

A SKETCH BY HENRY M. BURT.

Springfield, Mass., was the first town settled within the present limits of the State, west of Boston. A few Connecticut towns were settled at a slightly earlier date. Wethersfield and Windsor were a little more than a year in advance, but Hartford, where the most important settlement was begun, was simultaneous in its date of founding with that of Springfield. In 1634 and 1635 movements were begun looking toward making permanent settlements in the Connecticut Valley, but it was not until 1636 that the Hartford Colony under Hooker, and that under Pynchon, destined to locate at a place higher up the Connecticut, turned westward from the Bay settlements to found homes on the banks of the Connecticut. William Pynchon, the leader, and the founder of Springfield, who was one of the patentees of the grant to the Massachusetts Bay Company, came over with Winthrop in 1630, he settling at Roxbury, where he remained four years, until he removed to Agawam, the name given to what subsequently became Springfield. He had secured special advantages, and he went to the banks of the Connecticut to engage in the fur trade as well as to found a town. It had become known in the eastern settlements that along the streams running into the Connecticut River was an abundance of beaver, and the monopoly of the trade which had been given him promised to yield large and profitable returns. He was accompanied by a small number of settlers. Only eight names were affixed to the agreement made on May 14, 1636. These were William Pynchon, Mathew Mitchell, Henry Smith, John Burr, William Blake, Edmund Wood, Thomas Ufford, and John Cable. This agreement, under which the town was founded, is in the handwriting of Henry Smith, and is still in a good state of preservation in the office of the City Clerk. Pynchon, in his own hand, closed the agreement which precedes the signatures with the following: "We testifie to the ordr above said, being al the first adventurers & subscribers for this plantation."

Not one of the subscribers spent his life in Springfield, and only a few of them remained longer than a few months. Pynchon returned to England in 1652, and Henry Smith, who was a son-in-law of Pynchon, and the son of his second wife by her first marriage, went with him, or very soon afterward. John Burr, who was the ancestor of Aaron Burr, went to Fairfield, Conn. William Blake returned to Dorchester, and John Cable went to a Connecticut town. Mitchell, Wood and Ufford remained only a short time.

Among the very earliest settlers was Joseph Parsons, known to his many descendants by his military title of Cornet Joseph. The public records of his day and contemporary writings, still in existence, show that he was a man of unusual activity and force of character. Business enterprises brought him into familiarity with the country for many miles up and down the Connecticut River, which made his services of more than ordinary value to those with whom he was associated, in both public and private concerns. He had the courage and enterprise necessary at that time in a remote wilderness for the successful up-building of the towns which later became important frontier settlements. Besides successfully conducting his own affairs, he gave considerable time to public business. He served on various boards of Selectmen, was called to the business of establishing boundary lines and of laying out important highways, and into the military service when the towns were in great peril from the neighboring Indians and their allies.

As yet no evidence has come to the writer of sufficient authenticity to establish the precise time of his arrival in Springfield, nor as to whether he remained a permanent settler from the date of his first appearance up to the time of his removal to Northampton in 1655, a year after that town was founded. He was certainly in Springfield at a very early date.

Two months after the agreement to which Pynchon and his associates affixed their signatures the lands on both sides of the Connecticut, within a considerable distance of what is now Springfield, were purchased of the Indians, and on July 15, 1636, the title was transferred by the Indians to Pynchon, who secured it in behalf of the settlement. This deed bears the signatures, as witnesses, of Joseph Parsons, John Allen, Richard Everett, Thomas Horton, Faithful Thayler, and John Townes. In 1662, Joseph Parsons testified, at a court held at Northampton, that he "was a witness to this bargain between Mr. Pynchon & the Indians." He was a young man at this time—ten years before his marriage—and whether he came with Pynchon from the Bay, or subsequently followed him, or came from Windsor or Hartford, does not appear as yet to be fully established. Of the other witnesses, Allen, Thayler—this latter name evidently intended for Taylor—and Townes did not remain, as there is no mention of them in later records. From the time of his signing as a witness in 1636 up to 1646, Parsons' name does not appear. During this interval of ten years, whether he remained in Springfield or was in a Connecticut town, are still matters of conjecture. In 1646 he was made a fence viewer with Thomas Merrick, the year that he was married at Hartford. The birth of his first three children, Joseph, Benjamin, and John, are not in the Springfield records. The death of Benjamin is entered in the following words: "Benjamin Parsons, ye son of Joseph Parsons dyed ye 22 d. 4 mo. 1649." Henry Smith, the Town Clerk, was distinguished for minuteness in details, and apparently had unusual method in his transactions; and from all the facts as yet brought to light it would appear that Joseph Parsons did not remain long here between 1636 and 1646. Unmarried men who had come to settle were early given land, and their names appear as receiving grants, or as fence viewers, or highway surveyors, or constables. Yet, for all this conjectural evidence to the contrary, he might have been a resident of Springfield from the very first, but it would seem that one so active and so useful could not have remained ten years a silent witness and passed entirely unnoticed in the records. Whether he was or was not is of little importance in comparison with the service he rendered subsequently. He was the first of his name alike in Springfield, and in New England. The names of Hugh and Benjamin Parsons appear here at a later date, and their relationship, if any, to Joseph Parsons has been the subject of discussion with different members of the family. Colonel Chester, a distinguished antiquary in his day, claimed that Hugh and Benjamin were brothers, and were not nearly related, if at all, to Joseph. Later investigations prove that Joseph and Benjamin were brothers, and no relationship with Hugh is established. The probabilities indicate that he was not related to them.

William Pynchon, the magistrate, began early to hunt for witches, and Hugh Parsons and his wife Mary were the first victims. Many of his towns-people were summoned before him to give evidence. Their statements, taken down in Pynchon's own hand, which are still extant, have an important bearing upon the condition of the public mind at that period, showing conclusively that the belief in witchcraft pervaded all classes, and that the learned as well as the unlearned had brought to New England the beliefs of the Old World. Out of these examinations came much gossip concerning witchcraft. The wife of James Bridgman accused Joseph Parsons's wife of being concerned in the same business, and out of these charges Joseph Parsons brought a suit for slander. Benjamin Parsons was a witness, and in his evidence he refers to Joseph's wife as "my sister" and as "sister Parsons." As to the relationship which these expressions indicate there are other proofs. When William Pynchon came he opened a store, from which the settlers obtained their family supplies. When he went to England it was left to his son John, who was energetic in its management and had accounts with many living remote from Springfield as well as those residing in the town. He had extensive dealings with Joseph Parsons, and in one of the entries of the accounts is this: (March 12, 1656) "To Goodman Bissall I paid for you 10d more than I formerly accounted & the wheate *your Bro Benj* delivered me I accounted it ½ bushel to much." In 1658 there is another statement in the accounts, which reads: "By so much I Received of *your Brother Benjamin*, 12 shillings." The accounts from which these are taken are still in the possession of the Springfield City Library, and no more conclusive evidence as to the relationship of Joseph and Benjamin is needed to clear up a matter about which a difference of opinion had latterly arisen in some branches of the family.

Thomas Parsons was an early resident of Windsor, and was married in 1641. He had a large family of children, but heretofore nothing has been adduced to show that there was any relationship between him and Joseph and Benjamin.

When our ancestors left England the whole of Europe was but little more than an armed camp. Conflicts between contending factions made certain military duties necessary, and the military spirit prevalent in England was transferred to these shores as soon as the newcomers began to get a foothold. Training days, from the experience of the settlers, became a necessity. Under date of November 14, 1639, as found in the town records of Springfield, this entry was made: "It is ordered that the exercise of trayning shall be practiced one day in every month, and if occasions doe sometymes hinder, then ye like space of tyme shall be observed another tyme though it be 2 days after one another: And yt this tyme of training is referred to ye discretion of Henry Smith who is chosen by mutuall consent to be ye Serjant of ye Company, who shall have power to choose a Corporall for his assistant, and whosoever shall be absent himselfe without a lawfull excuse shall forfeit twelve pence, & yt all above 15 yeares of age shall be counted for soldiers and the tyme to begin the first Thursday in December next."

There is nothing left to show who were the rank and file of the Springfield train-band, which corresponded in the exercises, in the equipment, and in officers to those in England at that period. Pikes, in the absence of muskets, were used in some parts of New England in the various exercises, and those rude implements of warfare have sometimes figured in the inventories of the estates of deceased persons. The military service rendered by Joseph Parsons in the first years of the settlement is not known, but it must have been in accordance with the established rules. A place was set apart, at what is now the western end of Elm Street, in Springfield.

a few years after the arrival of Pynchon, for a burying-ground, and this also was used for many years for a training-field. Joseph Parsons's title of Cornet dates from October 7, 1678, shortly following the Indian disturbances in the Connecticut Valley. Under that date the General Court made the following appointments: " Leiftenant Philip Smith is appointed lieutenant to the troop of horse, of Hampshire County, under the command of Major John Pynchon, and Joseph Parsons Senr to be cornet of said troop; and Ensigne Joseph Kellogg leiutenant for ye foot company in Hadley." Smith and Kellogg were both residents of Hadley. This appointment of Joseph Parsons made him the color-bearer in the Hampshire cavalry, the third officer in command, corresponding at that time with that of ensign in the infantry or foot company. A military office was one of esteem, and gave those thus honored more than ordinary distinction. It showed to some extent the standing in the community of those who were placed in command, and their titles were afterward used in all records made concerning them. It is probable that Joseph Parsons had been actively engaged with Pynchon during the various attacks upon the settlements, in Hampshire County, in defence of those whose homes had become insecure after the ferocity of the savages had been thoroughly aroused.

" Before proceeding further, let us take a glimpse of the country to which our ancestors had come. When Pynchon and his little company emerged from the primeval woods through which they had threaded their way from the bay to the Connecticut, there was one vast wilderness stretching westward from the sea to the shores of the Pacific, with the slight exception of the unimportant settlements made by the Dutch colony along the Hudson. Bordering the Connecticut in various places there were open fields, made bare of timber by frequent inundations and by fires which were kindled annually by the Indians. These open spaces made clearing of the forests at the very beginning unnecessary, and the cultivation of the soil was begun at once under more favorable circumstances than attended the labors of the pioneers of Western New York, Ohio, and Michigan, where a generation passed away before there was more than the rudest com-

forts for those who had undertaken to subdue the forests.
These open fields extended along only the river bottoms, and
these at first were sparingly divided among every comer who
was regarded as one who would make a desirable citizen.
Character and capacity for making one's self independent of
aid from the town were the only requisites necessary. These
were exacted, and the town's proceedings show that many
of those who became permanent inhabitants gave bonds to
secure the town from liability of their becoming a public
charge from lack of ability to make themselves self-support-
ing. No one was permitted to harbor a stranger, and unde-
sirable comers were not infrequently warned to depart from
the town for many years after the first settlement was begun.
Idlers and dissolute persons found no favor at the hands of
the stern moralists who had crossed the Atlantic to found
communities based on the principles for which they had been
persecuted by intolerant authorities in Church and State.

Joseph Parsons married Mary Bliss, daughter of Thomas and
Margaret Bliss, at Hartford, Ct., November 26, 1646. Her parents were born in England, her father being the son of Thomas
Bliss of Belstone Parish in Devonshire. Thomas and Margaret had ten children, six of whom were born in England.
Thomas died at Hartford in 1640, and at some period subsequently Widow Margaret moved to Springfield. Four of her
sons, Nathaniel, Lawrence, Samuel and John, the latter the
youngest of the family, also became residents of the town.
In 1647 a rate was made for raising £30 for the purchase of
the lands of the Plantation. Nathaniel Bliss, who was here
at that time, was credited with having 51½ acres, and his rate
or tax was 7s 9d. The names of his mother and brothers do
not appear in the list. Joseph Parsons, whose name appears
for the first time in relation to being a land owner, was
included in this list of 42 persons, among whom were three
widows. Joseph held 42½ acres and his rate was 11s 9d. He
probably resided in that part of Springfield which is now
within the limits of Longmeadow. If not, he must have gone
there not long afterwards. The Book of Possessions, still in
existence and in the custody of the City Clerk of Springfield,
the entries of which were made by Henry Smith, prior to his

returning to England in 1652, states: "Joseph Parsons is possessed of a parcell of land in the Long meddow that *his house stands on*, bought of Alexander Edwards, being part of his lott, viz: in Breadth 10 rod, length 28 rod. Bounded South by yᵉ mill-lot, North by George Colton."

His other holdings of lands at that time are given below:—

"Also in the Long meddow Eighteen acres, more or less. Breadth 40 rod. Length extending from the East to the fence. Bounded North by James Bridgman. South by George Colton.

More, bought of George Langton five acres of meddow, more or less. Breadth 12 rod. Length 67 rod. Bounded North by Nath. Bliss. South by Widdow Bliss.

Also four acres of meddow. Breadth 10 rod. Length 69 rod, out of which he hath sold Alexander Edwards 10 rod in breadth & 28 in Length, soe the Length of this lott is 49 rod from the river East. Bounded North by Widdow Bliss, South by Jonathan Taylor.

In the back side of the Long meddow four acres, more or less, wᶜʰ is in Lue of his 3ᵈ division Lott over Agawam river, resigned into yᵉ Townes hand. Bounded North by Widdow Bliss, South by George Colton.

Over Agawam river five acres more or less, in the 2d division. Breadth 10 rod. Length from yᵉ river extending west 80 rod. Bounded North by Thomas Tomson. South by Jonathan Taylor."

Under date of May 12th, 1657, the recorder states: "All these several parcels of Land are by Joseph Parsons sold & for ever passed away to John Stebbins & by him yᵉ sd John Stebbins is passed away to Richard Fellows of Hartford." These lands were probably sold some time previous to this entry, when Joseph went to Northampton. Another entry of land is given below; date of purchase not stated:—" George Colton and Joseph Parsons are possessed of a lott in the Long meddow by purchase from Mr. William Pynchon, which was formerly part of the allotments belonging to yᵉ mill, viz: Twenty five acres, more or less. The Breadth is 26 rod, the length 160. Bounded North by Alexander Edwards, South by Roger Prichard and Benjamin Cooley."

This last was probably purchased at or near the time when Pynchon in 1652 went back to England. The above pieces of land are all that Joseph Parsons owned at one time, prior to his removal to Northampton, and the greater part had come to him by purchase rather than by grants from the town, as the larger share of the holdings had to the other residents. The comparatively few grants, and most of those in the 2d and 3d divisions, which were made to Joseph would seem to indicate that he had not been a constant resident of the town.

The first official position held by him in Springfield was that of highway surveyor. At a Town Meeting held January 8, 1646, the following entry was made in the records of the transactions of that day:—

" Thomas mirack and Joseph Parsons are chosen surveyors to make the way fro: yᵉ mill river to yᵉ long meddowe, who shall have power to call to yᵉ work, & in case any P'son shall refuse to come to yᵉ work, having had 3 days warninge before hand, shall be lyable to pay 2s 6d fine, except that they can alledge such an excuse as yᵉ magistrate shall judge to be sufficient; alsoe they are to see this way finished by yᵉ end of May next: alsoe if they give 3 days warninge to teames and they come not to yᵉ worke they shall be lyable to a fine of 5s for defects, except yᵉ magistrate shall allow of theyʳ excuse.

Nov: 2ᵗʰ, 1646. The same surveyors voted to continue yᵉ worke and finish it by yᵉ last of May, 1647, & in case yᵉ surveyors be defective In finishing by yᵗ day they are to pay 10s Pr weeke for every weeke after yᵉ day appointed."

This highway is in part the same as now follows near the Connecticut river towards the village of Longmeadow, only at that time the settlement was on the meadow not far from the present railway station at Longmeadow. After that location was abandoned and the home lots located on the high ground to the eastward, the southern part of the highway was changed to its present position.

November 5, 1650, " Joseph Parsons and John Clarke are chosen overseers of the fences from yᵉ meeting house downward, who are to take direction from yᵉ Townsmen for ordering these fences." In this connection it may be of interest to note that the first mention of Joseph's brother Benjamin in the town records is concerning his election to the same office. At the annual town meeting November 4, 1651, "James Bridgman & Benjamin Parsons are chosen veiwers of yᵉ fences for yᵉ lower end of yᵉ Towne."

The following year, at the annual meeting, Joseph Parsons was for the first time elected to the office of Selectman, a position of great honor and trust in those far-away days, and especially for a young man just entering upon a busy career in his own affairs. The terms Selectmen and Townesmen, refer to the same office. Frequently they are termed Select Townesmen in the records. They were regarded as capable and trustworthy citizens who would give faithful service, and were selected for their recognized fitness, and hence has come the name of Selectmen of New England townships, the highest offices in the gift of the people for the conduct of their own public affairs within the town. To show who served on the board with him the following is quoted:—

"November 2, 1652. At a Towne meeting It was Concluded to make choice of Seven Townsmen for yᵉ yeare ensuing, viz: John Pynchon, Samuel Chapin, George Colton, Henry Burt, Benjamin Cooley, Thomas Stebbins, Joseph Parsons."

"Nov. 22, 1652. Two of these Townsmen being sworne Commissioners for yᵉ Towne of Springfield were discharged fro: Townsmen & so yᵉ work rests upon yᵉ last five: To whom by yᵉ joint Consent of yᵉ Plantation is Given full power to order all yᵉ prudentail affaires of yᵉ Towne & to distribute Land this yeare & to act according to what is expressed in yᵉ Court orders: These to continue in this place for a year or till new be chosen."

"Court orders," refers to the law established by the General Court in reference to Selectmen. John Pynchon, Dea. Samuel Chapin and Elizur Holyoke were appointed in the preceding October Commissioners, or justices, to hear and "end small causes," and this was the reason for the withdrawal of Pynchon and Chapin from the board. Of this board, George Colton became known later to his descendants as "Quartermaster George Colton." Henry Burt was the ancestor of all bearing that family name in the Connecticut Valley. He was

on the first board of Selectmen and held the office of Clerk
of the Writs from 1649 to his death in 1662. Benjamin
Cooley was prominent in town affairs, and Thomas Stebbins
was later known as Lieut. Thomas Stebbins, a son of Rowland
Stebbins, who was one of the first settlers of both Springfield
and Northampton. Joseph Parsons was for five terms a Selectman at Northampton and again for one year in Springfield, on his return from his residence in Northampton, which
indicates that his services as a public officer were held in high
demand and regard.

At the town meeting November 1, 1653, "Joseph Parsons
& Miles Morgan were chosen surveyors of the highways for
the year ensuing." This was the last time he held public office before removing to Northampton. Clocks were unknown
to the first settlers of Springfield, and we find in the transactions of the Selectmen at a meeting held February 10, 1653,
that it was voted to give "Joseph Parsons 13 shillings for an
houre glass." It is probable that this hour glass was to note
the passing of time during the religious services at the meeting house on Sundays, or at public gatherings on other occasions.

It would appear that Joseph Parsons at or about the time
he moved to Northampton in 1655, had begun trade with the
Indians. His accounts were opened with John Pynchon in
1652. For several years afterwards his purchases at the Pynchon store indicate that they were mostly family supplies,
articles needed in his own household. Later a large share of
them were evidently intended for trade, and it is also evident
that his trade to some extent was extended to the settlers as
well as to the Indians. "Blew Trading cloth" was evidently
largely exchanged with the Indians for Beaver and other
skins, and most likely other items mentioned in these accounts
were also exchanged with them for such products as they had
for sale or barter. Wampum, largely made by the settlers
from shells of the sea-shore, were disposed of to the Indians.
and for many years served a good purpose in New England during the absence of a currency that had greater intrinsic value, .
but which disappeared like the fiat money of later times when
our commercial transactions concerned the world beyond our

own surroundings. Pynchon's special privileges gave him great advantage over every other settler. While they toiled in the fields and in the woods, his time was devoted to getting gain through the channels of trade. The Beaver and other skins which he bought were sent to England and there turned into cash. The wheat, peas and Indian corn were taken down to Warehouse Point or Hartford, and there sent around in sailing vessels to Boston, where they found a market. The first agreement that Pynchon made with Parsons for the Indian trade is copied from the Pynchon account books, and is as follows:—

"August 24, 1657. Agreed with Joseph Parsons for ye trade of Nolwotog & thence up the River, for which he is to allow for this yeare ensuing ye Sum of Twelve pounds to be p^d in Bever. Y^e winter Bever at 8s pr lb, ye spring at 9s, & I am to furnish him wth Trading cloth at 7s 6d pr yd, & wth shag cotton at 3s 7d pr yd, & to take of his Bever at 8s pr lb ye winter Bever, & ye Spring Bever at 9s pr lb, excepting the stag Bever & small skins, wch I am to take at such price as wee can agree at, & in case of not agreeing, y^t is to say, if I cannot yield to his price for ye stag & small skins, then he is at liberty to pay to me so much wheate as ye stag Bever comes to in leu thereof, he being otherwise ingaged to pay unto me all his Bever & likewise otter & musquashes."

Another agreement was made with John Webb concerning the trade at Nolwotog on "behalf of Joseph Parsons," as Pynchon states, but for some reason this was cancelled, for Pynchon writes underneath it "Void." It is here, however, given in full:—

"Septr 1st, 1657. Agreed with John web on ye behalf of Joseph Parsons: y^t he, ye John web, shal give foure pounds this year comeing for his liberty to trade at Nolwotogg, he being furnished from Joseph Parsons wth 200 yds of trading cloth, or 250 yds at 7s 9d, & 60 or 80 yds of Cottons at 3s 9d pr yd, wth a proportionable quantity of wampum & other smal things for trade, & cloth is to be marked out by mee, for John web, & of y^t cloth Joseph is to let web have his quantity. And John web Ingages to pay all the Bever, otters & furs wch he receives to mee or to Joseph Parsons, ye winter

Bever at 7s 9d pr lb, & spring Bever at 8s 9d, stag Bever, walsis excepted, wch is to be paid at such prices as Mr. Pynchon shall accept."

Nolwotog, was one of the Indian names of Northampton, but Nonotuck was more frequently used and has come down to us as the name in general use when that region was bought of the Indians. John Pynchon's orthography was never consistent with itself, and the same might in some instances be said of his book-keeping. His accounts often show that he made mistakes, sometimes in his own favor, but about as likely to be against himself. His " walsis " finds no explanation in our modern dictionaries, and may have been a word of John Pynchon's own coining. If it refers to small and less valuable skins the kind is not known.

In 1657 Pynchon reduced the price to £3 to Joseph Parsons for the Beaver trade, and " I pr'mise not to give or allow liberty to any more trade than to Edward Elmer." This privilege was renewed for several years, the price varying from £2 5s to £3 10s for each year.

That the Pynchon accounts may be more easily understood it may be well to state that his abbreviations and contractions were generally in accordance with the practices of his time. The orthography belongs to Pynchon. W^t stood for white, ye for the, y^t for that, and y^m for them. The foundation of these contractions is in the Saxon character resembling the letter " y," which stood for " th." Some of the other abbreviations used in these accounts to the casual reader are misleading. Wherever the letter " G: " precedes a Surname, as in G: Bliss, or in G: Parsons, it stands for " Goodman." * The use of Mister and Mistress seldom occurs in the writings of that time, only applying to people of distinction, or so regarded by the recorders who have saved to descendants what is known of the people who were the first to come to New England.†

---

* " Goodman, goodwife ; applied to the master and mistress of a house, implying some degree of respect." (Stormouth.) "The goodman of the house." (Matt. xxiv. 43.)

† " Our Northampton forefathers lived in a simple democracy. A very few only were distinguished by civil titles. Ministers, school-teachers, Justice Joseph Parsons, and Lieutenant William Clark had the honorable title of " Mr." (President Dwight : " Strong Family.")

These accounts, which extend over the greater part of Joseph Parsons' more active years, and during his commercial relations with the Indians, indicate his own progress in what was a most successful business career. His steady advancement in acquiring wealth is well illustrated in these purchases of Pynchon. His indebtedness to him frequently exceeded what would now be more than $3,000. Then, too, the large dealings in Beaver, Otter and Moose skins, for so many years unknown in the Connecticut Valley, carry us back to a very primitive period, making in some degree an almost forgotten past a reality to us.

The originals of these accounts are in a fair state of preservation and can be seen in the City Library at Springfield.

Page 91

Joseph Parsons Dr.

Septbr 1st 1652

Due to mee in my old booke.......................... 01 00 08
1 pr large wt Cotton stock......................... 00 02 06
1 pr knit... 00 04 02
1 yd ¼ holland at 3s 4d............................. 00 04 02
½ yd ½ qr at 6s 8d.................................. 04 02 02
½ yd ½ qr at 9s 6d.................................. 00 06 00
1 yd ½ Scot at 2s 7d................................ 00 03 10½
½ Lockr 1s 6d...................................... 00 01 06
4—col. Thrid 2—wted browne......................... 00 00 04
6 yds Manchester binding........................... 00 00 07½
1000 Pins 16d 1 Pa 5d.............................. 00 01 09
1 knot of tape..................................... 00 01 01
1 yd of wt fustion at 18d.......................... 00 01 06
3d yds of wt Cotton at 3s 4d....................... 00 10 00
6 yds of wt fillet & 8 laces....................... 00 01 05
1 knife 12d.. 00 01 00
9 yds of Red sh. Cotton at 4s...................... 01 16 00
3 sc. of ff thrid 3d............................... 00 00 03
2 knives 16d 2 knives 2s........................... 00 03 04
1 doz of Points 4d ½............................... 00 00 04½
4 yds of Rib. at 7d 4 yds at 6d.................... 00 04 04
Needles 2d a Remnant of fustion 18d................ 00 01 08
2 lb of Powder 4s 6lb of—shot 4 lb Bullets......... 00 07 04

Septbr 15 1652

You are to pay for Tho. Gun........................ 00 16 09
2 yds ¼ of greene kersy at 5s 6d................... 00 12 02

100 of Needles...	00 02 00	
1 Q of Pap...	00 00 06	
a Cord...	00 01 04	
1 yd & ½ of greene kersy.................................	00 08 03	
3 yds of sacking at 14d...................................	00 03 06	
2 yds of Red Cotton at 3s 10d...........................	00 07 03	
a warming Pan...	00 10 00	
½ lb of horsespice..	00 06 03	
2 oz of Cinamon...	00 01 04	
pd for you to Bro Davis...................................	00 07 08	
3 yds & ½ of wt shag Cot at 3s..........................	00 10 04	
2 se of silke 2d 1 yd yellow Tamy.......................	00 02 07½	
2 yds ¼ of flanel...	00 05 07⅓	
Pd for you to G: Branch for.............................	00 05 00	
100 nayles	00 00 11	
500 of nayles at 11d......................................	00 04 07	
300 at 4d pr lb...	00 01 00	
300 at 5d...	00 01 03	
1 Ell wt bone lace..	00 02 00	
1000 Pins 10d 1 Pap 4d...................................	00 01 04	
Pd your wolfe Rate 1651..................................	00 04 00	
pd your Countrey Rate 1652..............................	00 06 07	
6 aules 9 Needles...	00 00 10	
1000 pins	00 01 04	
¼ & Nayle of searge......................................	00 02 06	
5 Pills	00 00 10	
2 lb Shot...	00 00 08	
pd for you to Wm Branch.................................	04 00 00	
Due for Smithery worke...................................	00 16 00	
Sharpening a share..	00 00 02	

17 03 03

Reced 31 bush ¾ of wheat at 3s 10d..................	06 01 03	
Reced by bringing up ½ Tun of goods with G: Mirick in October last 1652 your halfe is..............	00 03 06	
Reced 37½ of wheat at 3s 10d for ye Purchase & to acot here 25 bush ½.................................	04 17 09	
Reced by Carrying down ye ffalls 61 bush Corne.......	01 00 04	
Reced by carting downe to ye foote of ye 40 bush of wheate at 3d per bush...........................	00 10 00	

12 13 03

1653

Acoted & Rests due to mee...........................	04 10 08	
And for John Porter you are to pay me............	00 10 00	

all is 05 00 03

Received G: Wariner Bill for Mr. Moxom £2 6s 0d
Received by Mr. Horshfords Bill to Mr. Moxon... 0 13 10

To Joseph Parsons

June 8th 1653

2 quts & 1 Pint of vinegar	00	01	10½
1 pr childr Stockens	00	01	02
Resting due to mee on ye other side	01	00	10
clouts for you cart & mend. a Cops Ring	00	01	06
for G: Thomas Cannoe ye first voyadge down you have not allowed for	00	03	00
Shutting a staple	00	00	02
2 quts of vinegar	00	01	06
1 pr shag stockens	00	03	06
1 knife 7d 1 C nayles 3d	00	00	10
Shooing a horse	00	01	02
1 lb of Powder 2s 6 lb shot 3s 1 awl 1d	00	05	01
1 bush of sowre apples 3s 4d ½ bush apples 2s	00	05	04
2 hats 6s & 6s 8d	00	13	08
3 yds blew linen at 18d	00	04	06
1 Tunnell	00	00	06
2 pr stockens	00	02	00
2 pr stockens	00	02	00
by Tho Stebbins you to pay	00	00	06
Needles 6d hooke & eys 4d 1 pce tape 12d	00	01	10
4 knives 2s 8d 1 Q Pap	00	03	00
pd for you to Wm Brooks wch you are to pay mee in wheate	01	13	06
3 yds ½ qr Kersy at 3s 11d	00	12	03
a hat	01	00	06
4 knives	00	04	00
8 yds canvas	00	17	00
4 yds ¾ red kersy at 5s 8d	01	06	11
3 yds ½ scarlet beys at 9s 4d	01	12	08
cotton rib Benja. took up for Holcomb	00	03	00

Novembr 14th (53)

pd for you to Wm Brookes wch you ingage to pay me in ye Spring in wheate	02	05	00
1000 hobs 3s 4d 6 awls 5d	00	03	10
2000 pins 2s 6d 1 paper pins 5d	00	03	01
4 yds red sh. cotton at 3s 8d	00	14	08
4 yd wt cotton at 3s 4d	00	10	00
2 doz points 9d 1 pr sissars 6d pr 11d	00	02	02
2 Combs 16d a tin bottle 12d	00	02	04

4 yds cotton rib 16d 200 hobs 8d 1000 pins 16d........ 00 03 04
6 doz thrid buttons 12d 2 yds ½ linnen 2s............ 00 07 03
2 pr stockens for G: Bliss.................... 00 02 06
½ lb Peper 2 thimbles............................ 00 01 07
1 pint bottle 2s 1 pint brandy........................ 00 03 06
2 lb coppris.. 00 00 08
                                                         _____
                                                         16 04 06

Recd in wampam..................................... 00 19 03
Recd by Wm Brookes.............................. 00 17 00
                                                         _____
                                                         01 16 03

      Decr 2d 1653
Acoted & is due to me............................... 14 08 03
making a pr hinges 4d new hooke 5d................ 00 00 09
a staple 00 00 09
pd for you... 00 00 09
1000 wormseed 00 01 06
600 hob nailes.. 00 02 00
you are to pay me for G: Merick.................... 00 07 00
You are to pay me g: S............................. 00 06 00
you are to pay me for G: Lyman.................... 01 00 00
you are to pay me for G: Lyman Edwards.......... 02 05 00
you are to pay for G: Cooper....................... 00 03 06
                                                         _____
                                                         18 14 09

Received 13 bushs & almost a peck of wheate at 3s 8d.. 02 09 00
Received 57 bush at ye falls 39 bush of it 4s per bush
  18 bush 3s 10d................................... 03 08 06
                                                         _____
                                                         06 07 00
Recd by carting this 57 bush....................... 00 09 06
                                                         _____

     April 3d 1654
Acoted & rests due to mee......................... 06 07 00
    Se page 204

    Se page 204

Page 204

Joseph Parsons Dr

     August 9th 1654
To 3 yds of wt fustion at 21d......................... 00 05 03
3000 of Pins 1 pap 4d................................. 00 04 04

```
2 yds ½ ½ of blew linnen 14d..................... 00 03 02
2 yds ff lockram at 3s 6d........................... 00 07 00
4 laces & 6 points................................. 00 00 10
2 pces tape........................................ 00 02 05
1 yd ¼ greene Say at 6s 8d......................... 00 03 04
2 pr wt Stock at 17d............................... 00 02 05
2 pr stock at 13d.................................. 00 02 02
3 yds ff lockram at 3s 1d.......................... 00 09 03
6 yds red penistone at 4s 2d....................... 01 05 00
6 leather points.................................. 00 00 06
2 pr stockens at 11d............................... 00 01 10
3 knives at 8d & 1 knife 7d........................ 00 02 07
1 yd holland....................................... 00 04 06
4 yd & nayl holland at 12s......................... 00 03 09
1 yd lockram 20d................................... 00 01 08
1 yd ½ greene shag at 3s 6d........................ 01 08 01½
3 sc ff thrid...................................... 00 00 03
4 yds wt cotton at 3s 7d........................... 00 14 04
18 yds cot rib..................................... 00 03 00
2—wt br thrd 4 sc ff thrid 6 yds bg................. 00 02 00
1 comb 8d 2 pr sissars 2 thimbls................... 00 02 01
1 pr stockens...................................... 00 02 00
3 yds yellow peniston.............................. 00 12 06
12 yds cotton rib.................................. 00 02 00
6 yds wt cotton at 3s 7d........................... 00 05 04½
2 doz of hookes & eyes............................. 00 00 08
1 pr stockens...................................... 00 03 00
1 pr stockens...................................... 00 04 02
¾ yd of greene shagg............................... 00 02 08
6 yds cotton rib................................... 00 01 06
1 lb Powder........................................ 00 02 04
6 yds of blanket at 8s 6d pr yd.................... 02 11 00
18 sc silk 2 yds ½ greene rib...................... 00 03 06
8 yds gallome 2 doz buttons 18d.................... 00 04 02
1 hat 18s.......................................... 00 18 00
1 yd ½ & ½ qr of kersy at 8s 9d.................... 00 14 03
1 yd ½ greene cotton 4s 6d......................... 00 04 06
1 lb Powder 2s 4d.................................. 00 02 04
2 lb Allom 12d 2 lb copperis 8d.................... 00 01 08
2 yds blew cotton 6s 4d............................ 00 06 04
300 doble tens 6s.................................. 00 06 00
5 yds ½ gallome 1s 10d Needles 7d.................. 00 02 05
1 pr sissars....................................... 00 00 05
1000 hobs ......................................... 00 03 04
3 yds red cotton................................... 00 09 06
1 Q Pap............................................ 00 00 06
1 Comb ............................................ 00 00 08
```

1 Ell binding..	00 00 01½
6 lb Sugar..	00 05 00
more, 6 lbs Sugar.......................................	00 05 00
1 lb Pepper...	00 02 04
1 qt of vinegar...	00 00 09
In Page 92 is...	12 15 07
	29 11 08

Reced 9 lb of Bever at 10s 4£ 10s; 6 lb at 9s 2£ 14;
    4 lb ¾ at 8s 1£ 18s................................ 09 02 00

June 14th 1655 Acotd & rests due to me............. 20 10 00
posted to p. 249

Joseph Parsons Dr

June 11th 1655

to 11 yds of wt trading cloth at 8s....................	04 08 00
to 7 yds of blew cloth at 8s..........................	02 16 00
9 yds ¼ of red shag cotton at 3s 10d................	01 15 06
125 mackrill hookes..................................	00 02 08
1 C (100) Needles....................................	00 01 06
5 doz awles at 10d p doz.............................	00 04 02
2 brass boxes wth glasses at 17d.....................	00 02 10
½ doz brass tobacco boxes at 10s.....................	00 05 00
½ doz tin boxes at 4s................................	00 02 00
6 waste coates at 7s 10d.............................	02 07 00
3 Shurts at 7s 4d....................................	01 02 00
a psell of wampam...................................	06 11 00
a sieth	00 04 08
6 lb Sugar...	00 05 00

July 17th (55)

49 yds of blew trading cloth at 7s 6d pr yd.......... 18 07 06

August 2d (55)

54 yds of red shag Cotton at 3s 8d pr yd.............	09 18 00
3 waste coates at 7s 10d.............................	01 03 06
3 lbs of Powder 2s 4d................................	00 07 04
16 lb of shot..	00 05 04
6 brass boxes wth glasses at 17d.....................	00 08 06
6 brass boxes at 10d.................................	00 05 00
6 pr of large Sissars at 5s 6d pr doz................	00 02 09
1 doz of smale sissars...............................	00 04 00

4 doz Points at 5d.................................... 00 01 08
6 caps 00 15 00
2 doz of wood boxes at 8s here is 8s set to much wch
    is abated on ye accot.............................. 00 16 00
1 doz of brass boxes wth glasse at 18s................ 00 18 00
To charges of your wheate I sent to Boston for you we
    I pd 00 09 00

                                                     119 04 05

Joseph Parsons Cr.

August 10 1655
By 14 lb of Bever at 10s pr lb........................ 07 00 00
By 10 lbs & ¼ at 9s pr lb............................. 04 12 03

October 31 1655
By 8 ¼ lb of Bever at 10s............................. 03 02 06
4 & ½ lb of Bever at 9s............................... 00 02 06
14 lbs Bever at 4s.................................... 02 16 00
12 lb musquash.. 00 06 00
2 otters 00 19 00
by 34 bushs & ½ of wheate, ye rest I had was sent
    for you to Boston................................. 06 06 00
by 20 lb cheese....................................... 00 10 00
by 38 lb of Butter.................................... 00 19 00

                                      posted below 28 11 03

Joseph Parsons Dr.

To so much due to me in page 204.................... 20 10 00
To the other side...................................119 04 05
To 1 doz red tape................................... 00 14 00
4 bunches wt tape at 16d............................ 00 05 04
1 gross of thrid points............................. 00 05 00
1 C of needles...................................... 00 02 00
6 brass Tobacco pipes............................... 00 07 00
10 yds of red shag cotton at........................ 01 18 06
32 yds of Blew Trading cloth........................ 12 16 00
1 Q of Paper.. 00 00 06
6 doz of knives at 6d............................... 01 16 00
1 yd ½ of Canvas at 6s.............................. 00 09 00
200 of doble Tens................................... 00 04 00

```
12 yds of wt shag Cotton at 3s 9d....................  02 05 00
2 doz & 3 knives at 6s..............................  00 13 06
1 pce of red Trading cloth 45 ½ yds at 8s...........  17 08 10
wt trading cloth, 20 yds at 7s 8d...................  11 02 04
2 yds of kersy at 10s...............................  01 00 00
6 brass boxes wth glasses at 18s....................  00 09 00
3 doz grt silk buttons..............................  00 02 06
3 doz for a doblet..................................  00 01 06
12 se of silke......................................  00 02 03
10 yds of red shag at 3s 9d.........................  02 17 06
3000 pins ..........................................  00 04 00
20 Lb Powder at 2s 4d...............................  02 06 08
1 gilt Bible........................................  00 07 00
1 doz hookes & Eyes.................................  00 00 04
¼ yd canvas 2s......................................  00 02 00
1 yd ¼ lock ram 8d..................................  00 02 08
```

Sept. 21, 1655

```
16 yds of wt trading clóffi at 8s pr yd.............  06 08 00
15 yds ½ of blew cloth at 8s........................  06 04 00
33 yds ½ of red shag cotton at 3s 10d...............  06 06 06
12 yds of wt shag Cotton at 3s 9d...................  02 05 00
3 doz of knives at 6s...............................  00 18 00
2 knives 2s.........................................  00 02 00
500 of Nayles.......................................  00 05 00
500 at 14d pr C.....................................  00 05 10
200 doble Tens......................................  00 04 00
Thrid ..............................................  00 03 00
1 doz awle blades at 10d............................  00 08 00
2 doz of glass boxes in wood at 16s.................  01 12 00
1 doz of wood boxes at 8s...........................  00 16 00
1 yd of Searge at 7s 6d.............................  00 13 03
6 waste coates......................................  02 07 00
3 yds ½ of wt Trading cloth at 8s...................  01 08 00
——mbr 26th 1655  In wampam by G: Thomas.............  00 08 04
1 pr stockens 3s 4d 1 pr 1s 8d......................  00 05 00
1 pr stockens.......................................  00 04 06
2 pr ...............................................  00 04 04
1 pr ...............................................  00 01 03
1 hat 21s 6d 1 hat 20s 12d..........................  02 02 06
4 yds ½ & ½ of red Searge at 8s 6d..................  01 19 04
3 pr Cot Stockens...................................  00 07 06
2 se. silke 1 comb..................................  00 01 01
2 yds red cotton....................................  00 07 08
3 yds ½ of red shag.................................  00 14 00
10 grss of Pipes at 8s 6d...........................  04 05 00
```

Pd for you to Goodm: Bissall........................ 00 07 00
I'd for you to John Gilbert........................ 00 06 00

17S 19 07
Received as above.................................. 2S 11 03

So Rests due to mee 150 03 04

---

posted over yᵉ leafe to yᵗ side on yᵉ right hand p. 250

Joseph Parsons Dr

To Accot made up yᵉ 21st of December 1655 for
    Severall paiculars as in Page 249............... £140 00 04
8 doz of thrid buttons at 2d, 3 doz pewter 3d........ 00 02 01
¼ ½ greene Cotton................................... 00 01 05

ffebr 27th 1655—(6?)
To 30 yds of trading Cloth at 8s..................... 12 00 00
6 yds of wt shag cotton at 3s 10d.................... 01 13 00
6 doz of points at 5d................................ 00 02 06
6 doz of pewter buttons at 3d........................ 00 01 06
6 wt wast coates at 6s............................... 02 08 00
2 made Coates at 18s................................. 01 16 00
1 doz of smale sissars............................... 00 04 00
6 pr large sissars.................................. 00 02 06
3 caps 00 07 06
1 Pap. booke.. 00 00 10

March 12th
15 yds & ¼ of trading cloth at 8s.................... 06 02 00
To Goodm: Bissall I pd for you 10d more than I
    formerly acotᵈ & the wheate your Bro Benj dlred
    (delivered) me I acoted it ½ a bushel to much.. 00 02 08
2 lb of steele 2s, 1 lb of Powder 2s 4d.............. 00 04 04
2 yds of Cotton ribban............................... 00 00 04

May 15th 1656
To 48 yds of wt Trading cloth at 8s.................. 19 04 00
56 yds & ½ of blew Trading cloth at 8s............... 22 12 00
one wt Coate of Thick cloth & broad stripes......... 00 17 00
2 made Coates at 18s................................. 01 16 00
12 wast coates at 8s................................. 04 16 00
6 caps 00 15 00
1 doz of brass boxes wth glasses.................... 00 18 00
4 doz thrid buttons................................. 00 00 08

5 yds of wt shag Cotton at 3s 10d.................... 00 12 00
57 yds ½ of red nape Cotton at 3s 9d................. 10 14 02

June 13th 1656
to 20 yds of blew Trading cloth...................... 08 00 00
6 yds of wt trading cloth............................ 02 08 00
6 greatwaste coates at 8s pr wastecoate.............. 02 08 00
2 Coates at 18s...................................... 01 16 00
4 pees of tape at 14d................................ 00 04 08
pd for your to D: Ashley............................. 01 11 06
1 lb Ginger 8d 1 lb starch 9d........................ 00 01 05
                                                    _____
                                                    262 13 05

Received by a psell of Beaver Summed up a little
    below to ye Sum of............................... 191 06 06

July 22 1656
Acoted & rests due to mee............................ 07 06 11

July 23 (56)
To 27 yds of blew trad. cloth at 8s.................. 10 16 00
30 yds of wt shag cotton at 3s 10d................... 05 15 00
24 yds of red Cotton at 3s 10d....................... 04 12 00
remanants of cotton & Trad. cloth.................... 01 08 06
4 waste coates at 8s................................. 01 12 00
To a psell of wampum................................. 04 00 00
1 C (100) of Needles................................. 00 01 08
1 C (100) of hookes.................................. 00 02 00
10 doz of points..................................... 00 03 04
10 doz of points..................................... 00 03 04
July 22th 1 knife 4 pr sissars & 1000 of Pins........ 00 02 07
    (Bottom of page in the Account Book cut out)

Page 250

Joseph Parsons Dr.

To 28 yds of blew Trading cloth at 8s................ 11 04 00
29 yds of wt Trading cloth at 8s..................... 11 16 00
30 shirts at 6s...................................... 09 00 00
3 quire of Pap....................................... 00 01 09
10 pr of Cotton Stockens at 22d...................... 01 13 00
52 yds of wt cotton at 3s 8d......................... 09 10 08
122 yds of red shag cotton at 3s 10s................. 23 07 08
25 yds of blew Trading cloth at 8s................... 10 00 00
23 yds ¾ of blew Trading cloth 8s.................... 10 00 00
24 yds ½ of blew.................................... 09 16 00

23 yds of blew.................................... 09 04 00
24 yds 09 12 00
45 yds of blew Trad. cloth at 8s................... 18 00 00
31 yds of red Trad. cloth at 8s.................... 12 08 00
30 yds of red...................................... 12 00 00
16 yds ½ of wt duffeild at 8s...................... 06 12 00
18 yds of wt....................................... 07 08 00
12 yds of wt....................................... 04 16 00
33 yds ½ of wt..................................... 13 08 00
28 yds ¾... 11 10 00
16 yds ½ of bilbo rugg at 11s 8d................... 09 12 06
20 doz of knives at 6d............................. 06 00 00
3 doz of smale sissars at 3s 8d 1 doz 5s........... 00 16 00
12 doz of looking glasses at 4s.................... 02 08 00
1 doz of brass glasses............................. 00 18 00
12 peces of wt tape at 17d p 6 pcs of red & 6 of wt at
    14d 01 11 00
6 pcs of cotton binding............................ 00 08 00

These   1 pce of Manchester...................... 00 03 08
goods   3—of cott. thrid at 5s 6 of of—bro. at 6s.... 01 17 00
coming 18,000 of Pins............................ 01 04 00
to 28£
are only 2 grss pewter buttons at 2s 8d............... 00 05 04
for Corne 1 bunch of silk....................... 00 03 00
&c all   23 yds of Kersy at 7s 8d................ 08 16 04
ye rest 3 canvas sutes........................ 01 10 00
for
Bever.   20 yds ½ of stone grey kersy at 7s 10d....... 08 00 07
       21 yds of red kersy at 5s 10d................. 06 02 06
10 waste coates at 8s.............................. 04 00 00
12 caps at 2s 6d................................... 01 10 00
    Coats at 18s................................... 02 14 00
                                   ————————
                                   258 12 07

on ye other side is................................100 00 00
more on ye other side at ye bottom of ye leafe is.... 024 15 07

                                   383 12 07

Joseph Parsons of Nolwotogg Dr

To 11 yds of red shag Cot.......................... 021 06 05
114 yds ½ of wt shag...............................020 10 04
52 yds of wt napt cot.............................. 09 06 04
106 yds ½ of red shag cot.......................... 19 01 08
18 yds ¼ of red napt Cot. 3s 7d pr yd.............. 03 05 05
48 yds ½ of blew duffeild at 7s 6d pr yd........... 18 03 09
48 yds of blew duffeild at 7s 6d................... 18 00 00
20 yds of wt duffeild at 7s 6d..................... 07 10 00

47 yds ½ red duffeild at 7s 6d........................... 17 16 03
34 yds ¼ of blew duffeild at 7s 6d..................... 12 16 11
1 pce of kersy.. 04 08 00
22 yds of Pink Peniston at 4s 9d..................... 05 04 06
a pseſſ of wastcoats, Petticotes & Gounds............ 35 00 00
3 childrens hats at 7s 4d............................. 01 02 00
1 hat 23s 1 hat 29 s................................... 02 12 00
1 pce of kersy.. 06 10 00
9 yds of Packing Canvas.............................. 00 11 00
2 ropes 00 01 06

October 13th 1657.

4 grss of Points at 4s p grss 2 grss at 5s............. 01 06 00
3 doz of glasses in wood frame at 2s.................. 00 06 00
3 doz of Tin box glasses at 3s....................... 00 09 00
½ doz of booke glasses................................ 00 06 06
400 of ordinary needles at 20d per 100 100 4s........ 00 10 08
18 seale rings 9s 2 doz of hoop rings at 5s.......... 00 19 00
½ doz of wosted girdling 9s ½ doz best 12 s......... 01 01 00
1 doz of cotton binding............................... C0 15 00
1 Pap. Manchester binding........................... 00 07 06
½ doz of gilt boxes in nests......................... 00 07 00
3 Inkhorns 00 01 04
3 grss of thrid buttons at 22d 1 grss at 16d.......... 00 06 10
1 Ivory Comb 18d 18 bone combs.................... 00 14 06
3 boxes wth burning glasses in ym &c............... 00 07 00
3 burning glasses at 3d.............................. 00 03 03
1 bunch of ff wt thrid................................ 00 02 10
2 lb cott thrid 10s browne thrid 4s 2 lb thrid 6s....... 01 00 00
1 pce (ferrit) hard as ribban......................... C0 15 06
1 pce Cotton rib...................................... 00 05 00
2 pcs of cul'd purple lace at 2s 6d.................. 00 05 00
3 grss & ½ of crewell lace at 16s pr grss............ 02 16 00
500 of mack. hookes 11s 500 wt 8s................... 00 19 00
1 grss of aules....................................... 00 13 00
18000 of Pins... 01 04 00
5 Paps of grt Pins at 5d............................. 00 02 01
1 doz thrid laces 13d wt tape & cold 5 pcs cold at 10d.. 00 11 01
2 grss of silke flagon coat Buttons at 6d............. 00 12 00
12 doz of ye largest knives 7s 8d 36 doz at 5 but alto-
    gether they are 48 doz at 5s 6d................... 13 04 00
1 doz of knives Iron hasts gilt...................... 00 05 00
4 doz of large sissars at 5s 3d...................... 01 01 00
6 doz of smale sissars at 3s 8d...................... 01 02 00
2 baggs 00 02 00
2 doz of red tape at 12s doz......................... 01 04 00

½—wted browne thrid........................ .... 00 05 00
16 yds of silke lace 7s 4d 13 yds green lace 3d........ 10 04 00
6 doz of silk lace at 5s 6d pr doz at 4s 6d 6 doz 3s 6d.. 04 01 00
12 yds of holland at 5s 10d..................... 03 10 00
3 yds of fſ holland at 10s.................... 01 10 00
8 yds of blew linen at 2s 7d..................... 01 00 00
10 shurts at 6s.......................... 03 00 00
8 yds of silke (wch G: Holton had)................. 00 04 00

251 12 08

Posted over ye leafe forward

    Octobr 7th 1657.
To 12 yds of Devonshire kersy at 12s 6d.............. 07 10 00
5 yds ½ of kersy pse Devonshire at 14s............ 03 17 00
2 yds ptector cold kersy at 12s...................... 01 10 00
3 yds ¾ of shag beys at 6d 6s 6d................. 01 04 03
8 yds of red kersy at 6s 4d pr yd................. 02 10 08
6 yds of kersy at 7s pr yd.................... 02 02 00
6 yds of yellow Tammy at 3s 2d.................... 00 19 00
silke 00 03 00
4 yds ¼ T. N at 14s.......................... 02 19 06
2 pr large mens stockens at 4s 6d................. 00 09 00
6 pr womens No. 6 at 2s 10d.................... 00 17 00
1 doz No 8........................... 01 07 00
6 pr No 9 at 2s 2d..................... 00 13 00
1 doz No 10....................... 01 04 00
½ doz No 14 at 16s pr doz No 16 10s 6d............. 00 18 06
1 Codline 4s 2 yds of shag beys at 7s 8d............. 00 19 04
2 yds of black Searge at 9s.................. 00 18 00
6 yds Canvas at 2s 6d 4 doz buttons at 7d........... 00 17 04
2 yds of Cornation Tammy at 3s 8d................ 00 07 04

    Nov 19 1657
To 47 yds of red duffeild at 7s 6d.................... 17 12 06
48 yds of bleu duff at 7s 6d.................... 18 00 00
45 yds ½ of Sad deep blew at 7s 6d.................... 17 01 03
27 yds of wt duffeild at 7s 6d.................... 10 02 06
106 yds ½ of blew shag cot at 3s 7d................ 19 01 08
50 yds ½ of red napt cot at 3s 7d.................... 10 01 04
4 yds ½ of kersy at 7s 4d.................... 01 13 00
2 yds ¼ of wt flan at 3s.................... 00 06 00
6 doz of hooke & eyes 3 doz of clasps 2s............. 00 02 00
silke 5s Buttons 2s 4d.................. 00 07 04
200 of 8d nayles 200 of 6d.................. 00 04 00
1 yd ½ qr of greene Say 6d................. 00 06 09

39 yds ½ of cold callicos at 2s...................... 03 19 00
2 Q of Paper 14d ¾ p'agon 3s 8d...................... 00 04 10
1 grss of awles 13 s 3 doz buttons 21d silke 12....... 00 15 09
3 yds ½ of Searge at 7s 6d 2 primers 12d........... 01 07 03
2 yds ½ gren rib 15d Needles 2s.................... 00 03 03
3 sc. silke 3 yds gallome........................... 00 01 05
¾ yd of wt flanell.................................. 00 02 03

132 18 11
on ye other side is ye Sum of.................... 251 12 03
in my old booke is ye Sum of.................... 249 09 07
To wt is due on a Bill for John Stewart....... 003 15 00

637 16 02

Receed by 53 lb of Bever at 8s pr lb this 4th of Febr
1657 is 21 £ 4s. Receed for wt I allow you for fetch-
ing your goods fro Hartford 15s, all is...........021 19 00

Febr 4th 1657. Acoted & Rests due to mee ye Sum of..615 17 02

Receed by what I allow you (besides former allowances) for wampam you had of mee before I went
to England weh you say is....................... 02 00 00

So ye rest due to mee............................. 613 17 02

Febr 5th 1657 To Tammy, Paper, shot, laces & bordering stuff 05 09 10
Tammy & lace delvrd to G: Cooper................. 00 07 05
1 lb of Powder.................................... 00 02 04
20 Shurts 05 00 00
10 yds of hambro.................................. 01 00 00
2 sieths 10s 2 sickles 4s......................... 00 14 00
3 yds ½ ½ qr of ff Searge at 8s..................... 01 09 00
2 doz buttons 14d 6 sc silke 9d...................... 00 01 11

June 16th 1658.
44 yds of blew duffeild at 7s 6d..................... 16 14 00
58 yds of red shag cotton at 3s 7d.................. 10 07 10

652 03 06

Deduct ye sun Reed as P Contra £288 01s 09d. So
Rests due to me of all acots made up —— July
1658 ye Sum of................................. 364 01 09

Joseph Parsons Dr

Joseph Parsons owes me on what I set off on his acot to much by Mr. Goodwin 8s. Mr. Goodwin not allowing so much as I set off in Josephs acot by 8s... 00 08 00

Due to me for ye trade of Nolwotogg & upward for wch you were allow me £ 12 in Bever for a yeare & ye yeare is Expired ye 12th of August 1658. This I Receed on an act forward 11L 12s 03d wch I acceptt & so cross it.

Octobr 26th 1658.

To 3 doz smale sissars at 3s 8d pr doz...............	00	11	00
To 3 C of ordi. Needles.............................	00	06	00
To 5 lbs, 1000 ff & browne thrid at 4s................	01	01	03
8 yds of narrow Callico at 22d........................	00	14	08
9 yds of brd. Callico at 2s 6d........................	01	02	06
6000 of Pins at 16d 1000 smal 15d 4 Paps at 5d......	00	11	00
3 grss of thrid buttons...............................	00	04	00
3 doz of lace at 5s 6d pr doz 6 doz at 2s 6d............	01	11	06
6 doz of Crewell lace at 16d..........................	00	08	00
2 yds ¼ kersy at 7s 6d...............................	01	00	08
16 yds ½ kersy at 6s 8d..............................	05	10	00
To 55 yds ¾ of wt shag Cotton at 3s 7d...............	09	19	10
To 29 yds ¾ of blew duffeild at 7s 6d.................	11	03	02
To 23 yds of blew duff. at 7s 6d......................	08	12	06
To 48 yds ½ of blew duf at 7s 6d.....................	18	03	09
24 yds of blew duff at 7s 6d..........................	09	00	00
23 yds ½ of blew at 7s 6d............................	08	16	03
24 yds of blew at 7s 6d..............................	09	00	00
45 yds ¾ blew at 7s 6d..............................	17	03	02
14 yds of wt duffeild at 7s 6d........................	05	05	00
49 yds of wt shag Cotton at 3s 7d....................	08	15	07
60 yds of blew shag Cotton at 3s 7d..................	10	15	00
119 yds of red shag cotton at 3s 7d..................	21	06	05
63 yds of red Shag Cotton at 3s 7d..................	11	05	09
54 yds of red shag cotton at 3s 7d...................	09	13	06
3 pcs wt tapes at 16d is 4s 1 green & blew...........	00	06	00
12 yds of filleting....................................	00	01	04
12 yds cotton rib.....................................	00	02	00
1 doz of hard as rib 6s, 1 doz & ½ at 4s 6d..........	00	12	00
½ lb woted bro thrid 4s, ½ lb 5s 6d ff thrid 1 bunch at 3s 6d	00	13	00
4 yds of ff Lockram at 3s 8d.........................	00	14	08
4 yds of holland at...................................	01	00	00
2 yds of shag holland................................	00	06	06

¾ yd of ff holland................................... 00 08 00
1 yd ¼ greene Say at 8s, 1 yd ½ at 5s pr yd........ 00 17 06
2 yds ¼ of Protector Cold cloth at 12s.............. 01 07 00
5 yds of kersy at 9s 8d pr yd...................... 02 13 02
16 se of silke....................................... 00 02 00
1 Testament, plain.................................. 00 02 06
1 yd of stuff for facing............................ 00 05 10
1 looking glass..................................... 00 02 00
12 yds of wt cotton at 3s 7d........................ 02 03 00
6 lb of Powder...................................... 00 12 00

184 17 06

Whereas upon my motion Joseph Parsons hath surrendred
up to me yt share of my land in Minhan weh he had agreed for,
being the lowermost 20 acres I do pmise him yt in case I should
sell it (before I have bin at any further charges either in building, fencing or Improving or otherwise) that then I will let
him have ye refusal of ye sd Twenty acres & at ye same price
wch was £6 10s this pmise I made him in June 18, 1658

Joseph Parsons Cr

By 21 Bushels & ½ of wheate....................... 03 15 03
By so much I Recd of your Brother Benja.......... 00 12 00
Aprill 27th 1658. By 219 lb of Bever at 8s pr lb....... 87 12 00
By 26 lb of Bever at 5s 6d.......................... 06 10 00
by otters mushquashes &c........................... 03 15 00

July 23 1658
By 259 lb & ½ Bever at 9s pr lb....................116 15 06
By otters 01 15 00
By Bever Cods....................................... 00 18 00
By Mr Dan. Clarke.................................. 34 00 00
By 5 bush Pease & 2 bush wheate delid into.......... 01 03 00
By Mr Holyoke 50s. By 42 bush wth Keny £8 8s..... 10 18 00
By Bill Mr Goodwin 12£ 4s, more by Mr Goodwin for
G: Howard 3£ 15 04 00
By 23 bush wheate G: Holton pd in to Mr. Goodwin.. 04 12 00

deduct this Sum Pr Contra....................288 01 00

October 26 1658
To 12 doz of knives at 6s 8d........................ 04 00 00
1 doz knives at 8s.................................. 00 08 00
1 doz of smale wt halfes silv shoulders.............. 00 05 00

1 doz of knives 6s 1 doz 8s............................ 00 14 00
1 doz of stockens no 1 10s 1 doz No 4 13 s........... 01 03 00
1 doz no 6 17s - doz no 7 18s....................... 01 15 00
2 doz of womens stockens at 3s...................... 03 12 00
25 shurts at 6s..................................... 07 10 00
4 Quire of Pap...................................... 00 02 00
4 yds of Searge at 7s p yd.......................... 03 03 00
1 pr stockens 4s 6d 2 pr mens 2 horn books.......... 00 05 08
54 lb of Iron....................................... 00 14 08
allowance to Bever.................................. 00 18 00
2 lb of nayles...................................... 00 02 00
3 doz Buttons 21d silk 12d.......................... 00 06 03
¾ Searge 6s, 2 yds ½ convas 7s 2d hookes........... 00 13 06

Jan 12th 1659

3 yds of cotton rib 4s 6 thimbles 12d............... 00 05 00
3 yds ¼ of Tuffted holland at 4s................... 00 13 00
1 yd dimity 22d 1 Q Pap 7d.......................... 00 02 05
¾ yd of holland.................................... 00 07 03
a cold. hat... 01 00 00
1 doz stockens 1 doz womens stockens 3s 4d pr pr.... 02 00 00
1 yd ¼ of scarlet shag beys at 7s 4d............... 00 09 03
6 yds of ½ Taunton Searge at 7s 8d................. 02 08 11
1 ff felt hat....................................... 01 05 00
1 doz of steele Tobacco tongs....................... 00 10 00
3 nayles of Searge dld to Thos. Noble............... 00 01 06
1 yd ¾ of holland at 7s 3d pr yd is................ 00 12 08
1 doz & ½ of Buttons............................... 00 01 09

July 12th 1659

To what you pay for John Bliss as pr your own
    letter ordering me to set it to your accot......... 08 16 00
more to John Bliss.................................. 00 02 08

                                             44 17 05
on ye other side is..............................184 17 06
& on ye former side is...........................364 01 09
4 yds ribban at 10d................................. 00 03 04

Nov: 21 1659.

To 55 yds of red shag cotton at 3s 7d 50 yds ½ of wt
    Shag at 3s 7d................................... 18 10 11
1 doz knives Needles worstead....................... 00 19 00
3 yds napt cotton at 3s 2d.......................... 00 09 06
28 yds of greene kersy at 4s 10d.................... 06 15 04
1 pr of cards....................................... 00 03 06

To so much pd for you to Mr fitch.................. 04 05 00
½ holland 2s 3d Needles 1 C 18d..................... 00 03 09
To 1 draft Bed................................... 02 00 00

Sept 26, 1660
1 yd ¾ Searge at 7s 6d........................... 00 13 02
6 yds Gallome 2s silk 8 scaines 12d.................. 00 03 00
To 1 lb of Colloured thrid 5s 6d brown thrid......... 00 09 06
ffor ye fur this yeare past viz to July or August 1660. 03 00 00

Decembr 12th 1660
To 46 yds of blew Duffeild at 7s 6d.................. 17 05 00
To 43 yds of red shag cotton at 3s 7d............... 07 14 01
16 lb of Iron (formerly).......................... 00 04 04
for ye Bever Trade this yeare to July 1661......... 04 00 00
To 2 peices of Red tape........................... 00 02 06
1 pce Cotton rib 6s 1 yd wt fustion 2s.............. 00 08 00
6 lb Plums 6s 1 swath 2s 8d....................... 00 08 08
1 pe wosted 2s 6 yds lace is 8d.................... 00 03 08

June 29th 1661
To 46 yds of red Trading cloth at 7s 6d............. 17 05 00
to 8 yds of wt blanketting at 7s 6d................. 03 00 00
To 6 yds of red shag cotton at 3s 7d............... 11 13 00
                                                 _____
                                                 693 16 11
Recd p Contra 567 10 00 rest to Ballance............126 06 11

June 29th 1661
Acoted, & of all acots is due to me to Ballance ye Sum
   of 126 06 11
To 1 doz of stockens 31s 3 pce of tape 3s 9d 3 peces
   girdling wostd girdling 5s.....................011 19 09
To a miscast on one of ye psells of Bever on ye other
   side & to what you pay for Medad Pomrey.... 11 12 06
                                                 _____
                                                 139 19 02
Recd p contra 93 14 02 rests 46 14 02

August 27th 1661. Acoted due to me fro: Joseph Parsons 46 14 02
& for 1 lb of Raysons............................. 00 01 00
   Witness his hand, (autograph) Joseph Parsons

Joseph Parsons Cr

By what Good: Mirick pays	02 10 00	
By 10 lb of Bever	04 10 00	
by 6 lb ¾ of Bever 7s	02 07 03	
By Bever at 9s	01 08 00	
By 2 otters	00 17 00	
	11 12 03	

This you pay towards what you are to allow for ye
    Bever Trade & I acquit it
ffor the yeare to come I have agreed wth Joseph Parsons Till
August 1659 about ye & for his Liberty to trade furs at Northampton wth ye Indians he is to allow me for this next yeare ye
Sum of three pounds & I pmise him not to give or allow liberty
to any more to trade than to Edward Elmer.

    Jan 12th 1659

By wampam to make the purchase of Lands for Hart-
    ford people (besides wt wampam you had) I allow
    you on accot and all busyness wth Chickwallop
    cleared 27 19 06
more, By what I pay you by Richard fellows Order
wch I allow him on Billings accot.................. 05 00 00
By what Goodm: Barnard pay me for Robt Bartlett. 01 05 00

ffebr 26 1659

By what John Stebbins pays me for you by a note
    under my hand to ffellows ye other 3L being set
    off on John Stebbins acot I allow you 40s, I say.. 02 00 00
By Deacon Chapins paymt of 20s..................... 01 00 00
By paymt of Alexander Edwards..................... 02 00 00

    May or June 1659

By 217 lb of Bever at 8s............................ 86 16 00
by 10 lb of Bever at 6d............................ 03 00 00
By 12 otters & 12 Musquashes....................... 04 15 00

    August 12, 1659

By 17 lb Bever at 10s............................... 08 10 00
45 lbs of Bever at 8s............................... 18 00 00
By 308 lbs Bever at 9s.............................138 12 00
By 63 of Bad Bever mostly at 6s 7s 10d............. 14 00 00
By 102 bush of wheate deld to Mr Goodwin......... 20 08 00

June 1, 1660

By 73 lb of Bever at 8s............................. 29 04 00
By 7 otters... 03 00 00
By 45 fox skins & 3 Racoone skins & others......... 03 13 00
By 30 musquashes &c................................. 00 13 00
By 23 bush of wheate................................ 04 00 06
By 10 Moose skins weigh 216 lbs at 12d............ 10 16 00
By 12 fad (fathoms) of wampam you pd Umpanche.. 03 00 00
By a coat to Umpanche & 5 fad. wampam............ 02 05 00
By 1 moose skin 22 lb............................... 01 02 00
By Mr Tyngs Atachmt................................. 00 01 00
By 48 lbs of Bever.................................. 21 12 00
9 Musquashes 00 04 06
98 Bush of wheat as you say into Jonathan......... 19 12 00
By G: Dumbleton 2 bush of wheate.................. 00 07 00

June 29th 1661

By 331 lbs ½ of winter Bever at 8s..................120 12 00
By 19 lb of Bever at 6s 8d.......................... 06 00 00
By 5 otters 2 being bad ones & Racoon skins........ 02 16 00
By 5 lb ½ Bever Cods............................... 01 00 00
By 2 Moose skins................................... 02 07 00
By 1 qt of Liquors.................................. 00 04 06
By ye Court charges at Northampton in March 1661.. 01 07 00
                                                   _____
                                                   567 10 00

August 16 1661 Reced 202 lb of Bever 9s............. 90 18 00
Reced 1 otter skin.................................. 01 10 00
By ffra. Hackleton.................................. 01 15 00
                                                   _____
                                                   93 05 00

Page 336

Joseph Parsons Dr

To 11 bush ¾ of wheat weh Jonathan Gilbert allows
   not of: he Red but 86 ¼ whereas you charged 98
   So yt you are to allow me for 11 bush ¾.......... 02 07 00
Apl 29 1662 To 3 Q of Pap............................ 00 01 09
To 1 lb ½ brown Thrid............................... 00 01 00
To 1 yd ½ of silk stuff at 7s........................ 00 10 06
To paymyt to John Bliss............................. 10 00 00

June 10th 1662

To 57 yds red shag cotton at 3s 7d................... 10 04 03
To 11 yds ½ wt stripd Duffeild....................... 04 06 03

To wheate fro: John King 40 bush.................. 08 10 00
To what you pay me for Mr fitch.................. 03 00 00

                                                  36 13 09

To rest on old acot p. 4 & 5........................... 46 15 02

                                                  82 08 11

June 11th 1662 Acoted & rests Due to Ballance....... 19 12 02
July 9th 1662 To a psell of wampam well strung and
    good ye white at 12 a Penny & ye black at 6 for
    good, thin skin Sumer at 10d pr lb ye wampam
    all is £30.. 30 00 00
To a psell of course wampam, sold ye Lump for £24
    in Summer Bever good at 10s.................. 28 00 00
To 2 shurts.. 00 12 00
To allowance for ye Bever Trade To July or August
    1662 .... 04 00 00

                                                  92 04 02

Reced pr Contra.......................£52 18s 6d
rests 29 05s 8d

August 4th 1662. Accoted & rest Due To Ballance.... 29 05 08
To 66 yds of red shag Cotton at 3s 8d.............. 12 02 00
To 3 doz knives...................................... 00 18 00

        Nov. 7, '62.
To 47 yds ½ blew Trading cloth..................... 17 12 00
58 yds red shag Cotton at 3s 9d..................... 10 17 06
13 yds ¼ of striped Duffeild at 8s.................. 05 06 00
yd 2 ¼ ½ ½ qr of kersy.............................. 00 17 11
8 doz lace 14s 1 C Needles 21d, 125 fish hooks 2s 3d.... 00 18 00
6 doz of Buttons at 13d.............................. 00 06 06
15 yds ½ North Kersy in remnants.................. 05 05 03
16 lb of Iron 4s 8d................................... 00 14 08
To 2s 6d you desired me to pay to G: Morgan for
    carrying Meale wch I pd since we reckoned...... 00 02 06
To 25 yds wt damaged Duffeild at 5s 10d............. 07 05 10
To ——— 5 ———...................................... 02 00 00

        April 6 1663
To 20 yds of red duffeild........................... 07 10 00

To 63 yds ½ of red shag betwixt you & Goodm: Wilton your halfe is 31 yds ¾ at 3s 9d.............. 05 19 01
To 24 yds of Trading Cloth......................... 09 00 00
To allowance for yᵉ Bever Trade the last yeare past
   vizt fro: July 1662 to July 1663................. 02 05 00

                              126 19 00

August 28th 1663 Acoted & rests due to Ballance.... 06 02 03
To paymt for you to G: Lyman....................... 01 08 00
To Compas 00 12 00
To Severalls brought fro: day Booke................154 04 03

                              162 06 06

Reced pr Contra.................................... 02 14 00
Novembr 10th 1663 Acoted and rests due to me yᵉ
   sum of.. 159 12 06
   Witness his hand (autograph) Joseph Parsons.

Joseph Parsons Cr

April 29 1662
By 5 otter skins................................... 03 00 00
By James Taylor 10s out of wᶜʰ I pay your Rate to
   Mr Glover 6s 4d & acots you.................... 00 03 08
By 20 Moose Skins 344 lb at 22d.................... 17 04 00
By 93 lb of Bever skins at 8s 6d................... 39 10 06
By Ensign Wilton................................... 04 15 00
By 3 Pints of wine................................. 00 03 07d

                              63 16 09

Accoted June 11th 1662
August 4th 1662 By 60 lb of Bever at 9s............ 18 13 06
By 4 otters.. 01 15 00

                              50 08 06

By 1 Moose—this moose being forgot to be summed
   up it is charged below By allowance on yᵉ Bever
   aforesd 01 00 00

                              51 08 06

By abatemt on yᵉ Course wampam Pr Contra...... 01 10 00

                              52 18 06

By 1 Moose Skin (forgot) 17 lb...................... 00 17 00
May 20th 1663 By G: ffeild 2 Pack of Bever 36 & 40 lb
    76 lb at 8s... 30 08 00
Moose skins, 190 lb at 9d........................... 07 02 06
July 14 1663 By 81 lb of Bever 9s 3d............... 37 09 03
By 26 otters.. 10 10 00
August 28, 1663 By a psell of Bever............... 24 10 00

                                                        120 16 09

    Octobr 13th 1663
By 5 ¼ of Bever.................................... 02 07 06
By 6 Musquashes & 2 Minks.......................... 00 06 06

                                                        02 14 00

    Memorandum, where Joseph Parsons & I made up this acot
I brought fro: Day booke but £154 4s 3d as Pr Contra when as
ye pticulars in day booke amounts to £57 4s 3d are so cast up
there, only I mistooke in Posting it & so have wronged myself
£3 wch will be evident in turning to day
Booke so yt Joseph Parsons is more Dr............. 03 00 00
                              wch add to 159 12 06

In all Joseph Parsons owes me ye full Sum of...... 162 12 06
Joseph Parsons Debt as it is one leafe back is..... 162 12 06
Reed towards it by Moose, Bever, otters, foxes and
    other smale skins & 1 Bundle of Bever this 20th of
    Sept 1664 .... 55 01 06
Reced by 500 Doble Tens............................ 00 08 00
Reed by wampam I take againe....................... 20 00 00

                                                         75 09 06

    Sept 20th 1664
Acoted & rests due to mee fro: Joseph Parsons ye
    sum of 87 03 00
                    Posted to New Booke
                    this 2d March 1664

                    Joseph Parsons Dr

To allowances for ye Bever Trade July 1663 to July
    1664 .... 03 10 00
To Severals dlrd Oc 22 (64)........................ 18 03 10
Nov. 1, 1664 To Severals........................... 53 18 00

To paymt for Tho Miller £16 in wheat at 2 paymts
    viz halfe at Spring & ½ spring com. 12 Mo....... 16 00 00
To 4 yds of silk lace sent Pr Wm Smead............ 00 02 08
March 2d 64 To 6 yds Gallome at 5d................. 00 02 06
To Ballance of ye acot in ye old Booke as it was made
    up Sept 20th 1664 ye Sum of.................... 87 03 00
April 7th 1665 To 2 Bonets at 18d 1 comb 15d....... 00 04 03
1000 of Nayles.................................... 00 03 00

    June 25th 1665
To 1 Sieth.. 00 06 00
11 yds filet 1s 5d, 1 pr stockens 12d.............. 00 02 05
1 Ivory Comb...................................... 00 01 08
To 1 bunch of tape................................ 00 01 08
Nov. 1665 To 32 yds of red shag cotton at 4s....... 06 08 00
To 4 yds ½ lace at 16d............................ 00 06 00
March 10, 65 To 3 knives at 9d.................... 00 01 06
May 1666 To 10s in Monny at Boston................ 00 10 00
June 20th 1666 To 1 sieth 5s 6d 1 point tape 15d... 00 06 09
Sept 27 To 1 pr smale stockens to G: Bliss......... 00 01 02
To allowance for ye Bever Trade for ye yeare 1664 &
    65, vixt fro: July 64 to July 65.............. 03 10 00
To ye Liberty of ye Trade July 65 to July 66........ 03 10 00
To ye Liberty of Trade fro: July 66 to July 67....... 03 10 00
To allowance for ye Bever Trade from July 67 to
    July 68 .... 03 10 00
Sept 8 68 To 3 doz silk & silk Buttons at 2s......... 00 06 00
ffeb 4th 1668 To 6 doz Buttons 12s 4 doz silk......... 01 02 01
6 yds black ribban................................ 00 06 00
To 8 doz silk Buttons at 16d 4 doz at 9d............. 00 13 08
                                  ————————
                                  204 00 02

Reced Pr Contra 184 10 06, Rest 19 09 08

ffebr 4th 1668
    Acoted & rests due to Ballance................... 19 09 08
May 1, 1669 dlrd to your Mother Bliss for you 12 lb
    of Sugar at 8d................................ 00 12 00
June 29 1669 To 1 yd ½ & nayle of Searge at 7s...... 00 11 00
Sept 27 69 To 11 yds of Bolter 11s 3d ½ yd Nayle
    Searge 4s 6d.................................. 00 15 09
                  ·
                                  ————————
                                  21 08 06
To neck Button Tho Stebbing Junr tooke up for you. 00 01 02

Joseph Parsons Cr

By wheate fro: Thos Copley........................ 01 11 06
August 22 1665 By 55 lb of Bever at 8s............... 22 00 00
By 7 otters at 7s 6d................................. 02 12 06
By wheat fro: Benjamin Parsons..................... 00 17 00
By due to you fro: ye Country; your fines &c dis-
    counted; the rests due you 1 14s wch I have al-
    lowed 01 14 00
Jan 28 65 102 lb of Bever at 7s...................... 35 14 00
By 3 otters... 01 01 00
By Benja Cooly...................................... 00 08 06
June 20th 1666 By 472 lb Moose..................... 23 00 00
By 69 lb of Bever at 7s.............................. 24 03 00
By 4 otters... 01 12 00
By John Hitchcock.................................. 00 10 00
By Nathanell Ely................................... 02 00 00
By Benjam Parsons.................................. 00 06 00
18 Jan 1667 By 80 lb of Bever at 8s................ 34 08 00
By 30 lb Bever at 4s................................ 06 00 00
By Musquashes &c................................... 00 10 00
By 288 lbs of Moose at 9d........................... 10 00 00
May 1668 By Monny at Boston....................... 07 00 00
By Goodman Bascomb................................ 04 00 00
ffebr 4 1668 By Geo Colton......................... 03 15 00
By 1 otter skin before winter....................... 00 08 00
                                                    ─────────
                                                    184 10 06

    Discounted all above Pr Contra this 4th ffebr 1688
March 3d 1668-69 By John Dumbleton in wheat...... 01 01 00
By Monny at Boston in May 1669.................... 01 01 00
By 25 bush of wheate fro: B Parsons................ 04 07 06
Nov 15 1669 By G: Parsons.......................... 01 10 00
By Ensigne Cooly.................................... 01 11 00
By allowance for 2 wolves of old 40s out of wch I pay
    your Rate to Mr. Glover, Town Rate & so allow
    you on acot here................................ 01 12 00
Aprill 1670 By your going to ye Bay wth ye votes for
    Nomination: for ye 36s, Courts pay, you accept
    25s 01 05 00
By Monny pd at Boston to my Son John Aug 30 1670. 05 00 00
ffebr 11 1670 By Reice Bedortha..................... 00 16 00
June 28 1671 By John Web........................... 02 06 00

At Northampton Joseph Parsons received many grants of land from the town. His homelot was on the North side of what is now Bridge street and extended from what is Market street to the present park in front of the Cemetery. The next lot north of his was granted to his brother-in-law, John Bliss. Joseph held at one time 81 acres besides his homelot. The Northampton Town Records contain entries of several grants that were made to him, as follows:—

"December 1, 1657. Voted & Granted to Joseph Parsons 6 acres of Swamp land at the Southerly Side of Mill River, towards the Millward, in Lieu of so much in Munhan."

"Frb. 8, 1658. Voted & Granted the day and year above said 3 acres of meadow to Joseph Parsons, for the Estate he had in his Irishman."

"December 1, 1659. Given & Granted by the Town to Joseph Parsons an addition of Land of two acres of upland joining to his 6 acres of swamp over the Mill River."

"February 19, 1660. It was voted & agreed the day & year above said that Joseph Parsons should have 10 acres near the common fence upon Pine Plain, 7 acres of it in lieu of his lot in little Rainbow & 3 acres in Venturers' field."

Other grants had probably been given him prior to these, and other possessions might have been by purchase. On the 5th month, 12th day, 1666, at a legal town meeting, "Joseph Parsons desiring that he might have liberty to run a fence from the great river (Connecticut) to the mountain at Pascomuck, to the hither end of his meadow & Soe up the path by the little milstone mountain to the great mountain (Mount Tom), the town have chosen Ens. John Lyman, Sergt. John King & Samuel Wright a Committee to view the place & give the Town Information concerning the Thing & these will consider of an answer."

This land was not far from the present Mount Tom station on the Connecticut River Railroad, and is now within the limits of Easthampton. The name of "Munhan," frequently occurs in the town records and refers to the original, or Indian name for the locality as well as the stream which runs into the Ox-bow of the Connecticut River. The latter is the Manhan river of the present time.

The first board of Selectmen were chosen before Joseph Parsons took active part in the town affairs of Northampton, but his name appears on the second board, having been elected in December, 1656, a year after his arrival in the town. He was also chosen in the years 1659, 1664, 1667, and in 1670.

At the February town meeting in 1656, " It was agreed that Joseph Person (Parsons) paying 20s shall be freed from any offis in the towne of Northampton for this yeare." The office in which he was desired to serve is not stated, but this vote indicates that office holding was not specially attractive to him and that he had more important affairs to attend to.

According to the town records of January 1659 Joseph Roote, Richard Lyman and Joseph Parsons were chosen Selectmen, and on the 11th of March William Holton, Arthur Lyman, and Richard Lyman were elected Commissioners to end small causes. A court had been established, composed of the six Commissioners from Springfield and Northampton, and a session was called to be held at the former place on the 29th of March. Among the cases presented was that of " Edward Elmer, Samuel Wright, Sen[r], Alexander Edwards, and John Stebbins, Plant. of Northampton, against the town of Northampton, Deft. in an action of y[e] case concerning their turning out some of the freemen from being Selectmen, to which office they were chosen."

When the Court came together the three men from Northampton, not being under oath, presented themselves by certificate, under the hand of the constable of Northampton. Several citizens objected to these three men because they had not been " legally appointed to the work," and had not been " allowed by any Superior Power as the law provides," which probably means that they had not been sworn, and that they were not freemen. After discussion the objections prevailed and no Court was held.

In May following William Holton appeared before the General Court asking for the appointment of Commissioners and Selectmen. The Court ordered that William Holton, Arthur Williams and Richard Lyman should be Commissioners, and that Joseph Parsons and Thomas Roote should be joined with them to be Selectmen. That settled the matter and Northampton was provided with five Selectmen instead of three, as had been the practice before. Among the jurymen at this Court is the name of Joseph Parsons. His associates on the board of Selectmen were always the leading men of the town. During the last year of his service the board was composed of Lieut. William Clarke, Dea. William Holton, Lieut. David Wilton, Joseph Parsons, and Medad Pomeroy. While he was strictly a man of business, he, besides attending to his own private affairs, gave in other respects time to public concerns not connected with the office of Selectman. Before narrating the various offices to which he was called, let us consider another event which concerned his wife Mary Parsons, more than it did himself.

The preliminary examinations at Springfield a few years before, which had been made by William Pynchon concerning the charge of witchcraft against the wife of Hugh Parsons, had evidently absorbed the interest of the public in general, and was the theme which had caused slanderous talk on the part of some of the settlers. In 1656, a year after Joseph arrived at Northampton, he brought a suit against Sarah, the wife of James Bridgman, for "slandering his wife, Mary Parsons." Much testimony on both sides was taken before the Commissioners, or Justices, for ending small causes in Northampton, and before John Pynchon and Elizur Holyoke at Springfield, the Commissioners in that town. Sarah Bridgman, as the result of these examinations, was held for trial before the Court of Assistants at Boston.

The slander consisted in the statements that Mary Parsons was a witch. Many of her friends and neighbors in Northampton and Springfield testified of their belief in witchcraft and named certain facts, the results of which they attributed to the use of witchcraft by Mary Parsons. Mrs. Bridgman's child had died and she said she thought Mary Parsons had bewitched it. Her eleven years' old son fractured his knee, which seems to have been very bunglingly set by the "chirugeon," and the little fellow, in his agony, cried out that Mary Parsons was pulling his leg off, and that he saw her on the shelf. When she went away he said that a black mouse followed her.

William Hannum testified that he had a "falling out" with Mary Parsons, about the use of her brother's (John Bliss) oxen. After that he lost by disease a "lusty cow" and a "lusty swine that had before been well and healthy. In a day or two after, while on his way to Windsor, with his cart and oxen, one of the cattle was bitten by a rattlesnake and died there. "These things," he said, "doe something run in my mind that I cannot have my mind from this woman."

The defendants also tried to show that Mrs. Parsons showed signs of being a witch while she lived in Springfield, bringing forward among others, Benjamin Parsons, brother of Joseph, to prove their allegation. She was said to have had fits, like the Moxon children, who were believed to have been bewitched. It was also certified that Joseph Parsons locked his wife in the cellar, to prevent her going out of the house in the night-time and wandering away. She was said to have frequently gone out in the night, dressed in her night-clothes, running until exhausted, and when she came to herself, did not know how she came there. On the other hand, testimony was introduced to prove that the child of Mrs. Bridgman had been sickly from its birth, and that Hannum's stock had died from natural causes.

All this testimony, and it was quite voluminous, was forwarded to the Boston Court, and the case tried there in October, 1656. The jury found a verdict in favor of the plaintiff, and the defendant was ordered to make "acknowledgment before the Inhabitants of the places where the said Partyes dwell, vizt: North Hampton and also at Springfield, at some Publick meeting at each place by order of Mr. Pynchon or Mr. Holliocke or eyther of y^m, and in such words and manner as shall be suitable satisfaction for such an offence and the same to be testyfied under the Hands of the said Mr. Pynchon and Mr. Holliocke, within 60 days next ensuing and in case of default, having notice of the time at each place, the said defendants, vizt: James Bridgman shall pay damages to the pl: ten pounds sterl: (sterling). Also this Court doth order that the Defft shall pay to the Pl. his costs of Court, vizt: seaven pounds, one shilling and eight pence."

This trial and its results evidently created a family feeling,

and eighteen years afterwards, Samuel Bartlett, who had in
1672 married Mary, daughter of James Bridgman, brought
suit against Mary Parsons for causing the death of his wife
by means of witchcraft. She died suddenly in 1674, and within
a few weeks Samuel Bartlett entered the case at the September court at Springfield. The Court was adjourned to the
18th of November, and on that day adjourned to meet at
Northampton January 5th, 1675. On this day the trial was
begun, and what follows is from the records of the Court:

"Mary Parsons, the wife of Joseph Parsons, Senr, Appeared. Alsoe Saml Bartlett whom this Corte ordered to produce ye witnesses in ye matter, referring to Goodwife Parsons
Suspition of witch Craft, And ye said Goodwife Parsons being
Called to speak for herself, she did assert her own inocency,
often mentioning it how Cleare she was of such a Crime, &
y^t the Righteous God knew her Inocency with whom she had
left her Cause.

Whereas Robert Old was ordered to appear at this Corte,
But not being warned, the Corte have now left y^t Case to y^e
Worshipfull Major Pynchon to Deale in y^t case as he sees
meete according to law. (He had probably been ordered as a
witness in this case but not summoned.)

There haveing beene many Suspitiousness of Witchcraft at
Northampton & severall testemonyes concerning the same of
Persons suspected, Exhibited to the Last County Corte in
September Last at Springfield, by Persons then & there Comeing Voluntarily, some to give Evidence & others there appearing also without Summonses to Cleare themselves of so exe-
crable a Crime. Also James Bridgman sending to ye Corte y^t
Diligent inquisition might be made Concerning the Death of
his Daughter, Saml Bartletts wife, whom both Goodman Bridgman & Saml Bartlett Suspect she Came to her end by some un-
naturall meanes, & for y^t Divers testemonys reflect upon Mary
Parsons ye wife of Joseph Parsons Senr, it being alsoe affirmed y^t there were many more witnesses y^t would Come in
y^t Case. The Corte then Thought meete to order Mary Parsons to appeare at ye Corte now hither adjourned, who accordingly appeareing as above sayd. Alsoe Saml Bartlett appeared, whom the Corte Ordered to Produce ye testemonyes

in ye Case, which being brought in & ye Corte finding them
many & various, some of y^m being demonstrations of Witch
Craft, & others sorely reflecting upon Mary Parsons as being
Guilty that way, Though the tryall of ye Case belongs not to
this Corte, but to the Corte of Assistants, yet Considering y^e
Remoteness, and ye Season of ye yeare & many Difficultyes if
not incapabilityes of Pearsons there to appeare, some being
soo weake, this Corte took ye more paines in inquiring into
ye Case, Appointed a jury of Soberdized, Chast woemen, to
make Diligent Search upon ye body of Mary Parsons, whether
any markes of witch Craft might appeare, who gave their account to ye Corte on oath of w^t they found, which with all y^e
testemoneys in ye Case ye Corte Orders to be sent to Boston,
to our Honored Governor by ye first opportunity, Leaving it
to his Wisdom & Prudence therein as they shal see Cause,
And ye Recorder of this Corte is accordingly to take Care y^t
all ye writings & Evidences in ye Cause be Ready & Delivered
to ye Worshipfull Major Pynchon who is desired to write to
ye Govern^r Concerning this matter.

It is further ordered y^t Mary Parsons shall make her appearance Before ye Governor or Magistartes or Corte of Assistants to answer to w^t she is suspected of in Case she be
called or required theretoo by Authority, & her Husband,
Joseph Parsons, to become Bound in a Bond of £50 for his
wives appearance accordingly, if required before ye 13th of May
next. And accordingly Joseph Parsons Senr, being sent for
& Comeing before this Corte acknowledged himself Bound to
ye County Treasurer for Hampshire in ye Sum of fifty Pounds
Sterling, that his wife Mary Parsons if required thereto shall
appeare at Boston Before ye Govern^r, magistartes or Corte of
Assistants or any Corte between this and ye 13th of May next,
to Answer unto w^t she is suspected of viz: Witchcraft, and in
Case of her non appearinge upon lawfull Sumons thereto,
Being sent to or left at ye House of ye sayd Joseph Parsons
then the sayd Joseph Parsons is to forfeite ye Sum of fifty
pounds as aforesaid to ye County Treasurer for ye use of y^e
County, this ye said Joseph Parsons Acknowledged in Courte
Whereupon his wife was Discharged further attendance at
Present.

Some testimony being Procured in Corte Reflecting on John Parsons ye Corte have Reade & Considered y^m doe not find in y^m any such weight whereby he should be Prosecuted on Suspition of Witchcraft and therefore doe discharge ye said John Parsons of any further attendance."

John Parsons was the second son of the accused. The case came before the Court at Boston in March, when the Grand Jury found a true bill against Mary Parsons and she was committed to prison to await trial, where she remained till the following May. The case was then tried, and she was found not guilty and discharged. Viewed in the light of the present, the charges and trials of witchcraft appear very ridiculous, but we should not forget that they belonged to an age quite different from our own, and that the light of experience and reason had not fully dawned upon the mental vision of the world. Our ancestors shared in the general beliefs of their childhood, and that which was general in England and throughout Europe when they came to New England.

At the March town meeting, held on the 12th, 1661, it was "ordered that Robert Bartlett, Thomas Mason and Joseph Parsons measure out 40 acres of land for Mr. Mather." This was Eleazer Mather, the first minister of Northampton and son of Rev. Richard Mather of Dorchester. This committee were also instructed to lay out a homelot for the ministry. They selected a lot on the south side of the present Main street, the front of which is now occupied by the principal stores of the place. At a town meeting held on the 12th of July of the same year, 1661, "It was voted and agreed by the Inhabitants of this Town that they would build a meeting house of 42 feet square, & that they would lay out about £150." This was the first meeting house built in Northampton and these six men were chosen and empowered to carry on and finish the work:—William Holton, Ensign Wilton, Robert Bartlett, Joseph Parsons, John Stebbins and William Clark.

In 1663 there was a movement to settle Joseph Eliot as an assistant to Mr. Mather in the ministry. He was a son of Rev. John Eliot of Roxbury, the Indian apostle, and it was voted that "the land that was Sequestered for the ministry is now granted & given by the Town to Mr. Joseph Eliot if he settle amongst us." Nine of the inhabitants dissented from this proposition, and among them was Joseph Parsons. The dissent was on the ground that the land had been given as a perpetual gift for the ministry and could not be disposed of as a personal gift. Mr. Eliot remained in Northampton only a few years.

The laying out and building highways was an important duty in the beginning of every New England settlement. In this work Joseph Parsons was frequently placed on committees and his judgment must have been considered extremely valuable by the many occasions that he was called upon to serve the town. May 24, 1661, Joseph Parsons, John Stebbins and David Burt were chosen to treat with Newtown men about a highway to Newtown over the river. Newtown was afterwards named Hadley. In 1670 the Town voted to "build a Cart bridge over Munhan River for the Carriage of our Carts and Trade to the foot of the falls." Lieut. William Clark, Joseph Parsons, and Robert Bartlett were appointed the Committee to execute the work. The first highway leading from the lower towns to Northampton was that built from Windsor. It crossed the Westfield river about mid-way between Springfield and Westfield and extended along the plain west of Mount Tom through what is now Easthampton. Travel from Springfield to Northampton went by the way of the road to Westfield until it intersected the road from Windsor to Northampton. The foot of the falls refers to the falls in the Connecticut river between Holyoke and South Hadley. This proposition concerned the first highway along the west bank of the Connecticut between Northampton and Springfield. At the County Court held at Springfield, Sept. 30, 1662, it was ordered in reference to highways and bridges between Springfield and Hadley, that Ensign Thomas Cooper of Springfield, Joseph Parsons of Northampton, and Nathaniel Dickinson of Hadley, be appointed a committee and impowered to consider the bridge, commonly called Batchelor's bridge, and other defective places in the said road and whether they shall be repaired by the County or by what particular place. They were given power, " with any one of the Hadley commissioners to issue warrants to impress men and carts out of either of those towns, as they shall judge needful for the work, provided they keep not any person or teams more than three days in a week: And the work is to be done either before winter or furtherest by the tenth of April next." The County Court in 1672 appointed Joseph Parsons and John King of Northampton and Samuel Porter and John Smith of Hadley "to lay out a highway from Hadley town to & over the Riverett called Fort River, towards the Bay, And therefore they are to take good view of the most convenient place for passage over that Riverett for the way to the Bay." This was the first road leading towards Boston from Northampton and Hadley and which intersected the Bay Path from Springfield to Boston in Brookfield. In this Joseph Parsons rendered valuable service to the community, and his active life no doubt brought him to notice the needs of such highways concerning which he was afterwards engaged to superintend, as one of the committee who were called to the work.

The Court records show that Joseph Parsons kept an "Ordinary," at Northampton, that is, a house of entertainment, what later would be called a tavern. He was licensed by the Court in 1661, which was renewed in 1662 and in 1664. The Court records say: "Joseph Parsons of Northampton is by the Corte Lycensed to keepe and Ordinary, or house of Comon Entertaynment, in the Town of Northampton, for the yeare ensuing: and he hath liberty granted him to sell wines or strong liquors for y⁰ same tyme: provided he keepe good rule & order in his house."

In 1665 he appears to have had some differences with Peter Hyndrix (or Hendricks) who brought a suit "about accounts." Medad Pomeroy pleaded for Hyndrix, presenting an account wherein he "charged Joseph Parsons with owing him £10 14s 6d." The jury found for the plaintiff in the sum of £4 9s 3d, "which was owned and proved in Corte; also the Costs of y⁰ Corte wᶜʰ is 20s & 6d." Following this, Joseph was presented to the Court for "breach of the Law in suffering Hendricks y⁰ Dutchman to Spend his tyme & estate in his the said Joseph's house, y⁰ Ordinary. He the said Joseph Parsons is by this Corte fyned to y⁰ County in y⁰ sume of 40 shillings, to be paid to y⁰ County Treasurer."

The year previous, 1664, Joseph Parsons and Robert Bartlett, the Constable, appear to have had a difference of opinion which the Court records do not explain. It appears in the record of the Court held at Springfield, Sept. 27, 1664, which says:—

"Joseph Parsons of Northampton was presented & complayned of to this Corte for opposing & resisting the Constable of Northampton in execution of his office & work, using means to Send downe the Countrey rate, violently taking away his "[Joseph's]" oxen & his Sack that were pressed "[by Bartlett]" for the Countrey service: Which act of the said Joseph being by this Corte judged high contempt of Authority, he was fyned to ye County in ye sum of five pounds: And for yt it appeared in the examination of things that the said Joseph Parsons & the Constable, Robert Bartlett, had Some Scuffling in the busyness whereby blood was drawn between them, they are each of them fyned to ye County in the summe of ten shillings apeace: The Severall fynes to be paid to ye County Treasurer. The Said Joseph Parsons upon passing the sentence of ye Court did immediately before the Court acknowledge his offence in affrunting Authority & intreated the Corte for abatmt of his fyne. The Corte well accepting of submission remitted twenty shillings of his fyne."

The "Countrey rate" refers to the Province tax, which was collected by the Constable, generally in wheat or corn, and taken down the river to Hartford and there shipped to Boston.

This fine of £4 10s was evidently paid in the sale of an acre and a half of land to the County, for there is in the record of Sept. 26, 1665, the following:—

"The County Treasurer propounding to this Corte whether the acre & ½ of land wch was taken last year of Joseph Parsons in paymt for a fyne shall not be accounted (being returned to him) as part paymt of the Countyes debt to him, according as it was then taken of him, vizt: at £4 10s, & whether his fyne of £3 at ye last Corte may not be sett off towards what the County owes him, ye said Joseph Parsons: This Corte declared yt such paymt is good & suitable & shalbe Soe accounted & ordered the County Treasurer to sett off Soe much with him ye said Joseph & to pay him the rest of the Counteys debt to his content."

With one having such wide business interests as did Joseph Parsons, it is not strange that he should occasionally appear in the Courts, as plaintiff or defendant. Then, too, in those early days our ancestors must of necessity have some amusement, even if it was only a suit at law. At the first Court held in Northampton, Sept. 28, 1658, " Joseph Parsons complaynes against John Webb for not delivering a Cow & Calf according to bargayne and thereupon Joseph demanded £4 of the said John wch the said John Owed him. Upon hearinge the busyness Joseph Parsons was content to accept of the Cow though the Calfe was lost, the said John allowing the said Joseph 5s wch he promised to allow & pay the said Joseph." At the same Court " Joseph Parsons was chosen Clarke of the Band, & took the oath accordingly for the due execution of his office."

At the Northampton court in 1665 Joseph Parsons brought a suit against Praysever Turner for non payment of a debt due by bill and damage of £30. This action was withdrawn and both plaintiff and defendant paid equal amounts for the entry of the action.

At the Springfield Court, Sept. 27, 1670, Joseph Parsons brought a suit against John Ingersoll of Westfield, but the parties agreed before the case was pleaded. He brought at the same time suit against Thomas Copley. This was also settled and the cost of the entry remitted.

At the Springfield Court, held Sept. 26, 1671, Joseph Parsons of Northampton was plaintiff in an action against Edward Blake, for " withholding a debt of £13 3s in money, for a hogshead of flax, wch he the said Blake received of Richard Goodall by order of the said Parsons, with due interest & all other due damages. In this action the attachment & evidences in ye case, wch are on file, being produced & read in Corte & committed to the jury they brought in their verdict, y^t they find for the plaintiffe, vizt: Joseph Parsons, that ye defendant is to pay him Six pounds one shilling & ten pence, to be paid in specie, vizt: in silver, & costs of Corte. The verdict is accepted, and costs as per bill as allowed is £1 9s."

At the Northampton court, held March 25, 1673, there is this record:—

"Joseph Parsons Senr, Plaintiffe, contra, John Abbott, Deft, in action of the case for fraudulent dealing in withholding, detayning & not delivering the writing, lease, or agreem^t wch was subscribed to by the said Joseph Parsons & John Abot, & two witnesses See Subscription & delivery. This writing, lease, Agreement, was respecting John Abbot taking the said Joseph Parsons Senr his farme at Pascomuck for a terme of yeeres, & to enter upon it the first of Aprill next ensueing, to ye damage of Twenty pounds. In this action between Joseph Parsons, Plaintiffe & John Abbott Defedt, the case being pleaded & heard & examined, & the Attachm^t & evidences in ye case (wch are on file) being produced & read in corte & committed to the Jury, they brought in a verdict that they find for the plantiffe, costs of Corte, & that the Instrum^t or writing detayned be delivered up in Corte. As soon as the verdict was given in it was declared that Plaintiffe & defdt were upon agreement by arbitration."

Hampshire County was created in 1662. The General Court "ordered that Springfield, Northampton and Hadley shall be constituted as a county, the bounds or limits on the South to be to the south line of the patent; the extent of the other bounds to be fully thirty miles distant from any or either of the aforesaid towns, * * * and further that the said county shall be called Hampshire & that Springfield shall be the shire town, & the Courts to be kept one time in Springfield & another time in Northampton." Two County Courts were held each year, the March term at Northampton and the September term at Springfield. The jurymen were drawn from both places, usually the greater number from Springfield. Joseph Parsons appeared quite frequently as a juror,—in 1667, 1668 and 1677 at Springfield, and in 1682 and 1683 at Northampton. The pay of a juryman at that period was 2s a day. The expenses of the jurors while serving appear to have been paid by the County, and they sometimes figure in John Pynchon's accounts. At a County Court held in Springfield, Sept. 25, 1660, the Judges were: John Webster of Hadley, the ancestor of Noah Webster, John Pynchon and Dea. Samuel Chapin of Springfield. The Recorder was Elizur Holyoke. The jurors were: Thomas Cooper, Henry Burt, Thomas Mirick, William Warriner, William Branch, John Dumbleton, Lawrence Bliss, Dea Benjamin Parsons, of Springfield, and William Janes, Arthur Williams, and Alexander Edwards of Northampton. After deciding the differences between man and man, and laying down the law, fancy these worthies with two Constables gathering around the dinner-table of the keeper of the Ordinary, Samuel Marshfield, and there spending an hour in social conversation concerning the great events of their time; and what it cost the County we still have the record in John Pynchon's own hand: "For ye Commissioners (the Justices), Jurors, & Constables, dinner on ye Court day, in all 18 persons, at 16d a peice, in all £1 4s, & 3 pints of wine, 3s 9d." There is also this entry in Pynchon's book, for the same Court expenses: "Sept. 25, 1660. To Sam. Marshfield, ye ordinary keeper, for ye Jurymen from Northampton, their suppers 2 nights, breakfast 2 mornings, Beds, Beere & 1 pint of wine, 14s 3d."

In the above we have a glimpse of court days in olden times and the gathering twice a year must have been an event of more than ordinary interest to those who dispensed justice and law in the beginnings of our Connecticut Valley.

The last case that Joseph had in the County Court was that brought against Benoni Stebbins of Northampton in Springfield Sept. 26, 1682, when he sued Stebbins for a debt of about 50 shillings. "The attachmt & evidence being produced & read in Corte, & transferred to the Jury they brought in their verdict that they find for the Plaintiffe, two pounds ten shillings in money & costs of Corte, wch as Pr bill allowed of in Corte: Thirteen shillings & six pence."

At the next Court held at Northampton, March 27, 1683, Stebbins brought a suit in Review, and the record states, "When upon account of sd Debt. as now may appear he had received & Improved one Barrel of Pork of said Stebbins in Boston, Porke being usually sold there then at between fifty & sixty shillings, or Three pounds a barrell, al which exposed the sd Plantiffe to the charge of about four Pounds ten shillings, besides charges in this Action. * * * Testimonys &

evidences In the Case being produced & read in Corte the Jury brought in their verdict y^t they find for the Plaintiffe, fifty three shillings in money & Thirteen shillings & Six pence in wheate (hereby reversing the former judgment) & Costs of Corte, which are as pr bill allowed, one pound seventeen shillings & six pence."

At a town meeting in Northampton, March 26, 1664, Lieut. David Wilton, Dea. William Holton, Joseph Parsons and Robert Bartlett were appointed to run the boundary line between Northampton and Hadley. At that time Hatfield was a part of Hadley and this line was between that town and Northampton. Six years later the Selectmen appointed John King and Samuel Wright to run the bounds between Hadley and Northampton. This refers to the line previously mentioned. They were to meet at Pontius, now Hatfield meadows, and "Joseph Parsons Seni^r is to go with them because he knows the way."

June 30, 1670, Joseph Parsons, Senior, Thomas Roote, Seni^r, Robert Bartlett, Isaac Sheldon, John King, David Burt, Samuel Wright, were chosen a Committee to order the settlement of all the highways in the meadow and rectify errors therein, "And because Joseph Parsons, Robert Bartlett, & Samuel Wright were absent on occasion the Town added to them Lt. William Clarke, Ensign John Lyman and Thomas Mason."

Connecticut proposed to exact a duty on all grain going down the Connecticut River from Massachusetts, first to establish and maintain a forte at Saybrook, and later to raise a revenue. To this Springfield and Northampton objected and petitions were sent to the General Court in relation to it, and finally the practice was abandoned. Northampton took action at a town meeting December 14, 1668, and appointed Lt. William Clarke, Dea. William Holton and Joseph Parsons a Committee " to consider the late order made by the Honored General Court with respect to Hartford in the excise of two pence per bushel." The doings of Connecticut created much feeling, but finally harmony was restored by withdrawing what would have been very unjust to the inhabitants of the Massachusetts towns along the Connecticut River, who had no other means of transporting the products of their farms to Boston.

In 1668 the town voted to give John King and Medad Pomeroy twenty acres of land on condition that they set up a sawmill, and keep it going four years. Failing to build it, " Joseph Parsons Senior, making a motion to build a Saw mill it was accepted & the land granted to him upon the same conditions as was given to John King and Medad Pumery, & the mill to go rate free so long as he keeps the mill going for the Town's use."

Trading with the Indians brought the subject of this sketch into friendly relations with them and he appears to have been consulted when important transactions were to be concluded. He was a witness to the deed from the Indians of Capawonk meadow in Hatfield and of the purchase of the lands in what is now Hadley. Wequagon and his wife Awonusk, and Squomp, their son, sold to John Pynchon, who transferred it to the inhabitants of Hadley, that piece of land on the East of the Connecticut from Hockanum to the Springfield bounds, taking in South Hadley and Granby. Some fifty or sixty acres in Hockanum were reserved, " being," Mr. Judd in his History of Hadley says, " mortgaged to Joseph Parsons." These Indians " owed him 80 beaver skins for coats, wampum and goods, and if it was not paid before the first of September, he was to have the land. This land was taken and afterwards sold by Joseph Parsons to the inhabitants of Hadley, for a considerable sum."

In 1664 the Indians desired to build a fort in Northampton, and " the men the town chose to deliver their mind to the Indians were David Wilton, John Lyman & Joseph Parsons. The Towns mind was declared to the Indians by us April 13, 1664." The terms as given were:—

" 1. First, they shall not break the Sabbath by working or gaming or carrying Burdens or the like.

" 2. They shall not Pawwaw on that place or any where else amongst us.

" 3. They shall not get Liquors or Cider & drink themselves drunk So as to kill one another as they have done.

" 4. They Shall not take in other Indians of other places

to Seate amongst them; we will allow only Nowutague Indians that were the Inhabitants of the place.

" 5. They shall not break down our fences & let in cattle
& Swine, but shall go over a Stile at one place.

" 6. The Murderers Callawane & Wuttowhan & Pacqual-
lante Shall not Seate amongst them.

" 7. They shall not hunt nor kill our Cattle or Sheep or
Swine with their Dogs; if they do they shall pay for them."

It is probable that Joseph Parsons had a more intimate
acquaintance with the Indians than any other inhabitant of
Northampton, or Hadley, as his trading with them must have
taken him to their villages up and down the valley. It must
have been a picturesque appearance that he and his dusky
friends made as they met to exchange commodities,—he to
take their Beaver skins and they the finery of John Pynchon's
store. It was this intimate relation that made him so valuable
when any transaction with them was to take place. It also
gave him a much more extended acquaintance with the country and of the most desirable lands. In the spring of 1671
he and a small party from Northampton, William Janes,
George Alexander and Micah Mudge, went on an exploring
expedition to what is now Northfield and there concluded a
bargain for a large and valuable tract of land. Sheldon, in
his history of Northfield, says:—

" They examined the location and ascertained that the na-
tives were ready and anxious to sell the tract." A bargain
was made and the deed conveyed to him, " for a valuable consideration a tract of land lying on both sides of the Great
River, (Connecticut) which is thus bounded: The Northerly
end on the west side of the Great River butting against Masa-
petot's land, and so running six miles into the woods on both
sides of the river." This covered the original and present
town plot of Northfield, and embraced 10,560 acres.

The second purchase was after the plantation was begun,
" comprising about 3,000 acres belonging to a Pacomptock
sachem, lying wholly on the west side of the river." This
deed was made on the 9th of the 7th month, that is, July
9, 1673, and reads: " between Joseph Parsons Senr and
William Clarke, both of Northampton, of the County of

Hampshire of the one party and Asogoa, the daughter of Souanaett, who was the true and proper owner of that parcel of land at Squakheag on the West side of the river called by the Indians Nallahamcomgon, or Natanas, and Mashepetot, and Kisquando, Pampatekemo, a squaw, which is Mashepetot's daughter—these four Indians above named of the other party, Witnesseth, that for and in consideration of the sum of two hundred fathomas of wampum in hand paid by the above Joseph Parsons and William Clarke, granted and sold all that parcel of land lying at Squheag, and is bounded with the Great River on the Easterly side; on the Westerly side a great ledge of hills six miles from the Great River, etc."

This deed was signed by the four Indians and witnessed by Timothy Baker and Sarah Clarke. It was assigned to the inhabitants of Squaheag June 15, 1675, and these two tracts comprise the territory of the town of Northfield during what is known as the First Settlement.

Joseph Parsons is entitled to the credit of being the first explorer and acted as the agent for the purchase. Sheldon says: "He received grants of a homelot and other lands, and bore his share of the charges of the first settlement, but appears not to have removed here in person. In 1683 he held a grant of 90 acres of meadow, which required him to settle three inhabitants."

His land at Northampton went to his widow in the division of the estate and was held by her heirs for many years. The town suffered from Indian depredations in the September following the assignment of the last named tract and the settlement was broken up, but resettled at a subsequent period.

From the date of Joseph Parsons' appointment as Cornet in the Hampshire County cavalry, 1678, it is evident that he entered actively into the suppression of the war which disturbed the entire settlements from Springfield to Northfield, but the records of that period are not sufficiently explicit to determine at this time the length of individual service. The County Treasurer in 1681 in his accounts makes this entry of payment: "To Cornet Joseph Parsons for a debt the County owed him for going after the Indians, &c., 5s 9d." Whether this was for military or in the nature of police service is not known.

The Indians when they were in possession of the country in and about Northampton were in the habit of burning the underbrush in the woods that they might more readily see and capture wild game, and for some purpose it would appear that the first settlers followed the example, for we find that the town appointed " Joseph Parsons to burn the woods on the Easterly and Northerly side of the Mill River, 2 or 3 miles above the meadow commonly called Broughton's meadow." Others were appointed to do a like service on the South and Westerly side of the river.

The town for many years gave a bounty for killing wolves of 10 shillings. The ears and sometimes the head was brought to the Constable, or to the Selectmen, as proof, but more frequently to the Constable, who gave a certificate of the fact which was handed to the Town Treasurer. In one year Joseph Parsons had six wolves to his credit. A few others were alike successful.

In 1664 John Williston of Windsor was admitted an inhabitant by Springfield authorities, " for Woronoco (Westfield) of this Township and hath liberty to build on his land there which he has purchased of Joseph Parsons."

In 1669, at a town meeting held in Springfield June 3, " a motion being made in Writing by Joseph Parsons of Northampton, for Liberty to Purchase a p'sell of land belonging to this Township, of Thomas Copley: wch land lys at ye foote of ye higher falls, his desire is granted, & also liberty to Build &c according to his desire."

This land was within the present limits of Holyoke and is occupied by some of the large manufacturing concerns of that thriving city.

After having a very active and busy life of twenty-four years at Northampton, when he had probably reached the age of about 60, he returned to Springfield to spend his remaining days. He purchased the lot of John Pynchon which was first granted to his (Pynchon's) brother-in-law, Henry Smith, and which was next south of the one granted to Elizur Holyoke. It was 20 rods wide and extended West from what is now Main Street to the Connecticut River. On the east side of Main Street was a lot of the same width extending across what was designated as wet medow, to the high ground. The eastern end, which must have extended nearly to the United States Armory grounds, was designated as wood-lot, and that where the house stood on the West side of the street as the homelot. These pieces embraced 27 acres, for which he paid Pynchon £130 pounds, nearly $650. This land is south of Bridge Street, the north boundary being not far from the south side of the street. Some years before he went to Northampton he resided at Longmeadow, but prior to his removing to that town he purchased a lot next south of that owned by his wife's mother, Widow Margaret Bliss, who lived not far from what is now Margaret Street. Whether he resided on that lot or in Longmeadow at the time he removed to Northampton is not now known. His Springfield real estate was sold a few years after his removal. On that purchased of Pynchon in 1679 he continued to reside till his death. The deed of this property is on record at the office of the Register and can be found on Page 53, Book A B. As this, after Joseph's death, became a subject of litigation, the deed is given below in full:—

"These Presents Testifie That John Pynchon of Spring-field in Hampshire, in the Colony of Massachusetts, for & in Consideration of the Sum of One Hundred and fifty Pounds of Lawful money of New England, to him paid & Secured to be paid by Joseph Parsons of Northampton, in Hampshire, in the Colony afores^d, Hath granted, bargained. & sold, & by these Prsents Doe demise, grant, bargaine, & sel unto the sd Joseph Parsons and unto his heirs & Assignes forever a Certaine Parcel of Land, Late Timothy Coopers, deceased, which said John Pynchon is Legally possessed of by Judgmt & Exe-cution, wch Land being about Ten Acres home Lot, with the Addition, & Seven Acres & halfe of medow, more or less, to-gether with a Wood Lott of Ten acres, more or less, al Lying between the Lot of Mr. John Holyoke on the North, & the Lot of Mr. Pelatiah Glover, on the South, & being in breadth Twenty Rod, the Length from the great River on the West, it Runs Eastward to the further end of the Wood Lotts, onely the Street or highway in the Town of Springfield runs or lyes across it, between the homelot & the Wet medow, wch said Alotm^t as before described of Ten acres homelot, Seven acres medow & Ten acres Wed Lot, be the parcels more or less, together with al the buildings, howsings, woods, wayes, waters, profits & Comodityes, with al the appurtenances & advantages thereof, & to the said Land belonging, & in any wise appertaining, the said Joseph Parsons, is to have & To hold, possessed, occupied & enjoy, for himself his heirs & Assines forever, & the s^d John Pynchon doth hereby Covenant & promise to & with the s^d Joseph Parsons, to Save the sd Joseph Parsons harmlesse from al manner of Claim of any Person or Persons Lawfully Claiming any Right in or Title to any of the Land above mentioned to be hereby sold from, by or under him, the s^d John Pynchon, his heirs, Executors or Administrators, or any unto him there belonging, & do herewith give possession of al the above demised premises, to him the s^d Joseph Parsons, to be to him the s^d Joseph Parsons his heires & Assignes free from al Incumbrances & molestations forever. In witness whereof the said John Pynchon hath hereunto set his hand & Scale this 20th day of November, 1679.

John Pynchon, with his Scale
affixt.

Signed Sealed & Delrd in the
presence of
John Holyoke
Benjamin Hinton."

The right of dower was released by Amy Pynchon, the wife of John Pynchon, to the above described property.

When the grants of homelots were made to the early inhabitants a majority of them were 8 rods in width on the street. That given to John Cable was 14 rods. The next south was 30, which was given to William Pynchon. Then came the lot of Elizur Holyoke, 20 rods wide. Continuing south the next was Henry Smith's, 20 rods; then came the ministry lot, first given to George Moxon, the first minister, who returned to England with Pynchon, which was 14 rods wide. With four exceptions all the other lots southward were eight rods wide. That of John Cable was sold to Thomas Cooper, later known to the people of his time as Lieut. Thomas Cooper, who was killed by the Indians when Springfield was burned by them in 1675. This lot he afterward sold and purchased the Henry

Smith lot. After Cooper was killed it passed to his son Timothy Cooper. When Timothy died he was in debt to John Pynchon, who obtained judgment and execution against his estate and took this property with other real estate, some of which was situated elsewhere in Springfield, some in Albany and some in New Jersey. Pynchon, as has been stated, sold this, the Henry Smith lot, to Joseph Parsons on his return to Springfield in 1679. After Cornet Joseph's death it went to his sons, Joseph and John. A suit was brought to recover right of dower to this lot, the particulars of which will be stated in another place. To make the locality clear to those who may have interest, the writer will state that the John Cable lot was located where the tracks of the Boston and Albany road cross Main Street. Then came the lot of William Pynchon, and the others in the order previously stated. The George Moxon lot was occupied by his successor in the ministry, Rev. Pelatiah Glover. Elizur Holyoke's lot after his death went to his son John Holyoke.

After Cornet Joseph returned to Springfield he was again called to the public service. In 1681 he and Jonathan Burt were appointed a Committee to examine the Selectmen's accounts, and his autograph is affixed to the report, which can be seen on Page 155 of the second volume of the Town Records. The same year at a town-meeting held in the following May it was "Voted that these three men, viz: Deacon Jonathan Burt, Samuel Marshfield & Cornet Parsons shall with any three of the townsmen make inquisition and search After ye overplus of all ye severall Country rates in the Severall yeares past since ye unhappy Indian war, & to endeavor ye recovery of it out of the hands of ye severall Constables, or any other person or persons, in whose hands they shall find ye said Monies. And the aforesayd Selectmen with ye Committee as aforesayd shall have power to take legall Course by suite at law or otherwise for ye recovery of the sayd overplus for ye use of the Town, or to Compound with any such persons or Constables where ye Money is found, as they shall see Cause."

The "overplus" of the country rate, was the amount collected to meet the Province tax in excess of requirement. In levying the tax (payment was generally made in grain, which included the expense of shipment to Boston) it sometimes happened that the Constable obtained more than was necessary, and this overplus was occasionally looked after. In this instance the Constable had a considerable amount in his possession and settlement was made by compounding,—that is, the authorities were satisfied to take what they could get.

At this meeting Deacon Burt, Cornet Parsons and John Holyoke were " chosen to joyne the Committee for Mr Glover his house, to examine & ballance the Townes debts and credits."

When Mr. Moxon left Springfield, his house and lands were purchased by the town to remain forever for the use of the ministry. When Mr. Glover came this property was given to him, but later the authorities, remembering the vote that had been passed, desired Mr. Glover to take other land instead. This controversy went on many years and was revived by Pelatiah Glover, Junr, after his father died, but finally this dispute was amicably adjusted. The subject had been submitted to the General Court, which decided against the elder Mr. Glover, and at a Town meeting " The Worshipful Major Pynchon, Deacon Burt, John Holyoke, John Dumbleton & Cornet Parsons were chosen a committee to treat with Mr Glover how to suite and accommodate him respecting the General Courts answer to Mr Glover our Reverend Teacher and the Townes petition concerning his Land; how he might have that wch may be just as satisfactory to him by other land the town did formerly give him & ye said Corte did determine not givable: & so make report thereof to the Town."

The fairness shown by the committee and their great desire to do justice to Mr. Glover, and afterwards the town to his son, who continued his claim to the property after the death of his father, were highly commendable and stamp them as men desiring to do what was exactly right.

In 1682 Cornet Parsons stood at the head of the board of Selectmen chosen that year. The full board was as follows: Cornet Parsons, Deacon Jonathan Burt, Thomas Day, John Hitchcock and John Holyoke. The next year, Feb. 6, 1683, he and John Holyoke were appointed a committee to examine the return of the accounts of the committee for building the new meeting house. This was the second meeting house built in the town. The present is the fourth structure in which the First Church society has from the beginning of the settlement worshipped. The committee found that the cost of the meeting house had been £400 5s, and that eleven shillings were due to the building committee, John Pynchon, Jonathan Burt and Samuel Marshfield.

The meeting house was built largely by contributions of labor and material, pretty generally distributed throughout the town. In the list is this: "To Cornet Parsons for 350 nailes, 5s 4d; 25 foot 4 Inch planks, 3s,—8s 6d."

His work was about over. He had been an industrious inhabitant of the two great towns, Springfield and Northampton, from a very early day. He had shown unusual talent whenever applied in directing the various affairs in these rude frontier settlements, and he had acquired a very handsome property, the largest, unless it be that of John Pynchon, of any one in Hampshire County, an indication of his foresight and enterprise. His death occurred October 9, 1683, little more than 47 years after he witnessed the transfer of the Springfield Indian lands from the Indians to the whites, the very beginning of the efforts to convert a vast wilderness into fruitful fields,—the beginning of that civilization which has made New England known and honored far beyond its limits. His place of burial is not known, but most probably it was in the burying ground at the foot of Elm Street, which was the first one laid out by the town. When the railroad from Hartford to Springfield was built it was extended through the west side of it, and in 1848 the town gathered all that could be found of the remains in those early graves, not removed by their descendants, and re-buried them in the present Springfield cemetery. Those having headstones, not reburied elsewhere, were placed along the eastern side of the cemetery, near the Pine Street entrance, and the long row of monuments along the path which can now be seen attest to the care that was taken in the transfer of the sacred remains of those who were the founders of the town. Such remains as could not be identified were buried in a single grave, and a stone erected which notes the fact. Very few of the very first settlers had head-stones at their graves, as it was almost impossible at that early day to obtain suitable material out of which to make them.

Mrs. Mary Parsons, Cornet Joseph's widow, survived him many years, her death occurring January 29, 1712.

The inventory of Cornet Joseph's estate shows that he had property to the amount of £2088 9s. The appraisers were John Dumbleton, his brother Benjamin Parsons, and John Hitchcock. With the exception of the estate of John Pynchon, who did not die until 19 years later, it was the largest probated in Hampshire County for many years. His brother Benjamin, who followed farming exclusively, had an average estate at his death in 1689, but that amounted only to £222 9s. A list made by the Springfield assessors in 1685 shows that John Pynchon held in Springfield over 2000 acres of land, the choicest in the valley, much of which had been taken by him for debt, largely by execution or foreclosure. Credit was easy to obtain and payment sure if the debtor held lands, at the Pynchon store. But there is little to show in the records to indicate that Cornet Joseph Parsons was an exacting creditor.

Inventory of Cornet Joseph Parson's Estate.

Of a County Court, held at Northampton, March 25, 1684, there is this record:

Mrs Mary Parsons, widdow, Relect to Cornet Joseph Parsons, Senr, late deceased of Springfield, presented to this Corte an Inventory of her late husbands Estate, to which she made oath, & power of administration is granted to ye said Widdow Mary Parsons, to Joseph Parsons, Eldest Son, & to John Parsons, 2d Son to ye deceased, And sd deceased dyeing intestate the Settlement of ye Estate is as follows: Here followeth a Coppy of ye Inventory of ye Estate of Cornet Parsons:—

Impr.	£ s d
To his purss & apparrell at.........................	09 15 00
To a house & homested in Northampton formerly mr ffitches & 23 acres of medow L'd in Northampton & moveable Estate, ded. to Joseph Parsons junr as his portion, all at..............................	225 00 00

To his homelot & orchard yt was mr Williams in
Northampton & 23 acres of Ld in ye meadow at
Northampton & moveable Estate, ded. to John
Parsons as his portion at....................... 160 00 00

To a homelot in Northampton & 23 acres of Ld in ye
meadow with moveable Estate ded. to Samll Parsons as his portion at........................... 160 00 00

To a homelot in Northampton & 23 acres of Ld in ye
meadow with moveable Estate ded. to Jonathan
Parsons as his portion at....................... 160 00 00

To 34 acres of Ld in ye meadows at Northampton at
£6 Pr acre... 204 00 00

To all his Ld in Pascomock within ye Lymits of Northampton 130 00 00

To all his Lds in ye place called Wesuakeage at...... 40 00 00

To ye houses & Lds in Springfield in ye Town and at
ye falls at... 230 00 00

To a house & Homestead in Boston & Remayns of a
place &c for a Warehouse, ye house being burnt
down, at.. 300 00 00

To Liveing Stock at £45 15s, Swine at 35s........... 47 10 00

To Cart wheels, plow, harrow, Chaines, timbr Chaine
fitrs, all at.. 03 10 00

To Corn & hay £10 6s, One ox hide 15s.............. 10 01 00

To shoes 15s, flax 30s, Penter Vessells at £10......... 12 05 00

To Tinn & glasses 10s, Earthen Ware 10s............. 01 00 00

To Brass Kettles, Skillets, Warming pann & other
Small things 08 10 00

To iron pots £6 10s, diapr Cloath at £2 5s.......... 08 15 00

To Lyning Cloath £45 13s, beds & bedding at £50... 95 13 00

To bedsteads 40s, Chest & trunks £8 15s............ 10 15 00

To boxes at 30s, tables at 40s, Silver plate at £5...... 08 10 00

To hats £4 5s, Sadle, bridle, pistols, holsters at £4
13s 08 18 00

To Chaires, Quishons & stooles at £4, baggs at 50s.. 06 10 00

To a Screw & Stilliards at £3, Cubbird Cloath & small
things at £4...................................... 07 00 00

To nayles £2, bees & honey at £3 15s............... 05 15 00

To a Cask & bolting mill at £2, other small tools 35s. 03 15 00

To Mauls 20s, Meale Sives & Corne Sives at 10s....... 01 10 00

To a Pannell & pillion with 3 yds Cloath £2 9s, 1 yd
Cloath 7s 02 16 00

To Indian Corn 2s, Carte rope & spring wheels at 29s. 02 13 00

To braided baskets & flasks at 15s, bees Wax at 10s... 01 05 00

To Cutlash, rapiour & silk Scarffe at................. 02 10 00

To pillions 30s, Guns 45s, green Say 40s, Linning Yaru
32s 05 07 00

	£	s	d
To iron tramels, pothooks, fire pann, Chaffing dish and irons all at......................................	04	00	00
To betle Wedges & a Chain 15s, bellows, hamʳ, slice, all at 8s..	01	03	00
To a Looking glass 8s, pork hooks, tallo, Chees, butter, Suiet	15	14	00
To a Cowle, half bushell Corn treys, dishes, trenchers, sithing dish	01	13	00
To a part of a Saw Mill at £30, Gun at 16s, hatchell 8s	31	04	00
To severall things at Josephs 40s, by severalls of yᵉ Estate in debts & Some thing Sold at £10..........	12	00	00
In John Parsons hands £86, in Samˡ Parsons hands £16 10s	102	10	00
In Jonathan Parsons hands £20, in debt due from D. Morgan £8.....................................	28	00	00
To a part of a Saw Mill at Haddam at..............	12	00	00
To Hats in Hadley at £4..........................	04	00	00

£2088 09 00

Taken Pr   John Dumbleton
Benj. Parsons
John Hitchcock.

A Statement of yᵉ Estate of Cornet Joseph Parsons, Senʳ, deceased

Whereas by yᵉ alwise disposeing hand of God (Joseph Parsons late of Springfield) is taken out of yᵉ Land of yᵉ Liveing, his awfull afflicting hand as we his Survivers desire Senceably to be affected with Soe humbly to Submit to his holy will & good pleasure & although sᵈ Joseph Parsons by his Precedent Care was thoughtfull & Studious Soe to dispose of wᵗ Estate God had blessed him with, Soe as might bee for yᵉ use & Comfort of his deere wife & Children Sirvivers as aforesaid, yet notwithstanding by Reason yᵗ yᵉ Last Will & testiment of yᵉ deceased afore-mentioned was made about seven yeares Since & attended with some imperfections wʳby it was doubtfull wheather it would stand in law yᵉ deceased had Concluded of Some alteration of sᵈ Testiment & acted accordingly So farr as he had libertie & Advantage So to doe & accordingly to his foure Sons had distributed while Living as in his book under his hand appeares & by a paper in order to a further declareing of his mynd to yᵉ disposall of his Estate then the

aforementioned will, wch was not perfected alsoe by Reason
of Weakness & ilness interposing incapacitating him accordingly & therein is expressed tend^r respect unto his deere Wife
& two his four daughters, alsoe appointing to s^d Daughters
£100 apeice & to his wife aforesd when all portions are payd
& set Out to Each Legatee aforementioned ye Remainder of
his whole Estate (debts being payed) to be her free & absolute dispose, And therefore we ye sd Sirrivers, have mutually
agreed & concluded as to a Setlem^t of ye Estate aforementioned, wch we intend humbly to propose to ye Cortes Consideration & determination, it shall be as followeth:—

That Joseph Junr Eldest Son to be deceased shall have Out
of his fathers Estate as his portion One Homelot with an house
On it which was formerly Bought of m^r Joseph Fitch as it is
Situate within ye Township of Northampton abutting On y^e
house Lot of Sam^ll. Wright Northerly, Town Street Southerly,
high way Westerly, & a house Lot of John Broughtons Easterly, & three acres of meadow Land in the tract of Land Com-
only called old Rainbow, Bounded by Land of John Lyman
Senr, Southerly, by ye Land of Deacon Judds, Northerlie, the
Raine bow hill, Westerlly, & ye River Easterly; Seven acres
& a halfe of Ld formerly Bought of John Bliss, Bounded by
Rainebow hill, Easterly, on a high way Westerly & Southerly;
by Land of John Woodwards Northerly; five acres of paster
Land Bounded by Land of Nenoenie Stebbins South east, &
Land of Jonath. Parsons, Northwest by a high way, North
west by Land of Nehemiah Allins South & land of Thomas
Bascomb. North & Easterly by an high way, & Westerly of
Isaack Sheldings; three acres of Grass Land in middle
meadow, Bounded by Joseph Roots Land South, the Re-
maynder of ye deceaseds Lot North, & a high way West & y^e
River East, & in moveable Estate to ye vallue of One hundred
twenty five Pounds wch he hath already Received.

To John Parsons 2d Son to ye deceased Land formerly
Bought of m^r Williams, a homelot and Ortchard Cituate
within ye Township of Northampton, Bounded by a homelot
of Christopher Smith South, & by a homelot formerly Henry
Cunliffs North, high way Westerly, & Land of John Langtons
Easterly; ten acres of meadow Land in Northampton meadow

bounded by a high way East & West, & Joseph Roots Land Northerlie, & Sam¹¹ Wrights Land Southerlie; five acres of grss Ld in middle meadow bounded by Ld of Sam¹¹ Bartletts Southerlie, & John Stebbins Land Northerly, high way west, & yᵉ River East; Eight acres & a halfe of Land bounded by Land of John Holtons Northerlie, & Land of Sam¹¹ Parsons Southerlie, a high way East & West, all wᶜʰ is vallued at £30.

To Sam¹¹ Parsons 3d Son to the deceased a homelot Cituate within sayd Township of Northampton, by estimation four acres, Bounded by a high way Westerlie, Easterlie by yᵉ Comons, by a homelot of John Parsons Southerlie, & by a homelot of John Alexander Northerlie; Eight acres of Land in yᵉ meadow, Bounded by yᵉ Town fence Westerlie, a high way East, by Land of John Bridgemans Southerlie & Ld of John Parsons North; three acres of Land in old Rain bow, Bounded by Wᵐ Millers land Southerlie, & Ld of Sam¹¹ Allins Northerlie, by a high way West & yᵉ River East; two acres & a halfe in young Rain bow, Bounded by Ld of John Hannums South, & Wᵐ Millers Land Northerlie, by a high way West & East; five acres of Land yᵗ was formerly Walter Lees Land, Bounded by Land of Isaack Sheldings Northerlie, & Land of Richard Lymans Southerlie, & by a high way West & East; One acre of Land in yᵉ meadow Commonly called Munhann, Bought of Capᵗ Cook; three acres & a halfe of Ld Bounded East & West by yᵉ high wayes, & by Ld of Widdow Goodmans Southerlie, & yᵉ Remayndʳ of sᵈ deceaseds Lot Northerlie, all vallued at £130 10s, & in moveable Estate wᶜʰ he hath already Recd £29 10s.

To Jonathan Parsons 4th Son to yᵉ deceased a homelot Cituate in the Township of Northampton, Conteineing two acres, bounded by a high way Easterly, yᵉ Comons Northerlie, & South by John Parsons homelot, & by a homelot of Sam¹¹ Parsons West, And Nineteene acres of meadow Land of Wᵐ Millers East, & Land of Mathew Cleasons West, And four acres of meadow in Munhann formerly Bought of Goodman Hantchet, Bounded by yᵉ River Easterlie, & Ld of Timothy Bakers Westerlie, & John Clarkes Land Northerlie & Land of Alexander Edwards Southerlie, all vallued at $125, & in moveable Estate wᶜʰ he hath already Recd to yᵉ full vallue of £35.

As alsoe to yᵉ Widdow Mary Parsons, Relict to yᵉ deceased all yᵉ Remaynder of her husbands Estae, both real & personall, wherever it is to be found, Either in Springfield, Northampton, Boston, Wesuakeage (Northfield), or Elcewhere, with all the privileges & appurtenances, Reversion or Reversions, to be at her free & absolute dispose, with this proviso, If she see Cause to make sale of any of yᵉ Lots, now at her dispose, then yᵉ Sons of sd Joseph Parsons Senr shall have yᵉ libertie before any other to purchase yᵉ sd Lands, agreeing with yᵉʳ mother, & not to be alienated to any other person or persons wᵗsoever till sd Sons all of yᵐ refuse to purchase sd Lands; as alsoe sd Widdow Mary Parsons Relict to yᵉ deceased aforementioned, to pay or Cause to be payd all debts due from yᵉ Estate, & to the sayd Joseph Parsons four Daughters One hundred Pounds apeice, to Mary Parsons One hundred Pounds, to Hannah Parsons One hundred Pounds, to Abigaile Parsons One hundred Pounds, to Easter Parsons One hundred Pounds, to be payd to yᵐ & Either of yᵐ in good Current pay & other goods out of yᵉ Estate, & at such tymes as the sd Mary Parsons Widdow, can Conveniently doe it, To all wᶜʰ as yᵉ joynt agreement & Conclusion of yᵉ Widdow & her childred as to a Setlment of said Estate, & an Issue of all further trouble, disatisfactions & disturbances as to any Rights, Titles, Claimes, any wayes Contrary or in Obstruction or Ejection of yᵉ aforsd pʳmises, but they may stand & abide as a full Setlment of sd Estate, & alsoe agree to pʳsent yᵉ premises as proposalls to yᵉ Countie Corte for their approbation & Confirmation, if they judge meete & Convenient Soe to doe, to wᶜʰ as our joynt agreement we sd Relict & Sirvivers have Subscribed this 5th day of January 1683 (new style 1684) as Witness our hands.

Mary Parsons	Samˡˡ Parsons	Abigaile Parsons
her mark	Jonᵗʰ Parsons	Easter Parsons
Joseph Parsons	Mary Parsons	under her marke
John Parsons	Hannah Parsons	

Witness to this agreemᵗ

John Pynchon   Samˡˡ Partrigg

Allowed & Confirmed as a Setlmᵗ of Cornet Joseph Parsons Senʳs Estate yᵉ above sayd, as attests at Corte this Mᶜʰ 25, 1684.   S. Partrigg, Clerke.

The death of Timothy Cooper brought a crisis in the financial affairs of the Cooper family, and the next year after the homestead was sold to Joseph Parsons, the widow of Timothy released her right of dower to Pynchon. The mother of Timothy, who married Lieut. William Clarke, of Northampton, set up a claim for her third interest in the estate, and the administrators of Joseph's estate brought a suit against Pynchon for recovery. A County Court was held at Springfield September 29, 1685. The judges were John Pynchon and Peter Tilton. What occurred in that Court is taken from the records of the clerk:

" Major John Pynchon, Esq in open Corte, ye Widdow Parsons being present sayd to her, the sd Widdow, that when he sold her husband Cornet Joseph Parsons the Land & house that Sometimes was Timothy Coopers Once of Springfield, the sd Major Pynchon told sd Parsons that he did not nor could not, nor would not Sell Goodwife Coopers thirds, ye Relict of Timothy Cooper her thirds, but Expressly Excepted it in Soe many words & sd that he would have it mentioned in the deed that he sold not widdow Coopers thirds & that Joseph Parsons Replyed & said you need not mention the Exception of thirds, Soe it be not expressed they are sold, because the law gives the Woman her thirds, & soe Major Pynchon Considering what hee sayd did not put the exception into the deed.

The clerk of this Corte being at Major Pynchons house when Cornet Parsons was upon purchase of the premises sayes that he Remembers their discourse about giveing a Sum of Money for the freedom of the thirds aforesd.

Moreover, the sayd Major Pynchon declared in Corte that after he had given the sayd Joseph Parsons the deed, he sayd Parsons desired ye said Major to buy out the sd Widdow Coopers 2ds, & what ever he gave for it costs he would repay it to sd Major Pynchon & further y^t sd Parsons offered sd Major Pynchon £20 to Cleare the 3ds which he refused, not knowing but it might Cost more, & further Major Pynchon sayd y^t Timothy Coopers Widdow being in Trouble Respecting her husbands great debts to sd Major Pynchon that he gave her a discharge of her husbands debt to him upon y^e

account of Joseph Parsons his Earnest desire that Major Pynchon would procure his freedom, intanglements Respecting thirds, & because sd Joseph Parsons had offered him £20 for it, but he demanded more & expected £25 in money, & told Widdow Parsons in open Corte that he would take his tyme to Sue for it, or Recover it if she did not Comply with him, & desired this to be recorded."

At the County Court, held at Northampton, the next session, March 30, 1686, there was further consideration of this suit, as appears by the records:

" The administrators to ye Estate of Cornet Joseph Parsons deceased, viz: Mary Parsons, the Widdow, Joseph Parsons & John Parsons, administrators aforesaid, Plaintiffe, & Major Pynchon Esq defendant, in an action of the case for the neglect of securing & defending sd administrators Right to Certain lands in Springfield according to a deed under his hand & Seale, In which sd administrators are Molested by a Writt of doweye to ye Relict of Lt. Thomas Cooper, alias Mrs. Clark, & all according to attachments. Entry Money 10 shillings.

" In the action depending in Corte Between Widow Parsons, Joseph Parsons and John Parsons, Pits, & Major John Pynchon Esqr defendant, the Testimoneys & Evidences in the case being produced & read in Corte & Comitted to the jury they brought in their verdict that they find for ye defendant Costs of Corte as Pr bill allowed of in Corte, 17 shillings."

This left Widow Mary Parsons without redress, although Pynchon in the deed had promised " to save Joseph Parsons harmless from all manner of claim."

CHILDREN OF CORNET JOSEPH PARSONS.

Births of these not on Springfield Records:
   Joseph, b. 1647; m. Elizabeth Strong of Northampton.
   Benjamin, died in Springfield, June 22, 1649.
   John, died young.
Born in Springfield.
   John, b. Aug. 14, 1650; m. Sarah Clark daughter of Lt.
      William Clark of Northampton.

Samuel, b. January 16, 1652.   Went to Durham, Ct.
Born in Northampton.

Ebenezer, b. May 1, 1655.   First on the list of Northampton
births.   Killed by Indians at Northfield, Sept. 2, 1675.

Jonathan, b. June 6, 1657; m. Mary Clark of Northampton, daughter of Nathaniel Clark, April 5, 1682; Benjamin Hastings about 1697.

David, b. April 30, 1659; died young.

Mary, b. June 27, 1661; m. first Joseph Ashley; second
Joseph Williston.

Hannah, b. August 1, 1663; m. Pelatiah Glover, Jr., son of
Rev. Pelatiah Glover.

Abigail, b. Sept. 3, 1666; m. John Colton.

Esther, b. Dec. 24, 1672; m. Rev. Joseph Smith.

Mary, Hannah, Abigail and Esther were married in Springfield.

Joseph's son Joseph had four sons,—Ebenezer, Daniel,
Moses & David, who married Springfield women, but only
Daniel stayed here.

The records of births, marriages and deaths in Springfield
were kept by Henry Smith from the beginning of the settlement up to 1649, when Henry Burt, by virtue of his office as
Clerk of the Writs, began to make the entries, and he continued to do so up to his death in 1662.   The record of the
death of Benjamin, and the birth of John and Samuel, is in
his handwriting.   The Hartford records were very poorly kept
at the beginning of the settlement there.   The birth, marriage
and death record is very incomplete; greatly in contrast with
what was done in Springfield.   In fact, the Springfield records of the general transactions of the town are much fuller
and more systematic than those of Hartford or of many of the
other towns.

II.

ON COLONEL JOSEPH LEMUEL CHESTER'S ALLEGED ENGLISH PARSONS ANCESTRY.

By ALBERT ROSS PARSONS.

"Col. Chester, a laborious antiquarian of the United States." (Dean Stanley: "Historical Memoirs of Westminster Abbey," p. viii.)

Colonel Chester, of New York City, collected a fee of $4,000 for making a search in England for the ancestry of the Parsons family of Springfield, Mass. The result we condense from the valuable and interesting "Hall Ancestry" (New York: G. P. Putnam's Sons, 1897), with comments of our own setting forth the facts of the case.

"Thomas Parsons was a country gentleman of Great Milton, Oxfordshire, England, of an heraldic family, and the progenitor of Deacon Benjamin Parsons' branch of the Springfield, Mass., Parsons family. The descent back to said Thomas is clear enough." (Hall, p. 63.) "Hugh, son of Thomas Parsons of Great Milton, had Hugh and Benjamin, who emigrated and settled at Springfield, where Hugh appears on the records in 1645. Benjamin came over with Hugh, or soon after." (Hall, p. 128.)

The New England Historical and Genealogical Register (vol. xii. p. 175), preserves the following letter of the Rev. Jonathan Parsons:

"Newbury Port, Oct. 20, 1769.—You write yt one Samuel Parsons from Martinico desires to know from wt part of England our Ancestors came. I will tell you as near as my memory enables me, (as I have no records of the matter but *what I heard from my parent*). I suppose my Great Grandfather Parsons came from Great Torrington about 20 or 30 miles from Tiverton and not far from Exeter. *He came over*

75

and brought my Grandfather Benjamin Parsons and other children about 130 years ago, perhaps 140 . . ."

J. Parsons.

Samuel H. Parsons, Esq., Lynn, Conn.

Conformably to this, Savage says (Gen. Dict., art. Parsons):

" Richard Parsons was at Windsor before 1640. He went to Hartford and probably returned to England."

At Hartford, Cornet Joseph Parsons was married. Thomas Parsons, married 1641, resided at Windsor, and gave to seven of his nine children identically the same baptismal names which Cornet Joseph and his brother Benjamin gave to their respective families. Samuel Parsons, born 1630 (probably the youngest brother), removed from the Connecticut River colony to Easthampton, L. I. He gave to four of his seven children the same names which were used by Cornet Joseph, Deacon Benjamin and Thomas Parsons, respectively. The name of Hugh Parsons, which first appears in the Springfield Records in 1645, or nine years after Cornet Joseph witnessed the Indian deed of lands at Springfield, is not found once in any of these families, nor among their descendants. The foregoing facts all combine to disprove Colonel Chester's " clear descent " from the Oxfordshire Hugh Parsons.

" Tradition has it that Benjamin was a brother of Cornet Joseph Parsons of Springfield. The English investigations of Colonel Chester, however, make it clear that the two were not brothers, as supposed, nor even related." (Hall, pp. 191-2.)

The original account-books of Pynchon, still extant in Springfield, in which books Pynchon charges against Cornet Joseph Parsons' account goods delivered to his " brother Benjamin " ; and Benjamin's testimony in court, in which he refers at least twice to Joseph's wife as his (Benjamin's) " sister " (i.e., sister-in-law), are not traditions, but facts of record, which no hypothetical pedigree framed at this late day by a baffled genealogist in England can obliterate.

" Colonel Chester says that in 1653, Benjamin proved his brother Robert's will in London, and the Springfield records show that he was married November 6, 1653, so he must have gone back to England, and after settling his brother's estate, returned to Springfield bringing with him perhaps the means which enabled him to marry in November." (Hall, pp. 191-2.)

Marriages in early Springfield do not appear from the records to have been noticeably dependent upon the possession of any considerable amount of means.

It may be safely affirmed that no other young inhabitant of Springfield ever made the long journey back to England either to prove a brother's will or to obtain the means to enable him to marry. If young Benjamin Parsons' resources were so limited as to hinder his marriage, why should the wealthy Oxford-shire Parsons family have required his presence in England simply to prove an English will? Further, where did Benjamin get the funds to enable him to go to England and obtain the means to return to Springfield and marry. Most genealogists would have concluded at once in the presence of these two 1653s, which Colonel Chester himself noted, that Deacon Benjamin Parsons of Northampton and the Benjamin Parsons of London were distinct.

" Colonel Chester infers from his investigations, that Hugh and Benjamin Parsons, in their intellectual and social status, were, in Springfield superior to those by whom they were surrounded." (Hall, p. 128.)

Plainly this inference was drawn in England, and not from the Springfield records still extant. As far as Hugh of Springfield is concerned, such superiority could hardly have been true of him save perhaps when surrounded by aborigines! Mr. Henry M. Burt states, after a thorough and minute study of the Springfield records, that no relationship can be traced between Hugh and the two brothers Joseph and Benjamin Parsons of Springfield. In a historic despatch to Boston for advice as to permitting the unhappy Mrs. Lewis to marry Hugh, the worshipful Pynchon describes her as having " falen into a leauge of amity with a bricke-maker;" * and in the

* Green's Official History of Springfield, p. 82.

witchcraft trials evidence was introduced concerning Hugh's alleged conduct in the capacity of bricklayer. As to Benjamin and Cornet Joseph Parsons, Burt writes: " Benjamin Parsons, who followed farming exclusively, had at his death an average estate, but that amounted to only £222 9s. The inventory of Cornet Joseph Parsons' property, on the other hand," (which, with his holdings at Springfield, Northampton, and vicinity, included a residence and a warehouse with a wharf at Boston) " amounted to £2,088 9s—the largest estate probated in Hampshire County for many years." The reader may be left to draw his own inferences as to the social status in early Springfield of the several settlers bearing the name of Parsons.

The true history of Colonel Chester's Parsons search remains to be written. As far as it has become known to the writer from the examination of Dr. Holton's MSS., and from extensive correspondence and enquiry, it is here set forth.

When that " laborious antiquarian " was commissioned by Dr. Holton to discover the English ancestry of the Parsons family at the instance of Judge Levi Parsons, who made a bequest of $60,000 to found a Parsons scholarship in Union College, documentary evidence was put in Chester's hands showing that Cornet Joseph and Benjamin Parsons were brothers and that Benjamin came from Devonshire, England, whence also came Jeffrey Parsons (born 1631 at Alphington, near Exeter), the ancestor of Judge Theophilus Parsons, termed by Savage, in his Genealogical Dictionary, " the most learned jurist that has ever appeared on our side of the ocean." Not finding, however, in Devonshire what he wanted as soon as he wanted it, Chester turned elsewhere. Had he met with the record of the marriage to the daughter of Sir W. Parsons of Black Torrington, Devonshire, of Colonel Abednego Matthew, born in 1629, whose father's cousin Alice, daughter of the mayor of Exeter (1552) and granddaughter of Geoffrey Matthew, Esq., had previously married W. Parsons (see " Devonshire Pedigrees "), perhaps he would have prosecuted his search longer in Devon. Under date of February 1, 1897, George W. Marshall, Rouge Croix, Herald's College, London, where Colonel Chester's papers are in custody, wrote to Professor Charles L. Parsons, of New Hampshire College:

" Colonel Chester did not examine registers at Black Torrington." And again (May 27, 1897), " I wonder that he did not look at them to make his search exhaustive."

Quitting Devonshire thus after but an incomplete examination of its records, Chester shortly after discovered a way to his handsome fee. Finding, namely, in a collateral branch of the family of Sir Thomas Parsons, of Oxfordshire, the names of Hugh and Benjamin, Chester, in defiance of positive and indisputable evidence, such as the letter of the Rev. J. Parsons before cited, Pynchon's autograph evidence and Benjamin's testimony under oath, declared, in effect, that neither Cornet Joseph, Benjamin, nor Pynchon knew what they were talking about when all three alike spoke of the first two as brothers. On the contrary, he boldly affirmed that instead of the wealthy Cornet and Deacon Benjamin Parsons having been brothers, it was the bricklayer and the Deacon instead; that they were born and baptized in Oxfordshire, and that there was no room for a Joseph in their family. The natural misgivings of his patrons, Dr. Holton and Judge Levi Parsons, both of whom were positive from documentary evidence that Joseph and Benjamin were brothers, Chester seems to have allayed by an artful appeal to enlightened self-interest and to convenience. Thus, Dr. Holton, the life-long collector of material for a Parsons genealogy, and Judge Levi Parsons, who found himself indebted to Chester to the amount of $4,000 for his work so far as it had progressed to that time, were descendants of Benjamin Parsons. To them Chester therefore reported that " Joseph Parsons' pedigree could be traced, but that if his descendants wished to have it, Judge Parsons should let them pay for it, since Joseph's descendants were as rich as Benjamin's." So obviously fair was this proposition, that it seems to have met with little or no resistance. The acquaintance with Chester's methods gradually formed by the writer of the present contribution to the history of applied genealogical science, led to his making inquiry of the custodian of Chester's papers, as to the meaning to be attributed to the statement that Joseph's pedigree could be traced. That is to say, whether it implied that Chester had a clue which warranted him in thus affirming the "traceableness" of said pedigree; or whether he simply committed himself to the proposition that, like anything else of the location of which absolutely nothing was known to him, Joseph's pedigree could be looked for! Addressing upon this point Chester's executor, George E. Cokayne, Esq., London, the following reply was received:

"College of Arms, London, August 24, 1888.—I find a neatly worked up pedigree of the Parsons family of Oxfordshire. In it Benjamin is called the fifth and youngest son of Hugh, and is said to have been baptized at Sandford in 1627-8. The names of the four elder brothers are given. There is, therefore, if Colonel Chester had grounds for *proving* that Benjamin was the youngest son, no room for a brother Joseph, not does the name of Joseph appear . . . in this pedigree, which is probably in print."

Similarly, Marshall writes:

"Herald's College, London, May 27, 1897.—I do not think Chester purposely left out Joseph. It is evident from his notes that he failed to find him."

From Chester's manuscripts now with the Herald's College, London, it is evident that Chester found no Joseph Parsons of English record to correspond to Cornet Joseph, but, finding two brothers in Oxfordshire whose ages approximated those of the Northampton Hugh and Benjamin Parsons, he asserted their identity, although the records showed sisters where Joseph should have been and in spite of the American evidence that Joseph and Benjamin were brothers.

History speaks of Cornet Joseph Parsons as "a man of action, of extraordinary energy, enterprise, and public spirit"; and of his brother, Deacon Benjamin Parsons, as "eminent in the church, an earnest worker, and of great purity in private and public life"—all "invaluable traits in the founders of a Christian state."

By the present *exposé* of the worthlessness of Col. Chester's English Parsons' pedigree, the breach which it created between the descendants of Cornet Joseph Parsons and his brother Deacon Benjamin Parsons from the Torringtons in Devonshire, and Jeffrey Parsons from the neighboring Alphington in the same shire, is closed, and the members of the reunited Parsons family of America (where they have not as yet traced their descent directly to some particular branch of the English Parsons, to whom a modification of the original arms of the Parsons family has been subsequently granted), may safely assume the ancient arms of Sir John Parsons of Hereford, among whose descendants, as will appear from our next chapter, are (1) the Norfolk Earls of Rosse; (2) the Oxfordshire Parsons, after whom was named one of the earliest settlements in the Barbadoes; (3) the Radnorshire Parsons from Springfield, Essex, England, whose Jeffrey alliance is commemorated in the name of Jeffrey Parsons of Devonshire, the progenitor of the learned Chief Justice Theophilus Parsons of Massachusetts, and his son Thomas Parsons, the American poet and translator of Dante; and (4) (a) Cornet Joseph Parsons of Springfield, Mass., ancestor of Captain Charles Parsons, who served under Washington at Valley Forge, Trenton, Monmouth, and Yorktown, and of Brigadier-General and Brevet Major-General Lewis Baldwin Parsons, from 1861 to 1865 Chief of Rail and River Transportation for the Armies of the United States; (b) Deacon Benjamin Parsons, progenitor of the intimate and "life-long friend of Washington," and subsequent chief justice of the Northwestern Territory, Major-General Samuel Holden Parsons, of whom Captain David Humphreys, in his poem "On the Happiness of America" ("Yale in the Revolution"), wrote:

> Shall I tell you from whom I learned the martial art,
> With what high chiefs I played my early part?
> With Parsons first, whose eye with piercing ken,
> Reads, through their hearts, the characters of men.

GARDEN CITY, LONG ISLAND, N. Y., U. S. A.,
September 16, 1898.

III.

THE NAME OF PARSONS.

1.

Dr. DAVID P. HOLTON.

" The name of Parsons occupies a peculiar position among English surnames.

" On the one hand are the names of landed gentlemen, derived from their estates, as Norton, Wedgewood, Lonsdale, etc. On the other hand are the names derived from trades, as Smith, Carpenter, Mason. Lower than these are Hayward (fence-keeper), Howard (hog-keeper), and Shepherd; while these are above mere Tom, Dick, and Harry and their offspring Thomson, Dickson, and Harrison, as these in turn are still above the nobodies—White, Black, Gray, Brown, and Green.*

" Unlike all of the foregoing classes of surnames, the name Parsons is derived neither from landholding nor from trades, etc. Parsons means son of the parson.† John and Mary Parsons mean the parson's son John and his daughter Mary."

---

* Thus, an act of Parliament passed in the fourth year of Edward IV. directed that all Irishmen within the English pale should adopt some English surname which should be either the name of a place, trade, color, or office.

† Celibacy (from cœlebs—unmarried) was preached by St. Anthony in Egypt, in 305. His only converts lived in caves until monasteries were founded. The doctrine was rejected in the Council of Nice, 325. Celibacy was enjoined on bishops only, in 692. The decree was opposed in England in 958-978. The Romish clergy generally were enjoined a vow of celibacy by Pope Gregory VII. in 1073-85, and its observance was established by the Council of Placentia in 1095. Marriage of the clergy was proposed, but negatived, at the Council of Trent in 1563. (Haydn's " Dict. of Dates.")—EDITOR.

82

2.

By F. MAX MULLER.

" The word parson comes from the Latin *persona*. In Latin, *persona* meant a mask made of thin wood or clay, such as was worn by the actors at Rome. Gellius informs us that a Latin grammarian, Gavius Bassus by name, who had written a learned work on the origin of words, derived *persona* from *personare*, to sound through. 'And because that mask makes the voice of the mouth clear and resonant, therefore it has been called *persona*.' Both the mask and its wearer came to be called *persona*, and hence a very important double development in the meanings of the word. While in some cases *persona* was used in the sense of the mask worn, we find it in others expressing the real character represented by the actor on the stage. When we read of *dramatis personæ*, we no longer think of masks, but of the real characters appearing in the play. After all, an actor, wearing the mask of a king, was, for the time being, a king, and thus *persona* came to mean the very opposite of mask, namely, a man's real nature and character. Thus Cicero, for instance, writes to Cæsar that his nature and person, or what would now be called his character, might fit him for a certain work. Nay, what is still more curious, *persona* slowly assumes the meaning of a great personage, or of a person of rank, and, in the end, of rank itself. This sense of *persona* prevailed during the Middle Ages, and continues to the present day. A man *magnæ personæ* means, in mediæval Latin, a man of great dignity. We read of *viri nobiles et personati*, also of *mercatores personati*, always in the sense of eminent and respected. In ecclesiastical language, *persona* soon took a technical meaning. *Personatus* meant not only *dignitas* in general, but it was used of those dignitaries who held a living, or several livings, but committed the actual cure of souls to a vicar. 'Persons are chiefly those who let their benefices and churches to be served by others.' These so-called *personæ* held very high rank. *Personæ habent dignitatem cum prerogativa in choro et capitulo.*" We read in a charter (anno 1227), 'A canon shall not have in our choir a stall in the row of the *personæ*, but shall have the first stall in the row of the priests.' As early as 1222, in a council held in Oxford, the question had to be discussed whether a vicar should fulfil the duties of the church or a *persona*. From this *persona* comes, no doubt, the modern name of parson, and it is strange that so learned a man as Blackstone should not have known this. For, though he knows that parson is derived from *persona*,* he thinks that he was called so because the church, which is an invisible body, was represented by his person. Blackstone, as a lawyer, was evidently thinking of another meaning which *persona* had assumed from a very early time. Anybody who had rights was, in legal language, a person, and slaves were said to have no person by law. In this sense, no doubt, the parson may be said to be the *persona* of his church, but this was not the historical origin of the ecclesiastical *persona*, as opposed to *vicarius*." (" Biographies of Words and the Home of the Aryas.")

* Thus, in the roll of possessions of the Abbey of Malmesbury, North Wiltshire (adjoining Oxfordshire), we find, A.D. 1307, the name of William le Person (English, Parsons) recorded as taxpayer to the Abbey. We further note, in Essex, the name of William Personne, gentleman usher of the Star Chamber, whose daughter Susanna was the wife of Sir Henry Maynard and the mother of Lord Maynard, baronet 1620.—EDITOR.

IV.

THE HONORABLE FAMILY OF PARSONS IN ENGLAND AND ITS CONNECTION BY MARRIAGE WITH SIR EDWARD PYNCHON, COUSIN OF WILLIAM PYNCHON, ESQ., FOUNDER OF SPRINGFIELD, MASS.

By ALBERT ROSS PARSONS.

" The honorable family of Parsons have been advanced to the dignity of viscounts and more lately earls of Ross." (Bishop Gibson, A. D. 1725, in 'Camden's Britannia').

" It does not appear that there has ever been any attempt to collect even the materials for a history of the English family of Parsons, notwithstanding there have been many individuals among them of great distinction, as knights, baronets, and noblemen." (New England Gen. Reg., 1847, p. 253.)

We learn from Guppy ("Homes of English Names," 1890) that Parsons is a striking example of a purely south of England name, not to be found north of the Wash. It is represented in most of the southern counties, but its great home is in Wilts, while it is also numerous in most of the counties around this centre, namely in Somerset, Dorset, Hants, Oxford, and Monmouth.

The following diagram represents approximately the relative positions and the latitude and longitude of the English shires in which the Parsons family has resided for 1,000 years or more. The figures in the squares show the number of persons of the name of Parsons to every 10,000 of population.

In order to realize the practical solidarity and near proximity to each other of the various branches of the Parsons family in England, it should be observed that the entire region represented in the said diagram is included in an area of about 200 miles east and west by 150 miles north and south,

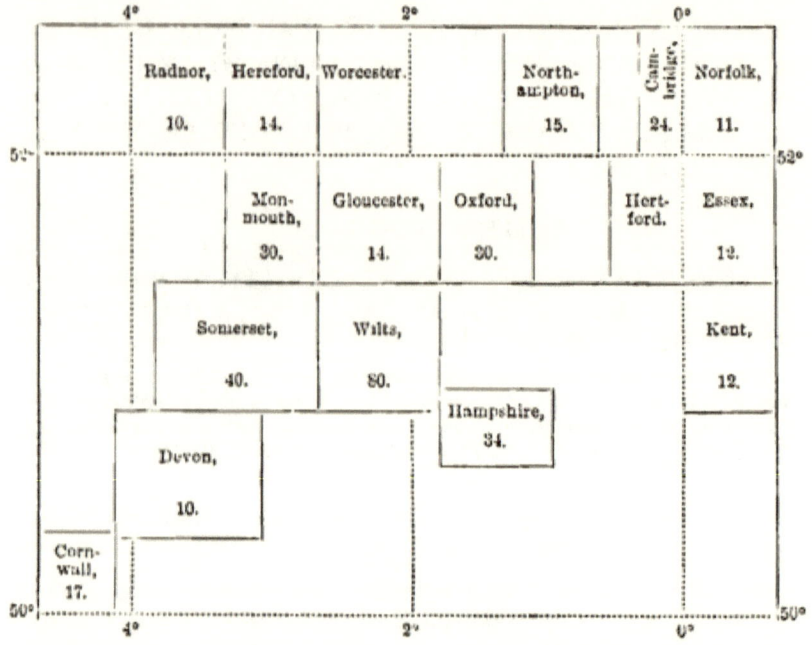

or less than one-half of the area of the New England States.
Thus, for instance, the Parsons of Oxfordshire and Devonshire, England, resided nearer to each other than the towns
of Springfield and Boston, Mass., in both of which places,
A.D. 1675, Cornet Joseph Parsons had residences, ware-
houses, and wharves, notwithstanding, at that time, outside
of scattered towns, New England was yet an unbroken wilderness. Emigrants *to* such a limited area of country as the lower
part of New England might be wholly unrelated to each other,
although they bore the same family name; but it would be
remarkable, indeed, if emigrants of the same family name *from*
so limited an area as that of the above handful of counties in
the South of England were not all more or less related as members of one and the same family of long-established prominence in the region whence they came.

In order to get a bird's-eye view of the ramifications of
the ancient family of Parsons in England, we may begin with
Herefordshire.

We note in this shire, in the Herald's visitation of 14 Edward I., as the most ancient representative of the family so

far discovered, the name of John Parsons of Cuddington, A.D. 1284. Two centuries later, A.D. 1481, Sir John Parsons was mayor of Hereford. In his armorial bearings is a leopard's head (symbolizing military service in the Orient) between three crosses (designating the crusades). The Parsons to whom this coat armor was originally granted may have gone to the Holy Land with Richard Cœur de Lion and Frederic Barbarossa in 1189, the last crusade that reached Palestine in force. This

PARSONS OF HEREFORD.
(A.D. 1096–1481.)

crusade, however, was a failure, as Cœur de Lion was only able to get within sight of Jerusalem, twenty miles away, without daring to attack the city, from which he retired, defeated, to imprisonment. Hence, in the light shed by the laws of heraldic symbolism upon the crusader's coat armor of Sir John Parsons, as it is further interpreted by the later arms of Sir Thomas Parsons of Oxfordshire, it is probable either, (a) that the original grantee was a knight who followed Robert of Normandy, son of William the Conqueror (1066), in the successful crusade of Godfrey of Bouillon, who, with one hundred thousand steel-clad knights, set out for the Holy Land in 1096, and, achieving the conquest of Jerusalem, set up in Palestine a Frank kingdom that stood until 1147; Godfrey being elected the first King of Jerusalem: or else (b) that he went with the expedition of Richard, Earl of Cornwall (brother of Henry III., and nephew of Richard the Lion-hearted), who, landing at Acre, "accompanied by the flower of the English chivalry," in 1239, remained in Palestine until the banner of the Cross was once more planted on the ruined walls of Jerusalem.* For,

* The crusading barons of England met at Northampton, and bound themselves at the altar, to lead their forces within the year (1238) to Palestine,

the arms of Sir Thomas Parsons of Oxford, which, like those of Sir John Parsons of Hereford, can only refer to the Crusades, place the leopard's head in the crest, surmounted by an eagle's thigh erased, symbolizing victory in the Orient, and display upon the coat armor two chevrons—a combination

PARSONS OF OXFORD.

signifying that the original grantee was eminent both as ecclesiastic and as warrior *—together with three eagles displayed,

taking a solemn oath " that they would not be hindered from fulfilling their honorable vow by the cavils of the Roman Church " (Et ne per cavillationes Romanæ Ecclesiaca honestum votum eorum impeditiretur . . . juraverunt omnes." Matt. Paris, 461-463). The renown of Earl Richard for personal prowess " struck the infidels with terror," and enabled him by their common awe of his name and reputation to extort from them a solemn and absolute cession of Jerusalem and the greater part of the territory of which the Latin kingdom there, in its best days, had ever consisted. Upon the execution of the treaty, Earl Richard quitted the shores of Palestine, and in his homeward progress through the states of Europe, was everywhere welcomed with honor as the deliverer of the Holy Sepulchre.

On his arrival in Palestine, Richard found that the Templars, and the Hospitallers had concluded discordant treaties with the Courts of Damascus and of Cairo, which by a single movement of the Christian host to Jaffa, he compelled the sultans of Damascus and of Cairo to abrogate. He had the satisfaction of receiving from the hands of the infidels all their Christian captives, among whom were thirty-three nobles, many Templars and Hospitallers, and five hundred knights and other crusaders.—EDITOR.

* The Crusaders' religious Order of the Knights Hospitallers, or Knights of St. John of Jerusalem, owed its origin to a hospice founded in Jerusalem in 1048, by merchants of Memphis, for the accommodation of pilgrims from Europe. An hospital was afterward added, which survived perhaps through the habitual respect of Mohammedans for charitable foundations. When Jerusalem fell into the hands of the Crusaders, A.D. 1099, the house was joyfully opened for the reception of wounded warriors, and many of the cavaliers joined the Order. In 1118, the Order of Knights Hospitallers of the order of St. John became a military order. The Crusaders of knightly rank who had enrolled themselves in the fraternity of the hospital *resumed their military, without discarding their religious garb and profession;* and thenceforth the banner and the battle-cry of the knights of St. John were seen and heard foremost and loudest in every encounter with the Paynim foe. The government of the Order was vested in the Grand-master and general council of the knights, all of whom were required to be of noble birth. When the

thus placing emphasis upon successive victories won. The arms of the earls of Rosse,* descended from Sir Richard Parsons of Norfolk, subsequently established in Ireland, bear three leopards' heads, while the crosses of the ancient crusader of Hereford reappear in the arms of the Parsons family of

PARSONS OF NORFOLK.

Radnorshire, Wales, whose connections with the Parsons of Essex and Devonshire will presently be shown, a further connection between this Parsons family in Wales, and the Oxfordshire Parsons, being indicated by the repeated appearance of the Welsh name Hugh in the Oxfordshire family.

PARSONS OF RADNOR.

Thus the heraldic indications of the Parsons arms and crest carry back the family patronymic, in connection with distinguished ecclesiastical and military services, to the time of William the Conqueror.

Adjoining Hereford, on the east, is Worcestershire, where,

Christians were driven from Palestine, the Knights of St. John settled in the island of Cyprus. In 1310 they departed to the island of Rhodes. From thence they went to Malta, which was given to them by Charles V. in 1530. Here their position has been retained to the present day and they bear the name of Knights of Malta. The Christian name, surname, and coat-of-arms of Sir John Parsons of Hereford, A.D. 1481, are all alike indicative of the period of military ecclesiasticism of the Crusade, and of the institution of the Order of Knights of St. John.—EDITOR.

* These earls take their title from Ross, in Wexford, the " e " being added by way of distinction from the Scottish earls of Ross.

prior to the time of Cromwell, Dorothy, daughter of Sir Charles Parsons, married Sir Charles Saunders, whose son, Sir Robert, married Arabella, daughter of Sir Marmaduke Humphreys and became ancestor of the Saunders' families of Devonshire and elsewhere.

The next county but one to the east of Worcestershire, is Northamptonshire where, about A.D. 1550, resided (1) Ralph Parsons, who had a son (2) John, who married the daughter of Esquire Cutler, and had a son (3) John of Boveny, who married Elizabeth, sole heiress of Sir John Kidderminster and had two sons; (4) I. Charles, b. 1625, d. without issue; (5) II. William, and three daughters. This William (5) married Elizabeth, daughter and heiress of Sir Lawrence Parsons, by whom he had two sons; one (6) a colonel, who died without issue, and the other, John (7), his successor.

William (5) was made a baronet by Charles II. He was somewhat conspicuous during the interregnum, as may be inferred from his giving a pass to a gentleman of the privy chamber to visit Ireland. This gentleman, being taken by the Parliament officers, was put to the rack.

Sixty miles farther east, in the county of Norfolk, toward the close of the sixteenth century, resided the Rt. Rev. Dr. Parsons, Lord Bishop of Norwich, who had three sons: I. Thomas, II. Sir William, III. Sir Lawrence. Of these sons, Sir William (II.) married the niece of Sir Geoffrey Lacy. Sir William was commissioner of plantations to Ireland under Queen Elizabeth in 1602; surveyor-general of Ireland in 1611; supervisor of crown lands (in conjunction with his brother Lawrence) in 1620; knighted in November of the same year; M. P. 1639; lord deputy 1640. From Sir Richard, the son of this Sir William Parsons, are descended the earls of Rosse.

Retracing our way, twenty miles west of Hereford is Radnorshire, where, in 1634, the high sheriff of the shire was Cecil Parsons, Esq., "descended paternally from the Parsons of Springfield, Essex Co." (the place of residence of William Pynchon, Esq., founder of Springfield, Mass.), "and maternally from the Jeffreys of Prior, Co. Brecon." This Jeffrey-Parsons descent reminds us that at Alphington, near Exeter, Devonshire, one hundred miles south of Radnor, was born, in

1631, Jeffrey Parsons, who came to America and settled at Gloucester, Mass. Meanwhile, it is but thirty miles from Alphington to the Torringtons, whence, according to Rev. Jonathan Parsons, came his grandfather, Deacon Benjamin Parsons, the brother of Cornet Joseph Parsons, of Springfield, Northampton, and Boston, Mass. Here is a clear connection, through Radnorshire, between the Parsons of Devonshire and those of Springfield, Essex, the seat of the Pynchon family.

In Devonshire, John Parsons was Burgess of Bideford in 1620. The daughter of the Mayor of Exeter, 1552, ——— Matthew, Esq., married W. Parsons, and Colonel Abednego Matthew, born 1629, married the daughter of Sir William Parsons of Black Torrington. Barton Bree Stapleton, b. September, 1771, married Sophia, daughter of William Parsons, Esq., of Plymouth, Devonshire.

Southeast of Herefordshire, where we found John Parsons, in the Herald's visitation of A.D. 1284, is Oxfordshire, in which appears the name of John Parsons, Forest of Wychwood, Oxford, 28 Edward I., A.D. 1300.

The name John Parsons survives in Oxfordshire in all branches of the family of Sir Thomas Parsons of Great Milton, who was knighted in 1634, by Charles I. From him were descended Sir John Parsons, Lord Mayor of London 1704, and Sir Humphrey Parsons, Lord Mayor in 1731 and again in 1740.

In the "New England Gen. Reg." for 1847 (p. 265), it is stated that "The grandfather of Sir Thomas Parsons was Thomas of Great Milton, who had three sons: I. Thomas, II. Hugh, and III. Richard. Richard (III.) had a son John, of London. Some of this family were among the early emigrants to America. The first of the name we find in New England is Cornet Joseph, Springfield, 1636. There appear, soon after, Hugh and Benjamin. And family tradition relates that Joseph and Benjamin were brothers, who, with other children, accompanied their father to New England, about the year 1630. It is probable they came over with Mr. Pynchon."

In connection with the family of William and Colonel John

Pynchon, and that of Cornet Joseph Parsons, whose respective wealth far exceeded that of all other inhabitants of early Springfield, there has been a persistent tradition that the Pynchons, of whom William was conspicuously prominent in the Massachusetts Bay Company,* and Cornet Joseph Parsons were in some way related.

It is well known that in the shadow of the Pynchons no one in early Springfield prospered greatly save Joseph Parsons, who, as a mere lad, was invited by Pynchon to sign, as witness, the Indian deed of lands. From the circumstances of the case it would seem to follow either that, his youth being considered, Joseph Parsons was, next to the Pynchons, the ablest business man in Springfield; or else that, for some sufficient reason, the Pynchons, who dominated and literally outstripped everyone else in the town, must have highly favored young Joseph Parsons † in permitting him so to benefit

* " William Pynchon was a man of broad and aggressive thought; he was remarkably complex in character. He loved both money and adventure; he also loved the Gospel in its purity; he hated political corruption, and at the same time he distrusted that phase of Puritanism which drifted away from royalty. What was the real motive that led him to leave the quiet walks of his Essex estate and to sail for the New World we will leave others to conjecture. After Charles Stuart had risen from his bed, where he had fallen in tears on hearing of the assassination of Buckingham, he continued the fight for the divine right of kings by adopting two equally memorable policies. The very month in which the king dissolved the Parliament which had bolted its door against the royal messenger, he signed the famous Massachusetts Bay charter, setting over, in liberal terms, the Massachusetts wilderness to Endicott, Pynchon and their associates. Mr. Pynchon's importance in the enterprise is evident from the first. He was not only an incorporator, but was named by the king a provisional assistant pending the regular organization under the charter. In May, 1629, he paid his " adventure money," and in October of that year he was placed on the committee to carry out the vote of the company to transfer the historic charter to America. The fleet of four vessels, which sailed in April, 1630, bearing the charter with the seal of England attached thereto by strings of braided silk, also bore Mr. Pynchon and his feeble wife with four children. He started a plantation at Roxbury, aided in establishing a church there, attended the first General Court at Charlestown, and was made treasurer of the colony. He planned at once an extensive beaver trade, and secured a license to trade in beaver-skins with the Indians. Many causes conspired to persuade him of the advantage of a still deeper taste of the Wilderness, and he resolved to settle in the Connecticut Valley." (Green's " Official History of Springfield.")

† This inference is strengthened by the peculiar fact, that after 1636, Cornet Joseph Parsons' name, unlike the names of other young settlers, disappears completely from the Springfield records for a period of ten years. In 1646, however, he suddenly reappears in the records and is thenceforth conspicuously active at Springfield, Northampton, Northfield, Boston, etc., until the very close of his life. During that long period of disappearance, obviously

by his own undoubted abilities that he became and " for half a century remained the richest man in the Connecticut Valley " (Dr. Holton), the " Worshipfull Col. John Pynchon " himself, perhaps, not excepted.

The tradition of a Pynchon-Parsons connection is further supported by the coincidence that (according to Green's " Official History of Springfield, Mass."), at the time when young Joseph Parsons appears in Springfield with the elder Pynchon, a younger son of Pynchon was in the Barbadoes, where a branch of the Parsons family of Great Milton, Oxfordshire, was among the earliest and most influential settlers, one of the Barbadoes settlements being named Parsons after this branch.

Hitherto, however, it has escaped notice that the Herald's visitations of Essex in 1612 and 1634 disclose a connection such as has always been surmised to have existed between the families of Parsons and Pynchon, namely, one by marriage. It is as follows:

William Hone, of London, one of the judges of Guildhall, had two sons, Thomas Hone, gent., and John Hone, doctor of civil law. Of these two brothers, viz., Thomas and John Hone, the son of Thomas, namely, William Hone, Esq., counsellor of the law, married Elizabeth Parsons, daughter of Thomas Parsons, gent., of Stortford, Essex; while the son of John, namely, Bartholomew Hone, married Jane Pynchon, the sister of Sir Edward Pynchon, kt., of Writtles, Essex, and first cousin of William Pynchon of Springfield, Essex, and Springfield, Mass. Thus Elizabeth, daughter of Thomas Parsons of Essex, was the sister-in-law of William Pynchon's first cousins Sir Edward and Jane Pynchon. Of this connection William Pynchon could not have failed to be cognizant. We have seen that William Pynchon of Springfield, Essex, was a puritan. We now note that among the pilgrims of the congregation of Rev. John Robinson at Leyden, prior to the sailing of the Mayflower, was Joseph Parsons of Colchester, Essex (father (?) or uncle (?) of Cornet Joseph). At Springfield, Mass., William Pynchon was a fur-trader. Cornet

he forfeited nothing in the way of a sure footing for his subsequent success; for upon his reappearance in 1646 he entered at once upon his career of remarkable prosperity.

Joseph Parsons also became a fur-trader, and Pynchon's successor in the trade.

At the same time we find recorded in Essex the marriage of Abigail, daughter of John Parsons. Cornet Joseph and Benjamin Parsons of Springfield, Mass., and Thomas Parsons* of Windsor, Conn., all had daughters named Abigail, and both Cornet Joseph and Thomas had sons named John, while the name of Richard Parsons, who went to Windsor, Conn., and returned to England (Savage: "Gen. Dict."), is that of several of the first earls of Rosse, originally from Norfolk, adjacent to Essex, England.

The only supposition capable of harmonizing the known factors of this Pynchon-Parsons problem, would seem to be, that Joseph Parsons and Pynchon's younger son left England at about the same time to seek their fortunes, young Parsons joining his Pynchon connections at Springfield, and young Pynchon accompanying or following his Parsons connections to the Barbadoes. Subsequently, the prospects of Cornet Joseph became sufficiently promising to induce his father (*vide* letter of Rev. Jonathan Parsons, quoted in the preceding *exposé* of Chester's alleged Parsons pedigree) to come from Devonshire to visit the settlements at Windsor, Hartford, and Springfield, bringing with him Joseph's brothers, Benjamin, Thomas of Windsor, and perhaps Samuel, subsequently of Easthampton, Long Island. Their Devonshire connection, Jeffrey Parsons, went first to the Barbadoes, and then settled at Gloucester, Mass.

Since this supposition fulfils all the requirements of a sound scientific hypothesis, it is entitled to be permitted to stand, pending the discovery of additional and determining facts in the case.

The England descent and affiliations of Cornet Joseph Parsons, a founder of Springfield, Northampton, and Northfield,

---

* Thomas is the distinguishing Christian name of the Parsons family of Oxfordshire, London, and the Barbadoes. In the churchyard at Great Torrington, Devonshire, are the names of Thomasine, daughter of Walter Parsons, Ambrose, son of William, Richard, son of Richard, etc. (See "New England Genealogical Register.") Meanwhile, John Parsons, sometime the celebrated organist of Westminster Abbey, had Thomasine, William, etc. The unusual name, Thomasine, thus forms an additional link between the Oxfordshire, Devonshire, and London Parsons families.

Mass., being thus indicated, this chapter may fittingly close with the following,—

ADDITIONAL ENGLISH PARSONS NOTES.

1290.—Walter Parsons, a resident of Mulso in Ireland. How long before this he or his ancestors went there we know not.

1481.—Sir John Parsons, mayor of Hereford.

1546.—Robert, afterward the noted Jesuit, was born this year, and died April 18, 1610. His father lived near Bridgewater, England, at a place called Netherstoway. Robert was educated at Balliol College, Oxford, and was early distinguished for his abilities, but being accused of some irregularities he forsook his country and resided for a time at Antwerp, Louvain, Padua, Rome, Paris, and Valladolid. Becoming a convert to the Romish faith, he propagated that doctrine with all his ability, and was no small instrument in stirring up the vassals of Philip II. to attempt the conquest of England.

He established an English college at Rome and another at Valladolid, for such of his countrymen as might follow him, or come otherwise into exile. He published several works, but that by which he is best known is "Leicester's Commonwealth" —a work of great ability. And although the pen of Sir Philip Sidney was exercised in its refutation, he is not considered to have completely effected his object. To the original edition of Father Robert's work is appended a poem entitled "Leicester's Ghost," a great literary curiosity. The following is an extract:

Let no man think I exorcised the Ghost
Of this great Peere that sleepeth in the dust,
Or conjured up his spirit to his cost
To presse with dispraise or praise unjust,
I am not partiall, but give him his due,
And to his soul I wish eternall health,
Ne do I thinke all written tales are true,
That are inserted in his commonwealth;
What others wrot before I do survive,
But am not like to them incenst with hate,
And as I plainely write, so do I strive
To write the truth, not wronging his estate,
Of whom it may bee said and censured well,
Hee both in vice and vertue did excell.

" Parsons, the wily Jesuit, was so doubtful how the Lady Arabella Stuart, when young, stood toward Catholicism, that he describes her religion to be as tender, green, and flexible, as is her age and sex, and to be wrought hereafter and settled according to future events and times." (Disraeli, " Curiosities of Literature.")

1556.—Francis was Vicar of Rothwell in Nottinghamshire. There is a wood called Parsons's wood in the hundred of Nassaburgh, in the same county.

1569.—Robert Parsons was organist of Westminster Abbey. He was a gentleman of the Chapel Royal, in the reign of Queen Elizabeth, and was drowned at Newark-upon-Trent in 1569. Many of his compositions are extant in manuscript and some of them have been spoken of in terms of high commendation. The following epitaph on Parsons is preserved in Camden's Remains:

> " Death passing by, and hearing Parsons play,
>   Stood much amazed at his depth of skill;
> And said, ' This artist must with me away,'
>   For death bereaves us of the better still.
> But let the choir, while he leaves time, sing on,
> For Parsons rests, his service being done."

1618.—Bartholomew Parsons appears as the author of three sermons—" First Fruits of the Gentiles," " Assize Sermon," and " Dorcas, or a Perfect Patterne of a True Disciple."

1624.—Sir Laurence Parsons, Puisne Baron of the Exchequer, Ireland.

1634.—Sir Thomas Parsons of Great Milton, Oxfordshire, knighted.

1640.—Sir William Parsons, Lord Lieutenant and Justice of Ireland. (This was eight years before Cromwell was appointed to the same office.)

1672.—Prior to this time Andrew Parsons, Gent., was of Somersetshire, and Phillip Parsons, Gent., of Worcestershire.

1690.—Philip Denzill Parsons, knight, sheriff of the county of Surrey.*

1704.—Sir John Parsons, Lord Mayor of London.

* " The sheriff of a county was a person of high consideration, called *spectabilis* in the old deeds, a ' man to be looked at '; a title intermediate between *illustris* and *clarissimus*. Under Edward II., the office became a royal emanation." (Victor Hugo: " The Man who Laughs.")

1731 and 1741.—Sir Humphrey Parsons, Lord Mayor of London.

1759.—Major-General John Parsons.

1767.—James Parsons, M.D., Fellow of the Royal and Antiquary Societies of London, published "The Remains of Japhet," being historical inquiries into the affinity and origin of the European languages.

1768.—Sir William Parsons, doctor of music, was from a very early period of his life instructed in the science of music. He attained the first rudiments of his professional knowledge in Westminster Abbey under the tuition of Dr. Cooke. Arduous in the pursuit of his scientific researches, he, in the year 1768, travelled in Italy to complete his musical education. We have not learned the exact time of his return to England, but find that on the death of Stanley, an event which happened in the year 1786, Parsons was appointed master and conductor of his majesty's band of musicians.

In the year 1790 he received from the university of Oxford the degree of doctor of music. He next went to Dublin during the administration of Earl Camden, in the year 1795, when that nobleman conferred upon him the honor of knighthood. In 1796 he was appointed by the Queen to instruct the princesses in music. In the same year his name was inserted in the commission of the peace for the county of Middlesex, in consequence of which he sat for several years at the public office, Bow Street.*

(Salisbury & Co., "History of Music," London, 1824.)

* In 1807, Sir William Parsons published a collection of poems in two volumes, concluding with the following sentiment:
"Thus we play the fool with the Time, and the spirits of the wise sit in the clouds and mock us" (Prince Hal).
Sir William's poetic confession is contained in the following,—

SONNET.
" O'er half the convex world the ocean spreads,
    Vast in its range and awful in its form;
The wild winds rage, the billows heave their heads,
    The calm, inconstant—dreadful is the storm!
The placid stream, in narrower channel, glides,
    With balmy breath the light-winged zephyrs play,
Green are its banks, unruffled are its tides,
    And shelt'ring groves o'erhang its silent way!
So Fame expanded bears an ample breast,
    Swept by the wild winds of the critic's rage;
So glides the humbler Bard, obscurely blest,
    Who bounds to Friendship's eye the sportive page.
Let bolder prows the boist'rous deep explore,
    I love the placid stream, the silent shore!"

To this sonnet he appends the following note: "When the author wrote

1806.—Sir Laurence Parsons, Commissioner of the Treasury for Ireland.

1813.—Right Reverend John Parsons, D.D., Lord Bishop of Peterborough (the same, Dean of Bristol, 1810).

1840.—The Right Honorable and Lord Laurence Parsons, Fourth Earl of Rosse, Knight of St. Patrick, Doctor Civil Law, LL.D., Fellow Royal Society, Irish Representative Peer, Lord Lieutenant Kings Co., High Sheriff, Chancellor of Dublin University, President Royal Dublin Society; seat, Birr Castle, Parsonstown, Ireland; Womersley Park, Pontefract, York; Carlton Club. Died, 1894. Son of Third Earl, President Royal Society, and a distinguished astronomer (" Lord Rosse's mammoth Telescope "). Heir; William Edward Parsons, Lord Oxmanton, b. 1873.

1855.—Rear-Admiral Robert White Parsons, retired.

1863.—Lieutenant-General James Parsons, C. B. (the same, Major-General, 1854).

1883.—Major-General Needham Thompson Parsons.

1886.—Major-General Clifford Parsons.

1897.—The Hon. Charles Algernon Parsons' invention, " the steam turbine-driven boat Turbinia made the speed of

this sonnet, he had a great aversion to publication of anything. His readers are at liberty to compare him to Benedick, who wisely remarked, ' When I said I would die a bachelor, I did not think I would live till I were married.' (' Much Ado About Nothing '—a title which well applies to Poetry, and to most other human pursuits)."

Sir William's political confession may be discerned in his—

SONNET ON LEAVING WEIMAR IN SAXONY, 1790.

Αγλαισεται δε και,
Μουσικας εν αωτω
Οια παισομεν φιλαν
Ανδες αυφι θαμα
Τραπεδαν. (Pindar, 1 Olymp.)

" Can I, by early independence train'd
  A stubborn foe to forms and etiquette,
Who long have bow'd, obsequious, nor complain'd,
  Forsake a Court—and own a deep regret?
Adieu! the spot, where Sov'reigns stoop to please,
Where, as of old, round Hiero's festive board,
Circles the harp, and triumphs letter'd ease,*
  And Genius feels his ancient rights restor'd!
Oft shall the Muse, with fond remembrance, tell
  With whom I stray'd these tasteful paths along,
Oft on the tender tales of Goethe dwell,
  Schiller's bold scenes, and Wieland's Attic song!
And, parting now, I scarce refrain from tears,
Here have I loiter'd months—and wish'd them years! "

* " Men of letters were on a much better footing at Weimar than in any other part of Germany. . . . The Duke has laid out a garden with more taste than the author has seen in any other part of the Continent."—Editor.

·32¾ knots an hour in an official trial in England on April 10th. This is about 37½ statute miles an hour.

" Turbinia is but 100 feet long and of 44½ tons displacement. It did not seem possible that a boat of these dimensions could be driven at such a terrific rate of speed by any sort of engine that could be floated in her, and incredulity was felt here until a report of the proceedings of a meeting of the Institution of Naval Architects, held in London at the beginning of the second week in April, was received. It contained a paper, read before the institution on April 8, by the Hon. Charles Algernon Parsons, the inventor of the engines which were used in the boat, and he gave a detailed account of the Turbinia and her performances.

" Mr. Parsons is an engineer of high repute and comes of an ancestor who did much in his time for science. Mr. Parsons is the youngest brother of the Earl of Rosse and a son of the third Earl of Rosse, the builder of the greatest reflecting tele-scope that was ever constructed. This was the great star-gaz-ing instrument, so big that a tall man could walk upright with-in its tube, which was set up a generation ago at Parsonstown, Ireland, the seat of the Earl of Rosse."

PARSONS ARMS.

" The crest is the highest part of the ornaments of a Shield of Arms. Its origin is probably more ancient than that of other heraldic bearings, since even the heroes of the Iliad are described to us as wearing ' crested helms.' The right to wear them was esteemed a very great distinction in the early days of Heraldry, because they could only be acquired by those who had, as Knights, seen actual service in the field. They were honourable distinctions conferred upon the officers only, and not upon the men. Coat armour became hereditary in the reign of Henry III., and crests began to be generally worn by Knights; they are thus purely of military origin. Ladies can neither bear, inherit, nor transmit them, and this rule is, and has always been, in force. Hence the only possible right a man can have to more than one crest is where more than one has been granted to his paternal ancestors." (Worthy's " Prac-tical Heraldry.")

Parsons. Viscount and Earl of Rosse (extinct 1764), con-firmed by St. George. Ulster, 1682, to Sir Richard Parsons, created 1718, Baron of Oxmantown, and Viscount Rosse. Gu. three leopard's faces or, Crest, a halbert's head or, embrued gu. Supporters—two leopards ar. spotted sa. collared gu.

Parsons, Earl of Rosse. Gu. three leopard's faces ar. Crest—

Out of a ducal coronet or, a cubit arm holding a sprig of roses all ppr. Supporters—Two leopards ar. pellettee each gorged with a collar gu. charged with four bezants. Motto—Pro Deo et Rege.

Parsons co. Hereford. Gu. a leopard's face between three crosses pattee fitchee at the foot ar. Crest—a halbert headed ar. embrued gu.

Parsons. Sir Thomas Parsons of Great Milton, Oxford, 1636, Sir John Parsons, Lord Mayor of London 1704, and Humphrey Parsons, Lord Mayor, 1731. Gu. two chevronels erm. between three eagles display or. Crest—An eagle's leg erased at the thigh or, standing on a leopard's face gu.

Parsons. Island of Barbadoes; borne by the Rev. John Parsons, M.A., of Begbrook House, co. Gloucester, vicar of Marden, co. Wilts, son of the late Daniel Parsons, Esq., M.D., of Barbadoes. Gu. two chevronels erm. between three eagles displ. or. Crest—A demi griffin sergeant ar. beaked and armed gu.

Parsons (Langley, co. Buckingham, Epsom, co. Surrey, and Stanton-on-the-Wolds, co. Nottingham, bart. extinct 1812; this family obtained a baronetcy in 1661, and became extinct in the male line on the death of Sir Mark Parsons, 4th and last baronet). Ar. a chev. betw. three holly leaves vert. Crest—Upon a chapeau gu. turned up erm. a griffin's head erased ar. beaked also gu.

Parsons, co. Buckingham. Az. on a chev. ar. betw. three oak leaves or. as many crosses gu. Crest—On a chapeau az. turned up erm. an eagle's head erased ar. ducally crowned or. charged on the neck with a cross gu.

Parsons. C'lanclewedog, co. Radnor. Quarterly, 1st, or. a chev. betw. four crosses crosslet fitchee gu. for Parsons; 2d, ar. two lions pass. guard. az armed and langued gu., for Hanmer; 3d., erm. a lion ramp. sa. armed and langued gu. a canton checquey or and gu., for Jeffreys; 4th, gu. three owls ar for Morgan. Crest—A demi-lion ramp. gu. Motto—Quid retribuam.

Parsons. Steyning, co. Sussex; granted April 23, 1661. Per fesse az. and sa three suns or. Crest—A garb of quatrefoils vert, banded or.

Parsons. Az. two swords in saltire blades ar. hilts and pomels or. pierced through a human heart ppr. in chief a cinque-foil az. Crest—A tower ar.

Parsons. Of Overbury, Offenham; also of Hemmerton Court, co. Gloucester, az. a chev. erm. betw. three trefoils slipped, ar.

AMERICAN PARSONS' ARMS AND CONNECTIONS.

Of the above arms, those of Sir Thomas Parsons of Great Milton, and Sir John Parsons and Sir Humphrey Parsons of London, were "stated by the Rev. Jonathan Parsons in 1769, in writing to his son, Major-General Samuel Holden Parsons, to have been the same claimed by some of the American family. Professor Theophilus Parsons, of Harvard University, in presenting Lewis B. Parsons, in 1867, with a copy of his memoir of his father, Chief Justice Parsons, wrote in it, ' from your friend and kinsman,' and stated that his family" (that of Jeffrey Parsons) " came from the same place in England as did Cornet Joseph Parsons, only at a later date, emigrating first to the Barbadoes and then to Gloucester, Mass." (Papers of Major-General Lewis Baldwin Parsons, privately printed.)

As the grandson of Cornet Joseph Parsons' younger brother, Deacon Benjamin Parsons, the Rev. Jonathan Parsons, born at West Springfield, Mass., November 30, 1705, was in a position to know from which branch of the English Parsons family his ancestors derived their descent.

V.

PARSONS GENEALOGIES.*

EDITED BY ALBERT ROSS PARSONS.

" A lively desire of knowing and recording our ancestors so generally pre-
vails, that it must depend on the influence of some common principle in the
minds of men. We seem to have lived in the person of our forefathers; our
calmer judgment will rather tend to moderate than suppress the pride of an
ancient and worthy race." (Gibbon's Memoirs.)

" The whole conception of immortality undergoes an important change if we
regard the personal consciousness, with its ego, as a mere partial and temporary limitation of a larger self, the growth of many seasons [generations],
as it were, of earthly life. The doctrine of transcendental individuality does
not conceive the soul to be wholly plunged into the successive bodies it con-
structs. We must not look for the consciousness of identity in the leaves of
successive seasons [generations] but in the tree which puts them forth. The
interest of the tree in last year's leaves is just the nutriment and growth
it derived from them. The experience and activity of one of our objective
life-times will be assimilated for results quite other, perhaps, than those
which the interest of the contracted ego proposed, and probably bear but a
minute proportion to the gradually accumulated psychical contents of the
whole individual. The constant aim of ethics is to bring the personal ego
to the point of view of the transcendental subject, to which the mere pleas-
ures of that ego are indifferent." (Du Prel: " Philosophy of Mysticism," pp.
xviii, xvii, xx.)

" All of us, and every one of us, ought to know how we have come to be
what we are, so that each generation need not start again from the same point
and toil over the same ground, but, profiting by the experience of those who
came before, may advance toward higher points and nobler aims. . . .
What history has to teach us before all and everything, is our own ante-
cedents, our own ancestors, our own descent. . . . The past is darkness
to him who does not know what those who came before him have done for
him, and he would probably care little to do anything for those who are to
come after him. Life would be to him a chain of sand, while it ought to be a
kind of electric chain that makes our hearts tremble and vibrate with the
most ancient thoughts of the past, as well as the most distant hopes of the
future." (F. Max Müller, 1889.)

" To the careful student of social forces and results, the family history
will plainly exhibit such facts as these: that families continue to bear, as
such, definite physical and mental characteristics from generation to genera-

* A plan has been arranged by which additions may be made to these
genealogies at any time by addressing the Editor, in care of the New York
Historical Society.

tion; that these are maintained and improved in their quality by thorough education, and that they inevitably degenerate without it; that hardships bravely met in one generation exalt the privileges and surroundings of those succeeding; that the physical and social surroundings of a family exert a long and a strong influence upon its whole future history. It makes generally quite as great a difference in the style of growth that a family exhibits, and often through long periods of time, where and how it is placed for its natural manifestation of itself, as where a plant is set, whether in much sunshine or in little, and with or without much exposure to sudden chills and storms." (Professor Dwight.)

I. EARLY EMIGRANTS FROM ENGLAND OF THE NAME OF PARSONS.

1. To America.

In early records the name Virginia does not necessarily refer to the region to which that name is now restricted. The purpose of the Pilgrims was to settle in the domain of the South Virginia Company "somewhere between the Delaware and Hudson rivers." But the captain of the Mayflower professed to be unable to land there. Hence, while lying off Cape Cod, November 11, 1620, the Pilgrims formed a body politic under a social compact to plant the first colony in "Northern Virginia," i.e., the present New England. It thus appears that the name "New England," given by Captain John Smith in 1614 to the northern coast, was, in 1620, not yet in general use. After the Pilgrims had officially styled the place where they landed Northern Virginia, naturally it would long continue to be customary to designate briefly ships sailing for the Pilgrim settlement as bound for Virginia. (See "The Colonies"; Thwaite.)

Joseph Parsons, of Colchester, near Springfield, Essex, England, the home of the Puritan * William

* "The most interesting phase which the Reformation anywhere assumes . . . is that of Puritanism . . . which came forth as a real business of the heart; and has produced in the world very notable fruit. . . . Look at American Saxondom; and at that little Fact of the sailing of the Mayflower, two hundred years ago, from Delft Haven in Holland! Were we of open sense as the Greeks were, we had found a Poem here; one of Nature's own Poems, such as she writes in broad facts over great continents. For it was properly the beginning of America; there were straggling settlers in America before . . . but the soul of it was first this. . . . These men, I think, had a work! The weak thing becomes strong one day if it be a true thing. Puritanism was only despicable, laughable then; but nobody

Pynchon and his cousin Thomas Parsons, was in the congregation of the Rev. John Robinson at Leyden, Holland. The Rev. John Robinson and Joseph Parsons were among those members who did not sail in the Mayflower. This Joseph Parsons is held by some to have been the father, and by others the uncle, of,—

1   CORNET JOSEPH PARSONS, who is the first of the name of Parsons in the New England records.

2   John Parsons sailed in the Marygold, 1619, and was enrolled February 16, 1623, among those then living at the eastern shore of (South) Virginia.

3   (a) Thomas Parsons, aged 30, sailed January 2, 1634, in the Bonaventura, bound from London to Virginia. (b) Thomas Parsons owned an estate in Boston in 1639. Savage says he may have been the same as (c) Thomas Parsons of Dedham and Medfield. (d) Thomas Parsons married Lydia Brown at Windsor, June 28, 1641. Stiles says he may have been the same as Thomas (a) above. He was an owner in Palisado Plot, 1650; agreed to keep the Rivulet Ferry, 1652; served in the Pequot War and received fifty acres for services then rendered; and died September 23, 1661. According to the foregoing data, Thomas (a), (b), (c), and (d) may all be one and the same person.

4   (a) William Parsons sailed from Southampton, April, 1635. (b) William Parsons, a "Fifth Monarchy man," was admitted to the church in Boston, April 20, 1644. Savage says he may be the same as William (a).

5   Henry Parsons, aged 14, and—

6   Phillipp Parsons, aged 10, both sailed, June 23, 1635, in the America from Gravesend (a port on the Thames for Essex) bound for Virginia.

7   (a) Joseph Parsons, aged 18, sailed July 4, 1635, in the Transport, from Gravesend (a port for Essex), bound for Virginia. On account: i, of the correspondence of his age with that of (1) Cornet Joseph Parsons;

can manage to laugh at it now. Puritanism has got weapons and sinews: it has fire-arms, war-navies; it has cunning in its ten fingers, strength in its right arm; it can steer ships, fell forests, remove mountains; it is one of the strongest things under this sun at present!" (Carlyle: "Heroes," IV.)

ii, of the date of his sailing; iii, of his embarking from
a port near the Essex home of Pynchon; and iv, by tradi-
tion, Joseph (a) is identified* with (b) Cornet Joseph
Parsons, (1) who, in his 18th year, signed as witness the
Indian deed of land at Springfield, to William Pynchon,
July 15, 1636.

8   (a) Robert Parsons was made a freeman of Lynn, 1638.
Savage says he may have been the same as (b) Robert
Parsons who died at New Haven prior to 1648.

9   (a) Richard Parsons was at Windsor before 1640;
went to New Haven and probably returned to England.
(b) Richard Parsons appears in the Suffolk deeds, 1640,
1642, and 1643, as "captain and commander" of the
"pinnace St. John," also styled "a certain ffrigot called
the John." According to the data aforesaid, Richard
(a) and Richard (b) may be the same.

10   (a) Hugh Parsons appears on the Springfield Records
in 1645, when he married Mary Lewis of Wales. He
died, June 18, 1675, at Watertown. (b) Hugh Parsons,
born 1613, was made freeman of Portsmouth, R. I., in
1663; he enlisted in a troop of horse August 10, 1667,
and died in 1684. His family became extinct.

11   Samuel Parsons, aged 20, from the New Haven Colony, united with the settlers at East Hampton, L. I., in
1650; he died October 3, 1728. The names of his children suggest that he was a younger brother of Thomas
(3, d) and Cornet Joseph (1).

12   Deacon Benjamin Parsons, brother of Cornet Joseph
(1), was one of a committee to organize a new settlement at Longmeadow, 1651; he married, i, Sarah Vore
of Windsor, November 6, 1653, and ii, Sarah Heald
Leonard of Springfield, February 21, 1677; he died
August 24, 1689.

13   Jeffrey Parsons, born at Alphington, Devonshire,
England, 1631, was at Gloucester, Mass., 1657, in which
year he married Sarah Vinson; he died August, 1689.

14   Mark Parsons, of Sagadhock, Maine, appeared, with
other inhabitants of the east side of the Kennebec

* See note on page 118.

River, to take the oath of supremacy and allegiance September 5, 1665.

15   George Parsons of Boston, Mass., married Eliza Wheelwright, and had a son, Joseph, born August 18, 1667.

16   John Parsons, of York, had a son, John, born July 31, 1677; took oath of allegiance, 1681.

2. To the Barbadoes.

17   William Parsons, Barbadoes, buried in the parish of St. Michaels, January 4, 1679.

18   (a) Edward Parsons was buried in the parish of St. Michaels, Barbadoes, August 5, 1679. (b) Edward Parsons and wife, of St. Michaels parish, Barbadoes, registered in 1680 as having two children, two hired servants, and twelve slaves; February 22, 1692, Edward Parsons, Esq., was appointed Secretary of St. Christopher's, Nevis, Mountserrat and Antegua, and other Leeward Carribee islands.

19   Frances Parsons sailed May 8, 1679, from the Barbadoes for London.

20   Captain Daniel Parsons, at the Barbadoes, bought two convicted political prisoners ("rebels") from Weymouth, March 25, 1685.

21   Thomas Parsons was transported to the Barbadoes for complicity in the Duke of Monmouth's Protestant uprising, September 23, 1685.

22   John Parsons was transported from Taunton to the Barbadoes, October 12, 1685, for complicity in the Duke of Monmouth's Protestant uprising.

II. DESCENDANTS OF CORNET JOSEPH PARSONS.

1

Cornet Joseph Parsons "was born about 1618, according to his testimony given in court in 1661-2, when he stated that he was 17 years old at the time when he witnessed the Indian deed of lands at Springfield, Mass., in 1636." * September 24, 1653, the Indians gave a deed of the land at Northampton to Capt. John Pynchon, and shortly after Cornet Joseph Parsons removed here from Springfield. May 15, 1675, he purchased a warehouse and dock, with privileges, in Boston, where he had a dwelling-house and lot in Marlborough Street. Thus he became a merchant of Boston. His name appears on the rolls of the Ancient and Honorable Artillery Company of Boston in 1679.† November 20, 1679, he bought a home lot from Capt. John Pynchon in Springfield, where he died October 9, 1683. On November 26, 1646, at Hartford, Conn., he married MARY BLISS, who was born in 1620 and died at Springfield, January 29, 1711-12.‡

CHILDREN OF CORNET JOSEPH AND MARY BLISS PARSONS.

23 I. JUDGE AND CAPTAIN JOSEPH PARSONS, b. 1647, d. Nov. 29, 1729, m. March 17, 1669, ELIZABETH, dau. of Elder John and Abigail (Ford), STRONG of Northampton. She was born at Windsor, Conn., Feb. 24, 1648, and

---

* Thus writes Mrs. Frances Holton, widow of Dr. David P. Holton, and his collaborator in the Winslow and the Parsons genealogical searches. Mr. H. M. Burt has failed to find this evidence in the Springfield Records. Whereupon Mrs. Holton makes the following statement: " The items we gathered were hastily written with pencil, but were always carefully compared with the originals before leaving them. I regret to find that the authority was not noted down in this case, but do not doubt the fact." General Lewis Baldwin Parsons's records state that Cornet Joseph thus testified at the March term of court at Northampton in 1662.

† A revised roll of this company, recently printed, transfers this membership to " Joseph Parson, merchant of Boston, who married Bethia Brattle." In 1679, there were two persons in Boston named Parsons and Parson, viz., Cornet Joseph, and Joseph, born August 18, 1667 (Savage). Cornet Joseph did not marry Bethia Brattle, who was born December 13, 1666, married 1685, and died July, 1690, aged twenty-four (Savage). In 1679, when the name of Joseph Parsons appears on the above roll, the other Joseph Parson, and future husband of Bethia Brattle, was twelve years old. Obviously this was not the merchant of Boston then enrolled.

‡ The Bliss family was reported to have been great friends of Oliver Cromwell, after whom one or more grandsons were named. Thomas and Margaret Bliss first settled at Braintree, Mass. Leaving there in 1636, they journeyed through the wilderness, living on wild berries and the milk of their cows, until they reached the site of the present city of Hartford. There the father died. Two of his sons joined a company that settled at Springfield. Thomas

died May 12, 1736. They celebrated their golden wedding. Joseph Parsons, Jr., went as a boy with his father to Northampton. He was one of the earliest lawyers in Western Massachusetts, several years justice of the peace at Northampton, and twenty-three years judge of the Hampton County Court, being first commissioned October 16, 1696. He was a deputy to the General Court fourteen years, twelve from Northampton and two from Springfield, beginning in 1693. In 1696, and again in 1718, he was appointed Commissioner of Oyer and Terminer. He inherited valuable lands at Boston and Northampton from his father, and was a man of unusual wealth and prominence. He held many commissions from the General Court for public improvements in his part of the colony.* Elizabeth Strong Parsons was the daughter of Elder John Strong, the progenitor of the Strong family in America.†

Bliss was the first to introduce potatoes. Previous to this the English turnip occupied the place on the table now accorded to the potato. ("History of Brimfield," p. 371.)

Margaret, the widow of Thomas Bliss, was "very resolute and capable. Two or three years after her husband's death she removed, with all of her children except Thomas and Ann, to Springfield, where she died August 28, 1684. Of her nine children, Ann married, in 1642, Robert Chapman of Saybrook, and Mary married Cornet Joseph Parsons."

* "Esquire Joseph Parsons was very prominent as a lawyer and justice of the peace, was first judge of Hampshire county court, 1698, of extensive business, largely connected with political and military life." ("Northampton Antiquities," Clark.) In 1711, he was commissioned by Governor Dudley as captain of a foot company in the New Hampshire regiment commanded by Colonel Partridge.

"In the year 1708, Joseph Parsons was directed to intercede with the governor against the proposed calling away of Springfield men to defend other towns, and to ask for a garrison for Springfield itself."

"At a Legall meeting of the freeholders and other Inhabitants, May ye 16, 1706: It was agreed and voted; that the Selectmen should, in ye name of ye Town, request, or desire the Worshipfull Joseph Parsons Esq. to be helpfull to you, in yt affair in refference to their taxes, and bounds, wch hath so often been managed in the Great, and Generall Assembly; but as yet brought to no comfortable Issue for ye town." ("Town Acts of Suffield," Sheldon, p. 154.)

† The Strong family of England was originally located in the County of Shropshire. One of the family married an heiress of Griffith, of the County of Caernarvon, Wales, and went thither to reside in 1545. Richard Strong was of this branch of the family, and was born in the County of Caernarvon in 1561. In 1591 he removed to Taunton, Somersetshire, England, where he died in 1613, leaving a son John, then eight years of age, and a daughter Eleanor. John Strong was born in Taunton, England, in 1605, whence he removed to

24   II. Benjamin Parsons, born January 22, 1649, died June 22d, in the same year.

25   III. John Parsons, born August 14, 1650, died April 19, 1728. He married Sarah Clark, daughter of Lieutenant William Clark.*

26   IV. Lieutenant Samuel Parsons, born 1652, died ———. He married, 1st, in 1677, Elizabeth, daughter of Major Aaron Cook; † 2d, in 1691, Rhoda Taylor.

27)
28 }   Lieutenant Samuel Parsons had, among other children, Ithamar, who was the grandfather of Judge Anson
29   V. Parsons of Philadelphia, and Aaron, who was named after his first wife's father, Major Aaron Cook. Both of these sons were children by his second wife, Rhoda Taylor.

London and afterward to Plymouth. Having Puritan sympathies, John Strong sailed for the new world March 20, 1630, in company with 140 persons, and among them the Revs. Messrs. John Warham and John Maverick and Messrs. John Mason and Roger Clapp, in the ship Mary and John (Captain Squeb), and arrived at Nantasket, Mass., twelve miles south of Boston, Sunday, May 30, 1630. In 1635, after having assisted in founding Dorchester, John Strong removed to Hingham, Mass., and, March 9, 1636, took the freeman's oath at Boston. December 4, 1638, he was an inhabitant and proprietor of Taunton, Mass., and a freeman of Plymouth Colony. He was deputy from Taunton to the general court in Plymouth in 1641, 1643, and 1644. From Taunton he removed to Windsor, Conn., where he was appointed, with four others—Captain John Mason, Roger Ludlow, Israel Stoughton, and Henry Wolcott, all very leading men in the new colony—"to superintend and bring forward the settlement of the place." In 1659 he removed to Northampton, Mass., where he lived forty years, and was a leading man in the affairs of the town and church. The church records at Northampton tell us that, "after solemn and extraordinary seeking to God for his direction and blessing, the church chose John Strong ruling elder." He was ordained June 24, 1663, by the imposition of the hands of the pastor, Rev. Eleazer Mather. Elizabeth Strong's mother was Abigail Ford, whose father, Thomas Ford, came to America on the ship Mary and John, and founded, with the rest of the company, the new Dorchester of the new world. Great pains were taken to form this company of such materials as should compose a well-ordered settlement containing all the elements of an independent community. Several gentlemen past middle life, with adult families and good estates, were added. Henry Wolcott, Thomas Ford, and four others were of this class. ("History of Dorchester.") Thomas Ford was one of the early settlers of Windsor, Conn.

  * Lieutenant Clark, with his wife Sarah, was a member of the Dorchester Church as early as 1637. In 1659 they removed to Northampton, five years after its first settlement.

  † Major Aaron Cook, whose second wife was a daughter of Thomas Ford of Northampton, was at Windsor, Conn., in 1640, and appears at Northampton in 1661, where he was chosen representative to the General Court, as also at Hadley, whither he subsequently removed. He was a man of great energy, and a devoted friend to the regicides, Goffe and Whalley.

30 V. Ebenezer Parsons, born 1655, died September 2, 1675, aged twenty years. He was the first white child born in Northampton, and was killed at Northfield, in a fight with the Indians.

31 VI. Jonathan Parsons, born 1657, died 1694. He married Mary, daughter of Nathaniel Clark.

32 VII. David Parsons was born 1659 and died young.

33 VIII. Mary Parsons, born 1661, died 1711. She married, 1st, Joseph Ashley, born 1651, died, 1698; and 2d, Joseph Williston. Their son, Joseph Williston, Jr.,* born December 28, 1700, died August 21, 1747, married, 1727, Hannah Stebbins, daughter of Thomas Stebbins and Sarah Strong, who was born August 17, 1706.

34 IX. Hannah Parsons, born 1663, died 1739. She married Rev. Peletiah Glover † of Springfield.

---

* Joseph Williston, Jr., had, among other children, Rev. Noah Williston, born 1733; Yale College 1757; died at West Haven, Conn., 1811. Rev. Noah Williston married Hannah Payson, daughter of Deacon Joshua Payson of Pomfret, Conn. Rev. Noah Williston had, among other children, Rev. Payson Williston, 1764-1856, who was the father of Hon. Samuel Williston of Easthampton, Mass., born June 17, 1795. Hon. Samuel Williston married, 1822, Emily Graves of Williamsburgh, Mass., daughter of Elnathan Graves and Lydia Pomeroy. Hon. Samuel Williston was State Senator 1841-42; founded Williston Seminary at Easthampton, to which he gave $250,000, and founded two professorships at Amherst with $50,000, etc. Sarah Williston (sister of Hon. Samuel) was born January 21, 1800, and died July 1, 1833; she married, December 4, 1818, Josiah Dwight Whitney of Northampton. Among their children were Professor Josiah Dwight Whitney, of Harvard College (born November, 1819), Professor of Geology and Metallurgy; and Professor William Dwight Whitney, of Yale College (born February, 1827), Professor of Sanscrit and Comparative Philology. Sarah Williston, born June 14, 1765, the second child of Rev. Noah (born 1733), married, August 30, 1763, Rev. Richard Salter Storrs (son of Rev. John Storrs of Mansfield, Conn., and Southold, L. I., and his wife, the widow Eunice Howe, née Conant, daughter of Shubael Conant and the daughter of Rev. Eleazer Williams of Mansfield). This Rev. Richard Salter Storrs settled at Longmeadow, Mass., where he died in 1819. His son, Rev. Richard Salter (2) Storrs, born February 6, 1787, settled at Braintree, Mass., July, 1811. He married, 1st, in 1812, Sarah Strong Woodhull, daughter of Rev. Nathan Woodhull; 2d, in 1819, Harriet Moore of Boston; and 3d, in 1835, Anne Stebbins, daughter of Rev. Stephen Williams Stebbins of Westhaven, Conn., and Eunicia, daughter of Rev. Nicholas Street. His son, Rev. Richard Salter (3) Storrs, born August 21, 1821, has been, since 1846, pastor of the Church of the Pilgrims, Brooklyn, N. Y.

† February 3, 1685, the inhabitants of Springfield, Mass., in dividing the common lands among the 123 heads of families or legal citizens, included by a special vote a gift of land to " our reverend teacher, Mr. Peletiah Glover." " In 1661, a young minister named Glover was settled over the Springfield church, after nine years vacancy in the pulpit. He was a worthy instrument in the hand of Providence for the advancement of the community. The dark interim closed, and the people must have felt the old confidence return with

35 X. Abigail Parsons, born 1666, died 1689. She married John Colton, and died shortly afterward, leaving a daughter, who married Francis Griswold * of Windsor, Conn.

36 XI. Esther Parsons and } born and died September
37 XII. Benjamin Parsons, } 11, 1672.

XIII. Esther Parsons, born 1674, died 1760. She
38 married Rev. Joseph Smith, who taught school at Hadley and at Springfield, was ordained Presbyterian minister, and installed first at Brookfield and then at Middletown, Conn.

CHILDREN OF HON. JOSEPH AND ELIZABETH   23
(STRONG) PARSONS.

39 I. Rev. Joseph Parsons, b. June 28, 1671-72; graduated at Harvard 1697.

40 II. Lieutenant John Parsons, b. January 11, 1674; d. September 4, 1746.

41 III. Captain Ebenezer Parsons, b. December 31, 1675; d. July 1, 1744.

42 IV. Elizabeth Parsons, b. February 3, 1678; d. April 17, 1763.

43 V. Rev. David Parsons, b. February 1, 1680; graduated at Harvard 1705.

44 VI. Josiah Parsons, b. January 2, 1682; d. April 12, 1768.

45 VII. Daniel Parsons, b. August, 1685; m., June 17, 1704, Abigail Cooley.

the renewal of the stated means of grace." By 1678 the " Rev. Mr. Glover, a man of great energy and studious application, had contributed materially in the direction of the town's activities." " Mr. Glover was a man of great tenacity of purpose." Mr. Glover early " opened an account at the Pynchon store, and not only traded out Mr. Pynchon's ministry rates, but anticipated the money due from others of the congregation, which, sad to relate, were often allowed to go unpaid until the town stepped in and made the minister good." His death, in 1692, left the Springfield pulpit vacant for two years.

* Francis Griswold was born in England and came to America with his father, Edward, in 1629. Edward Griswold, born in England in 1607, was the brother of Matthew Griswold, progenitor of the two governors of Connecticut of that name, who came to America with him.

46   VIII. Moses Parsons, b. June 15, 1687; d. September 26, 1754.

47   IX. Abigail Parsons, b. January, 1763; d. August 17, 1763.

48   X. Noah Parsons, b. August 15, 1692; d. October 27, 1779; m., January 17, 1712, Mindwell Edwards.

CAPTAIN EBENEZER PARSONS was born at Northampton, December 31, 1675. He married at Springfield, December 15, 1703, MERCY STEBBINS, born February 12, 1683, died November 1, 1753. Ebenezer Parsons inherited the military spirit and prominence in town affairs which both his father and his grandfather had possessed. He served almost continuously from 1721 until his death as selectman of Northampton. He held an ensigncy in the militia in defence of Northampton as early as 1723, and afterward he arose to the command of a company, for, although no record of his appointment has been found, he is designated as captain on the Northampton town records, in his will, and on his gravestone. He was one of the three citizens who, in 1721, purchased the whole of Northampton's portion of the entire £50,000 Province Bills "lately ordered to be made by the Government" by reason of "the scarcity of money and the want of other medium of commerce." He was the owner of the original Parsons Homestead in Northampton.

Mercy Stebbins Parsons (French, Kinsley, Bartlett descent) was the daughter of Samuel Stebbins and Mary French. Her great grandfather was Rowland Stebbins of Stebbing, Essex County, England. Her grandfather, John Stebbins, was the only person who escaped unhurt from the Bloody Brook massacre at Deerfield.

CHILDREN OF CAPTAIN EBENEZER AND
MERCY (STEBBINS) PARSONS; ALL
BORN AT NORTHAMPTON.

41

49   I. Mercy Parsons, b. January 1, 1706; m., November
30, 1732, Moses Kinsley.

50   II. Ebenezer Parsons, b. August 1, 1711; d. November 4, 1711.

51   III. Ebenezer Parsons, b. January 7, 1713; d. young.

52   IV. Simeon Parsons, b. April 27, 1716; d. May 27,
1727.

53   V. Elihu Parsons, b. March 14, 1719; d. August 22,
1785.

54   VI. Rachel Parsons, b. July 14, 1721.

55   VII. Lieutenant Benjamin Parsons, b. October 2,
1723; d. April 1, 1777.

56   VIII. Lydia Parsons, b. July 28, 1726; d. 1727.

57   IX. Simeon Parsons, b. February 11, 1731.

LIEUTENANT BENJAMIN PARSONS, born at Northampton, Mass., October 2, 1723, married, 1746, REBECCA
SHELDON, born December 6, 1727; died October 28,
1811. He was early engaged in military affairs, and in
1745 was a private in Captain William Williams's company at the siege of Louisburg. In 1747 and 1748 he
was stationed at Fort Massachusetts as "sentinel" in
the company of Captain William Lyman, engaged in the
defence of the then Western frontier. He was also a
soldier in the French and Indian War, and was there
promoted to a lieutenancy. In 1776, being enfeebled
and too old to take an active part in the Revolution,
he removed, with his sons Ebenezer, Solomon, Silas, and
Benjamin, from Northampton to Goshen, Mass., where
he took up an allotment in the so-called "Chesterfield
Gore," a grant of land given to the descendants of a
portion of the 840 soldiers who took part in the Narraganset Expedition in King Philip's War to satisfy

55

those to whom " Narragansett township No. 4 " had been given, and which had proved unfit for settlement. He died of smallpox within a year of his removal.

Rebecca Sheldon (Strong, Ford, Clapp, Holton, Marshfield, Wright, Woodward, Hinsdale, Johnson, Cheney, Blott, and Woodford descent) was the daughter of Benjamin Sheldon and Mary Strong of Northampton. Her great-great-grandfather was Isaac Sheldon of Dorchester, England, who settled with his son Isaac in Windsor, Conn. Her great-great-grandfather Robert Hinsdale was a member of the Ancient and Honorable Artillery Company of Boston, and both he and his son Samuel Hinsdale were killed at the Bloody Brook massacre at Deerfield.

CHILDREN OF LIEUTENANT BENJAMIN AND REBECCA (SHELDON) PARSONS. 55

58   I. Jerusha Parsons, b. September 22, 1750.

59   II. Ebenezer Parsons, b. December 26, 1751.

60   III. Mercy Parsons, b. November 29, 1753; m. Jed. Buckingham.

61   IV. Hannah Parsons, b. July 1, 1755; m. Cyrus Lyon.

62   V. Susannah Parsons, b. December 1, 1757; m. Colonel Nehemiah May.

63   VI. Rev. Justin Sheldon Parsons, b. July 19, 1759.

64   The Rev. Justin Sheldon Parsons had, among others, Lucretia
65 Parsons and the Rev. Levi Parsons, who died young in Alexandria, Egypt, while visiting the missionary stations of the East in behalf of the American Board of Foreign Missions.

  Lucretia Parsons (64) married the Rev. Daniel Oliver Morton, and had, among others, Levi Parsons Morton, Vice-President of the United States from 1889 to 1893.

66   VII. Rev. Silas Parsons, b. September 26, 1761.

67   VIII. Solomon Parsons, b. August 28, 1763; d. January 26, 1815.

68   IX. Rebecca Parsons, b. August 4, 1766; m. Thad. Naramore.

69   X. Rev. Benjamin Parsons, b. February 20, 1769.

SOLOMON PARSONS, born at Northampton, Mass., August 28, 1763, married, November 25, 1790, LUCINDA PACKARD, born April 8, 1765; died July 6, 1850; daughter of Joshua Packard. He kept a tavern in Goshen, 1791, and was selectman 1802 and deputy sheriff for several years.

Lucinda Packard's (Howard and Bryant descent) ancestor Samuel Packard came from England to Hingham in ship Diligent, in 1638. The family resided in East Bridgewater, Mass., until her father, Joshua Packard, who had been a soldier in both the French and Indian and Revolutionary wars, finally settled in Goshen.

CHILDREN OF SOLOMON AND LUCINDA (PACKARD) PARSONS.

70   I. Theodore Parsons, b. September 14, 1791; d. January 19, 1865.

71   II. Jerusha Parsons, b. June 23, 1793; d. February 15, 1820; m. Cyrus Joy.

72   III. Willard Parsons, b. July 20, 1795; d. May 6, 1876.

73   IV. Ebenezer Parsons, b. January 24, 1798.

74   V. Wealthy Parsons, b. February 26, 1800; d. September 18, 1832; m. Frank Naramore.

75   VI. Lucinda Parsons, b. April 12, 1802; m. Francis Lyman.

76   VII. Lyman Parsons, b. May 1, 1894; d. August 28, 1831.

WILLARD PARSONS, born at Goshen, Mass., July 20, 1795, married, June 6, 1820, TRYPHOSA NARAMORE, born July 8, 1797; died January 20, 1876; daughter of Alpheus and Mercy (White) Naramore. Her maternal grandfather was Captain William White of the Revolution.

CHILDREN OF WILLARD AND TRYPHOSA (NARAMORE) PARSONS.

77   I. Sophia N. Parsons, b. April 15, 1821; m. Amos Stone of Goshen.

78   II. Alpheus N. Parsons, b. July 2, 1823; d. April 29, 1851.

79   III. Benjamin F. Parsons; b. November 7, 1827; living 1897.

80   IV. Julia Parsons, b. December 8, 1831; d. March 29, 1863; m. M. N. Hubbard.

81   V. Helen Parsons, b. May 19, 1834; m. William Wells.

82   VI. Lyman Parsons, b. March 1, 1839; m. Octavia French; both living 1897; no children.

83   VII. Edward Parsons; b. September 5, 1842; d. September 17, 1845.

BENJAMIN FRANKLIN PARSONS, born at Goshen, Mass., November 7, 1827, married at Colchester, Conn., December 20, 1859, LEONORA FRANCES BARTLETT, born October 9, 1839, at Natchez, Miss. Benjamin F. Parsons graduated from Williams College in 1857, and was immediately appointed Principal of Bacon Academy, at Colchester, Conn. Here, two years later, he was married to Leonora Frances Bartlett. Together they became principals and proprietors of South Berkshire Institute, at New Marlboro, Mass. In 1870 they moved to Hopkinton, Mass., and in 1877 they took up their residence in Hawkinsville, Ga., where they still reside.

Leonora Frances Bartlett was daughter of John Chandler Bartlett and Lucy Ann Lathrop of Lebanon, Conn. She descends from eleven passengers of the Mayflower, two colonial governors, five governor's assistants, and several officers and soldiers of the colonial wars. This line has been carried back through several branches to the original pioneers, and, as with this Parsons line, no ancestor has been found who landed later than 1640, and none who were not English.

CHILDREN OF BENJAMIN F. AND LEONORA [79] (BARTLETT) PARSONS.

[84] I. Charles Lathrop Parsons, b. March 23, 1867, at New Marlboro, Mass.

[85] II. William Naramore Parsons, b. October 11, 1869, at New Marlboro; m., October 8, 1895, Miss Carrie Waterman, at Hawkinsville, Ga.

CHARLES LATHROP PARSONS, born at New Marlboro, [84] Mass., March 23, 1867, married, December 29, 1887, ALICE DOUGLAS ROBERTSON, born at Bluffton, S. C., June 20, 1870, daughter of James Douglas Robertson and Anna (Guerard) Robertson.

Charles L. Parsons graduated from Cornell University in 1888. Immediately after graduation he accepted the position of Assistant Chemist to the New Hampshire Experiment Station. In 1890 he was appointed Professor of General and Analytical Chemistry in the New Hampshire State College, at that time a department of Dartmouth College. In 1893 the New Hampshire College was, by act of the legislature, removed to Durham, N. H., where he now (1897) resides.

Alice Douglas Robertson was born at Bluffton, S. C. Her father, James D. Robertson, was born in Scotland, and is of the family of the Robertsons of Strowan. His grandfather, Lieutenant James Robertson, died from wounds received at Waterloo, and his great grandfather, Lieutenant-General James Robertson, was a prominent English officer of the Revolution and was Royal Governor of New York in 1779. Her mother, née Anna [84] Richardson Guerard, is descended from the two Landgraves Thomas Smith, Sir John Barnwell, the De Veaux's, Screvens, Bedons, Guerards, and other well-known South Carolina families.

CHILDREN OF CHARLES L. AND ALICE (ROB-
ERTSON) PARSONS. |84

86   I. Leonora Elizabeth Parsons, b. Hanover, N. H., October 3, 1888.

87   II. Charles Lathrop Parsons, Jr., b. Hanover, N. H.,
November 9, 1889.

88   III. Anna Guerard Parsons, b. Hanover, N. H., January 11, 1891.

89   IV. Alice Inez Parsons, b. Durham, N. H., March 26,
1895.

90   V. Priscilla Bartlett Parsons, b. Durham, N. H., September 18, 1897.

NOTE TO PAGE 105.

* " I think there is little doubt that this is an erroneous conclusion, for, in
the first place, the original record of this Parsons is written JO: which has
been fully decided to be an abbreviation, at that time, for John, and not for
Joseph, and also because he sailed for Virginia. In the early '20's the term
Virginia was often used to mean America, but by 1635 Massachusetts Bay
Colony and Virginia had become clearly differentiated. I do not believe that
we have any record of Joseph Parsons whatever previous to the Indian deed,
and I believe that when it is found it will include Richard Parsons and the
whole family. Personally, I have little doubt that his father was Richard,
and Thomas and Samuel his brothers." (Professor Charles L. Parsons.)

CHARLES L. PARSONS

DANIEL PARSONS

was born August 18, 1685, and died January 27, 1774. 45
June 2, 1709, he married, at Longmeadow, ABIGAIL
COOLEY, born February 22, 1690, died June 8, 1763.
She was the daughter of Lieutenant Joseph Cooley (son
of Ensign Benjamin Cooley*) and Mary Griswold
(daughter of George Griswold, son of "Mr." Edward,
son of George, son of Francis Griswold of Lyme Regis,
England).

"Daniel Parsons, b. 1685, who located at Springfield
as an innkeeper, probably ranked in public estimation
among the foremost of that influential family. At that
time only the choicest characters in the community, gentlemen in the technical sense the word then had, only
such received license to be innholders. As thus licensed
may be cited such names as Cornet Joseph Parsons,
Captain Henry Dwight, the distinguished Colonel Partridge. Daniel Parsons, therefore, stood as to high moral
worth probably second to none of his six brothers."
("Antiquities of Northampton"; Clarke.)

Daniel Parsons appears on the list of tax-payers holding property in the Chicopee part of the town in 1738.
He was not a church member. Such a change had come
over the spirit of Springfield that at this time the
Pynchons and Glovers were not represented on the lists
of church members on the male side, and even the wife
of the minister, Eunice Breck, daughter of the previous
minister, and her mother were not members.

* " The family of Cooley is of English origin. The name is borne by many
very respectable families, and by families also of illustrious rank. Arthur
Wellesley, Duke of Wellington, was the son of Garret, created Viscount
Wellesley, son of Richard Cooley, as the heir to his first cousin, Garret
Wellesley, who left him all his large estates, his arms and name. This
Richard Cooley was grandson or great grandson of Sir Richard Cooley,
sometimes spelled Cowley, and Colly, of Rutland County, the home, from
time immemorial, of the Colleys." (" Genealogy of the Early Settlers of
Trenton and Ewing, N. J.," by Rev. Eli F. Cooley, D.D., and Prof. Wm. S.
Cooley.)

Ensign Benjamin Cooley was born 1620, was a resident of Springfield,
Mass., of which he was selectman in 1646. He was a man of wealth, and
left large landed estates in Springfield and Longmeadow, besides other
property. He died, 1684, six days before his wife, Sarah.

CHILDREN OF DANIEL PARSONS AND ABIGAIL COOLEY.

91   I. Daniel Parsons was born, it is recorded, in 1709. This son must have died soon, for the church record shows a "second son of Daniel Parsons," born 1710, also named Daniel.

92   II. Daniel Parsons, Jr., was born in 1710 and died in 1760. He went to Wilbraham in 1737. May 29, 1741, Daniel Parsons (Jr.) "moderates" the meeting called to arrange for the place of ordination of the Worthy Mr. Mirick as minister of the new parish in Wilbraham. November 4, 1745, Daniel Parsons and Nathaniel Bliss are directed to wait upon a committee to determine the place of building the meeting-house, and to show them the land. November 16th they are voted each one pound five shillings "for Rideing with the committee two days and a half." (The smallest service rendered by any inhabitant of the precinct is paid for by the community.)

   The meetings on Sunday having been held in Daniel Parsons' house, he was paid for its use for the year ending March 22, 1746, "two pounds, old tenor." *

---

* "After many delays, about Christmas, 1748, the meeting-house was used for public worship. As our fathers went up to Wigwam Hill to worship God, the land lay spread out before them. From the meeting-house door the whole valley of the Great River, from the mountains on the north, Holyoke and Tom, to below Hartford on the south, was visible. The open fields of the first settlers were under their feet; and on to the west, over forests and meadows, could be seen the blue line of vapor signalizing the homes of the old settlers in Springfield Street, or the white cloud of fog, lying low along the tree-tops, indicating the course of the river from its gateway between the mountains to the settlement at Middletown. And beyond, more than twenty miles away, rose the blue ridges of the Green Mountains, tipped with gold in the morning, veiled in purple in the evening; and when the frost touched the forests in the autumn, how the red maple flamed among the trees, and the green of the pines, and the yellow of the walnuts, caused the whole vast landscape to appear like a gorgeous carpet woven in the loom of the gods.

"Winding their way, when the Sabbath morning comes, through field and bridle-path and cart-road, they turn to the right up the hill, climbing the mountain through the woods—a timid deer now and then pausing a moment to gaze at the strange sight, and then bounding away among the trees; a frightened partridge breaking the silence by whirring off through the bushes; till the procession, on horseback and on foot—for the young

Daniel Parsons, Jr., had (1) Daniel, born October 26, 1733, died January 20, 1734; and (2) Daniel, 3d, born July 15, 1735, died January 18, 1797. This Daniel Parsons, 3d, was First Lieutenant of the company of Captain Daniel Cadwell, in Colonel Timothy Robinson's detachment of militia from Massachusetts, which served at Ticonderoga from December 5, 1776, to April 2, 1777.

1742, Dec. 9. "Granted to Daniel Parsons, jr., 10s lawfull money for a bear killed by him Las Summer for old Tenor £2."

1738, March 14. "Voted that a Cart Bridge be built at twelve Mile Brook, in the Country Rhoad, at the Charge of the Town, and Dan'l Parsons, Obadiah Cooley, and John Hitchcock jr., Chosen a comtee to build the same at the Cheapest Rate they can."

93   III. Aaron Parsons, born June 2, 1712; died August 4, 1795.

men and maidens thought the walk most delightful—reached the road that came up from the east side of the mountain.

"Continuing on to the place of the sanctuary, they made their horses fast to the trees about the meeting-house, and after Christian inquiries for such news of their households and the precinct as their curiosity compelled and reverence could not restrain, they entered the sanctuary, of which, if they could not exclaim with David 'How amiable are thy tabernacles,' they could cry out with the royal poet, 'The sparrow hath found a house, and the swallow a nest for herself, where she may lay her young, even thy altars, O Lord of Hosts, my God and my King.'

"After they were as comfortably seated as possible on the benches, in such order as had been prescribed, the 'Worthy Reverend Noah Mirrick' with wig or powdered hair and cue, bands and small clothes and silk stockings, and shoe buckles of silver, entered the house, the congregation all rising as a token of respect. He reads a hymn, then hands the book over the top of the pulpit—for there was but one hymn-book in the precinct, and that was the minister's—to Deacon Nathaniel Warriner, who named the tune, the pitch, read one line of the hymn, and commenced singing it, the rest following after, as ability and strength permitted, the deacon considerately, and as became the service of God's house, waiting before he gave out another line, until the most dilatory had finished. When the hymn was ended, the minister solemnly prayed, the congregation reverently rising. When the prayer was over, another hymn was sung in the same manner. Then the sermon was preached, not seldom interspersed with the twittering of swallows above, or the crying of babies below. At last the benediction is pronounced, and the minister leaves the pulpit and passes out first, the congregation all standing, as when he entered. The families now gather about to eat their frugal dinners from the logs and stumps which are abundant. The short intermission over, the afternoon service follows, similar, in all respects, to the morning, after which they mount their horses —their wives on the pillions behind, and the baby on the pommel before,

94 | IV. Noah Parsons, born 1714; died young.

95 | V. Abigail Parsons, born 1718; married Benjamin Horton, Jr.

96 | VI. Miriam Parsons was born in 1721. She married Captain James Warriner* of Springfield.

In April, 1775, Captain James Warriner " marched in defence of Ammerican liberty on ye alarm occasioned by ye Lexington fight." †

Captain James Warriner was town clerk of Wilbraham

the young men and maidens going on foot, and finding the way all too short—and so all reach their homes again at the going down of the sun." (" Wilbraham Centennial.")

* William Warriner, who died in 1676, first appears in Springfield in 1640-43. He had a son, James, who took the oath of allegiance in 1678, and who in 1664 had married Elizabeth, daughter of Joseph Baldwin of Milford. In 1705 he was sent to Boston with Judge Joseph Parsons, to answer the " west-siders " in the contest over Springfield church-rates.

† " General Gage, commander of the British troops in Boston, had determined to get possession of the ammunition and arms of the province, which he heard were stored at Lexington and Concord. On the night of the 18th of April the troops stole out of Boston, hoping to reach Lexington without being discovered, but the preconcerted signal flashed from the spire of the New North Church, and Paul Revere was instantly on his way from Charlestown to Lexington, rousing the inhabitants along the road, so that when Major Pitcairn, who led the advance of the troops reached the Common, he found the ' minute-men ' of Lexington drawn up in arms before him. He ordered them to disperse. They stood their ground. He ordered his men to fire. That volley opened the Revolutionary War. Couriers were dispatched on the fleetest horses to arouse the people everywhere, and carry the flaming torch of alarm through the country. On the 20th, just as the sun was passing the meridian, a rider was seen coming down the Bay Road to Wilbraham at full speed, his horse dripping and smoking with sweat. He barely checked his horse before Samuel Glover's door, announced the fight, called upon the minute-men to hasten to the rescue, and was off and out of sight on his way to Springfield. Blood had been shed! Glover mounts his horse and rides, as he never rode before, down by Jones's and Bliss's, calling on them to come on, as he goes. Brewer and Merrick, and James Warriner, the captain of the minute-men, rush in from the field. The long roll is beaten by Charles Ferry, so that the mountain answers it from Oliver Bliss's to Noah Stebbins's. Merrick mounts his horse and flies down the west road by the Scantic; and Burt tells his most vigorous son to cross the mountains by Rattlesnake Peak as swift as the winds ever swept over them, and not to stay his speed till all the men of the south valley were summoned to the march; then to return without delay along the east road, and over the mountains home. ' Edward,' said Isaac Morris to his son, ' bring the horse.' As soon as he had slung his powder-horn over his shoulder, put his bullets into his pocket, and taken down his trusty gun from its hooks, the faithful steed was at the door. Breathing a prayer for his heroic wife, standing in speechless submission, he was off at full speed. Before the mountain ceased to glow with that day's departing sun, thirty-four men, with the blessing of their wives, and the prayers of the fathers who were too old to go to battle, were on the ' Great Bay Road,' hastening to defend, and if necessary, to die for, their rights."

1773-78; Noah Warriner 1779-80; and James, again, 1781-85.

97   VII. Gideon Parsons was born 1723, and died ——.

98   VIII. Abner Parsons was born in 1725, and died in 1798. He married Mary Abbot.

"Wensday July 18th. Wim. Hancock and Abner Parsons came up today." (Samuel Warner's Journal, Expedition to Crown Point, 1759.)

99   IX. Eunice Parsons was born in 1728, and died in 1771. She married Abel Hancock.

Abel Hancock marched from Springfield, April 20, 1775, in the company commanded by Lieutenant Gideon Burt. On April 24th this company was reorganized for three and a half months' service. Aaron Parsons, Jr., nephew of Eunice Parsons Hancock, was one of the sergeants of this company.

AARON PARSONS, 1st,

was born June 2, 1712, at Five-Mile Pond, near Springfield. He married (1), October 2, 1732, Mercy (daughter of John and Dorcas) Atkinson, born 1713, died July 11, 1750; (2) February 19, 1752, Experience Robinson, d. May 14, 1789, aged 67. Aaron was named after his father's cousin, Aaron, son of Lieutenant Samuel Parsons, who married the daughter of Aaron Cook, the devoted friend of the regicides, Goffe and Whalley. 93

Aaron Parsons went to Wilbraham, where his mother owned land in both the second and third divisions of land "on the East side of the Great River in Springfield" as the locality was designated, in 1737, at the same time with his brother Daniel Parsons, Jr. Both Aaron and Daniel Parsons were among the signers of the following paper:—

"We the subscribers, who are settlers on the Lands called the Outward commons Dwelling Some in the Second and Some in the Third Division of Said Commons In Springfield on the East Side of Connecticut River do hereby appoint and Impower Thomas Mirick 2nd & Abel Bliss Settlers on the Said Place to Prefer a Petition to the Next General Court that we with our Lands and theirs together with all the Lands within Said Divisions being In the whole in length Eight Miles and in weadth four Miles May be Set of a Separate and Distinct Precinct and that all the Lands Lying in said Divisions may be taxed at Such Rate as the General Court shall think Proper the better to Enable them to Settle a Minister Build a Meeting House and other Public Charges so that we may be enabled to Maintain the Gospel among us. Witness our hands May 7th 1740."

In January, 1738, the name of Aaron Parsons is found on the valuation and assessment list intrusted to Constable John Hitchcock for property in the Chicopee part of Springfield town. He was a member of the Springfield church at that time.

Aaron Parsons was a member of Captain Luke Hitchcock's company in the French war, which was in service from April 3, 1755, to January 3, 1756. They were in battle near the southern extremity of Lake George, with Baron Dieskau. In this battle, private Noah Grant, the great grandfather of General U. S. Grant, was killed. In the war of the Rebellion, 1861-65, a descendant of Noah Grant, viz., General U. S. Grant, commanded the armies of the United States, while a descendant of Aaron Parsons, Major-General Lewis Baldwin Parsons, was Chief of Rail and River Transportation for said armies from 1861 to 1865.* (See No. 161, page 152.)

The inscription on his gravestone is: "In memory of Mr. Aaron Parsons, who died Aug. 4, 1795, æ 83 years."

* "About five miles beyond the village of Glen's Falls, N. Y., the road passes Williams' Rock, a large bowlder which marks the scene of the 'bloody morning scout.' On September 7, 1755, when the French army, under Dieskau, was marching down from Crown Point against the Anglo-colonial army under General Johnson, Colonel Ephraim Williams (the virtual founder of Williams College) was sent out with 1,200 men to engage the French vanguard; 200 of his men were Mohawk Indians, under command of their noble white-haired chief Hendrick. The detachment marched into the very centre of the invading army (which was marching in a great half-moon curve), and was speedily enveloped and crushed by the enemy. A terrible massacre ensued (in a ravine still called the 'bloody defile') and Williams and Hendrick fell, with most of their men. The bodies of the slain were thrown into Bloody Pond, a quiet pool in a glen near Williams' Rock. Dieskau then advanced rapidly to attack the colonial camp at Lake George. Johnson had fortified his position, and the Indian and Canadian auxiliaries in the attacking forces were soon put to flight, by the fire of the batteries, while the French regulars suffered heavily and were finally repulsed with a loss of 700 killed and wounded. Dieskau was wounded and made a prisoner, while Johnson, though wounded, was made a baronet of

THE CHILDREN OF AARON PARSONS AND (1) MERCY ATKINSON PARSONS.

100   I. Mercy Parsons was born in 1733, and died in 1750. She married Abner Sikes.

101   II. Lucy Parsons was born in 1735, and died ——. She married Joseph Adna Abbott of Tolland.

102   III. Sergeant Aaron Parsons, jr., was born February 14, 1736, and died February 20, 1799.

103   IV. Deacon Reuben Parsons was born in 1739, and died in 1799. He married Margaret Granger.

104   V. Zenas Parsons was born in 1740, and died in 1818. He married Isabel Woodbridge of Stockbridge.*

Great Britain, and received the thanks of Parliament." (History of New England.)

"I want to say to you, comrades, that I am indebted to the private soldier for all the credit that has come to me. He was the man who did the fighting, and the man who carried the musket is the greatest hero of the war, in my estimation. I was nothing but an agent. I knew how to take care of men. I knew what a soldier was worth, and how to put him in a battle when one occurred; but I was simply the agent to take care of him, and he did the work. Now, comrades, these are common-sense things, and I can't say them in flowery language; but they are true nevertheless, and they are true not of me alone but of everybody else. It is to the common soldier that we are indebted for any credit that comes to us." (General Phil. Sheridan, at a reunion of veterans at Cresson.) "The private soldier was a man, not a musket." (General W. T. Sherman.)

* The great elm tree on the southeast corner of the present Court-house Square in Springfield once gave shade to the best known tavern of its day, that of Zenas Parsons, there being just room between the elm and the hotel veranda for the "stage wagon." There were extensive barns and sheds in the rear. Here auctions were frequently held, and on training day young men tried their powers of wrestling. Over the sheds was a long dance hall much used by the young people. Here Zenas Parsons offered lodging, October 21, 1789, to General Washington, and the old building is honored accordingly. In his diary, Washington mentions that "Colonel Worthington, Colonel Williams, Adjutant-General of the State of Massachusetts; General Shepard, Mr. Lyman, and many other gentlemen, sat an hour or two with me in the evening at Parsons' tavern where I lodged, and which is a good house."

"We can hardly realize the full place which the tavern occupied in those days, when the famous Zenas Parsons held sway. The English were naturally a tavern-haunting people. The tap-room was comfortable, informal, and conducive to the interchange of fact and opinion—three qualifications that appealed strongly to the English before the advent of the new and tremendous agency, journalism. Parsons retired with the century in which he was born; but many an anecdote remains of those days of flip-irons and toddy. A party once put up with Parsons after learning from him that he took Continental money, then hopelessly depreciated. The surprise was unbounded when a bill of several hundred dollars was presented. They asked

> " In the winter term of the Court of Common Pleas in 1784, Zenas Parsons, Moses Bliss, William Pynchon, Luke Chapin, Isaac Morgan, Jonathan Dwight, etc., were crowding on each other's heels to secure judgments against debtors."   (Green's " Springfield.")
>
> Isabel Woodbridge Parsons was the daughter of Judge Joseph Woodbridge* and Elizabeth Merrick of Springfield.

Parsons if he had not told them he accepted Continental money, and he replied that he did, and ' a lot of it, too '!

" On Fridays (1783) the Hartford stage-wagon left for Parsons' Inn at Springfield, and returned Saturdays. A little later Reuben Sikes ran a line of stages from New York to Boston, through Springfield, three times a week in summer, the fare being three shillings per mile. The arrival and departure of such ladies and gentlemen as were able to meet the expenses of the travel, was an event of no small importance. It was not permitted everyone to own a carriage. They were heavily taxed. Among those thus taxed in 1791 were, Captain Pynchon, Jonathan Dwight, Colonel Williams, Alexander Bliss, Zenas Parsons, etc. At the close of the year 1782, there were so many crimes against property that a society was formed for the pursuit and conviction of thieves; but this did not prevent a descent upon Zenas Parsons a year later, when much plate and other valuables were secured. One of the last events in the history of Parsons' tavern was the visit of President Monroe to Springfield in 1817. It was a very important occasion politically and socially for Springfield Valley and for Massachusetts also. The bitterness in politics occasioned by the embargo had been carried even to the breaking up of families. But Monroe had been so well received in New York and elsewhere, that by the time he reached Springfield bridge, he was greeted by a thoroughly cordial community. Ascending the west bank of the river, he found sixty Springfield citizens on horseback, many of them in military uniform, as well as scores in carriages, making a procession half a mile long. As they approached the village, Captain Warriner had assembled his company of artillery at the bridge, where also a crowd had gathered. The church bells were rung and a salute was fired. A formal address was presented the President when he arrived at the Parsons tavern, then kept by Captain Bennett; there was a visit to the armory, and a review of four hundred and ten school children. President Monroe was much interested in the little ones, and he said to the committee of entertainment standing beside him on the veranda of Parsons' tavern, ' I am much pleased and gratified with their appearance, and pray God to bless them, and you to carry your good designs for them into effect.' They say men fraternized after the Monroe visit, who had not spoken to each other in years."

* Rev. John Woodbridge of Stanton, northeast part of Wiltshire, England, had son John, born 1613, bred at Oxford, but left there on account of the Act of Uniformity. He was brought to this country, with his cousin, Rev. James Noyes, by his uncle, Thomas Parker, in 1634, in the ship " Mary and John." He married in 1634, Mercy, daughter of Governor Thomas Dudley, and in 1645 was ordained first minister at Andover. He returned in 1647 to England, and continued there sixteen years, being called to serve on the parliamentary commission for treating with the king in his prison on the Isle of Wight. As his Presbyterian views were opposed to those of Cromwell, he was finally excluded from the pulpit by the Bartholomew Act. He

105 VI. Captain Charles Parsons was born in 1742. He married Lucy Baldwin in 1785.

Captain Charles Parsons enlisted in the Revolutionary Army as orderly sergeant, Eighth New York regiment, Colonel Van Schaick. He was promoted Lieutenant, November 21, 1776, and Captain in 1778. He commanded two years at Ticonderoga, and was mustered out in 1782. He was at Valley Forge, and was wounded at Monmouth. He was present at Cornwallis' surrender at Yorktown. After the war he engaged in agricultural and commercial pursuits at Williamstown, Mass.*

106 VII. Elijah Parsons was born in 1744, and died in 1796. He married (1) Eunice Cadwell; (2) Eunice Jennings.

returned to Boston in 1663, and died in 1677. His son, Rev. John Woodbridge of Killingworth, born at Andover, married in 1671, Abigail, daughter of Governor William Leete. His son, Rev. John Woodbridge, born at Killingworth in 1678, graduated at Harvard College in 1694, was minister at West Springfield. His son, Rev. John Woodbridge, born 1702, Yale College 1726, was minister at Windsor, and afterwards at South Hadley. He was said to be the ninth Rev. John Woodbridge in uninterrupted succession from Rev. John Woodbridge, a friend of Wickliffe. The family in America is distinguished by a long line of clergymen reaching down to the present time.

Thomas Dudley, long time Governor of Massachusetts, and afterward Major-General (1630-53), had his estates and mansion at Roxbury, and here Joseph Dudley, Governor 1702-15, was born.

* The winter of 1777-78 was the darkest season of the Revolution. Washington went into winter quarters at Valley Forge. Congress had no money. Many of the soldiers were without shoes, and in their marches over frozen ground they left blood in their tracks. Some of the poor fellows sat up by the fires at night, for want of blankets to keep them warm. The first result of the alliance with France was the recovery of Philadelphia. Sir Henry Clinton was afraid that the French might blockade the Delaware, and thus shut him up in Philadelphia. He therefore retreated across New Jersey to New York, pushed by Washington's army. During this retreat the battle of Monmouth was fought. The Americans gained a partial victory, the English retreating under cover of the night. With the coming in of the year 1781, American prospects began to brighten. In the severe battle of Guilford Court-house, Cornwallis, who was the ablest of all the British commanders in America, drove the Americans from the field at the close of the day, but his army was so badly shattered that he was forced to begin a prompt retreat to the seacoast, leaving his wounded in the hands of the pursuing Americans. Reaching Virginia, Cornwallis pushed the work of fighting and destruction with his usual vigor. Lafayette, who was in command of the Americans, showed much ability in avoiding a battle. Washington now marched his forces to the southward, in company with a French army under Rochambeau. The French fleet blockaded the troops of Cornwallis at Yorktown, and the American and French armies laid siege to the place. On the 18th of October, 1781, the British army under Cornwallis surrendered, prisoners of war. The surrender took away from England the last hope of subduing America.

Elijah Parsons was one of the signers of the pledge of non-consumption of British goods, in 1774.* (" History of Wilbraham," p. 109.)

In the " Muster Roll of the Minit Company that came from Wilbraham under the command of Capt. Paul Langdon," it is recorded that, " Elijah Parsons of Wilbraham, private, marched April 20, 1775, discharged May 2, same year."

The whole State was startled in September, 1777, by what was called the Bennington Alarm, and a company of fifty-two men under Captain James Shaw, left Wilbraham September 24th, for the seat of danger. They were present on the opposite side of the river at the surrender of Burgoyne at Saratoge.†

Elijah Parsons was a member of Captain Shaw's company, which was "detached for the Regt. whereof Col. Charles Pynchon Esq. is colonel, and ordered to join Gen. Gates army for thirty days unless sooner discharged." In the exciting time of Shays' Rebellion, convention after convention assembled to devise measures of relief; and in November, 1786, Elijah Parsons was chosen to represent the town of Wilbraham at a convention to be held at Hadley the next day.

* " There being no other alternative between the horrors of slavery or the carnage and desolation of a civil war but a suspension of all commercial intercourse with the island of Great Britain, we do solemnly covenant and engage with each other (1) that from henceforth we will suspend all commercial intercourse with said island of Great Britain . . . and (2) that we will not buy, purchase or consume or suffer any person by for or under us to purchase or consume in any manner whatever any goods, wares, or merchandize which shall arrive in America from Great Britain, . . . and that we will break off all trade commerce and dealings whatever with all persons who, preferring their own private intrist, to the salvation of their now perishing country, shall still continue to import goods from Great Britain or shall purchase from those who do import and (3) we agree to purchase no article of merchandize of any who do not sign this pledge."

† (Journal of a private in the company, Dr. Merrick): " A day never to be forgotten by the American States. About 11 o'clock A.M., General Burgoine with a number of other officers rode out, escorted by sundry officers of the Continental army and a little south of the church was met by General Gates, and after a polite compliment proceeded to head-quarters; about two the army began to march out. I tarried till after four when I returned. They not all then marched out, but I believe nearly, the number can by no means ascertain but should be inclined to think between five and six thousand, but I am by no means a competent judge, tho I had a good view of them. The Lord be praised for this wonderful token of divine favor, for which we cannot be sufficiently thankful."

107   VIII. Miriam Parsons was born in 1746. She married Enoch Chapin, Captain of a West Springfield company, which sprang to arms the day after the battle of Lexington.

108   IX. Lieutenant Eli Parsons was born in 1748. He married Pansy Graves.

In the "Muster Roll of Captain Thomas Seward's company of artillery in the service of the United States of America, commanded by Col. John Crane," are the following records:

"Eli Parsons, 1st Lieut., wounded Oct. 4, 1777; on furlough November and December, 1777."

Lieutenant Eli Parsons was a promoter of Shays' Rebellion and issued over his own name a stirring proclamation urging the people to resist being wrongly reduced to beggary, and to take up arms to secure for themselves and their children the fruits of the war for independence which they had successfully waged against Great Britain.*

* In a recent novel, Shays's Rebellion is treated as belonging in the category of outbreaks of socialistic envy and discontent. The history of the time in which it occurred, puts the affair in a different light. It is as follows:

" It became more and more difficult to raise money, and the town, in their perplexity and distress, went so far, May 12, 1783, after the treaty of peace had been signed, as to vote to 'instruct their representative not to grant Congress the impost requested by them for the express purpose of raising a revenue independent of the States, nor to supply Congress any way until the half-pay to the officers of the army in the communication thereof be settled and entirely given up.' The war closed, but not the financial difficulties. Paper money sank in value rapidly—sank to worthlessness very soon. It would not pay debts, nor buy bread! Creditors began to press their helpless debtors. Silver, the only legal tender, could not be had. The unprincipled took advantage of the times and forced the payment of debts, securing liens on real estate worth immensely more than the real indebtedness. The courts were thronged. It is said that 1,200 suits were presented at one term of the court in Northampton. There was no peace, though peace was proclaimed. Men who had poured out their blood, either from their own veins or from those of their sons, were now to be deprived of the farms they had cleared, the houses they had built. The blessings of liberty and prosperity, for which they had fought, seemed to be escaping their grasp. Their own friends seemed to have become foes. The people were enraged, and their rage was fanned into a consuming flame, especially by one Samuel Ely, a discarded minister who had preached for a time in Somers. As early as 1781 there was an article inserted in the warrant for April meeting to see if the town ' would send a member or members to the county convention to be held at Hatfield as requested,' but no action was taken. February 22, 1782, ' Deacon John Hitchcock, Dr. John Sterns, and Abner Chapin were chosen delegates to set in a county convention, to be holden at Hatfield on the first Tuesday in

109 | X. Silence Parsons was born July 11, 1750, and died August 2d of the same year. Her mother, Mercy Atkinson Parsons, died the day Silence was born.

April next.' The same month, a mob led by Ely disturbed the holding of a court at Northampton. He was arrested and imprisoned at Springfield, but was released by a mob. Suits became more and more vexatious, and money more and more worthless. In October, 1783, another delegate was chosen— Dr. John Sterns—' to set in a county convention to be holden at Hatfield, at the dwelling-house of Colonel Seth Murray.' The tumult increased in different parts of the State, and arms were not seldom resorted to by the mob. April 25, 1786, Captain Phineas Stebbins and Mr. David Burt were chosen delegates to sit in a county convention at Hatfield; and in August of the same year, ' Lieut. Noah Stebbins is chosen to represent the town ' in another convention to be held at the same place; and in the ensuing November, Elijah Parsons is chosen to represent the town in a convention to be held in Hadley the next day. At the February session (1784) of the court, one Daniel Shays, of Pelham, ' Gentleman,' was defendant in a suit brought by John Johnson, ' yoeman,' for the enforcement of a promissory note for £12. Shays did not appear, and judgment and costs were entered against him. Shays was a hired man at Brookfield at the opening of the Revolution. He entered the army as sergeant, being under Washington near New York. He received one of the swords which Lafayette distributed to American officers. He eventually became Captain in the Fifth Massachusetts regiment, commanded by Rufus Putnam, and his record at Bunker Hill, Stony Point, and Saratoga was creditable. Being a judgment debtor, he did not allow the sales of property under judgments in Pelham to pass without protest. Taking specimen cases, and using round numbers, a man owing £24, had to pay £7 for the privilege of having the sheriff sell enough of his goods to raise £24. The sale of the bedding of a sick woman gave Shays a good text for tavern harangues at Pelham, East Amherst, and West Springfield, where Luke Day —legislator at large, and Captain in the Seventh Massachusetts regiment— talked by the hour. The legislature was flooded with petitions from suffering towns. Meanwhile, Shays and Day took a bold step at Springfield, September 26th, by interfering with the session of the Supreme General Court. The court adjourned, and also abandoned the October term at Great Barrington. Three weeks later, Shays proceeded to Rutland, and superintended the interruption of the courts at Worcester and elsewhere in December. He turned up in Springfield on the 22d of that month, and found the judges of the Court of Common Pleas an easy prey to the clubs, guns, drums, and threats of his men. In January, 1787, Shays essayed the difficult feat of capturing the federal arsenal at Springfield. He made a dash from Rutland with 1,000 men, indifferently armed, and on the 24th spent the night at Wilbraham, quartering his men on the inhabitants. Ely Parsons, with 400 insurgents from Berkshire, was at Chicopee, while Luke Day rested under arms at West Springfield with 400 more, whom he kept in good temper by occasional orations on the oppressions of government. Shays sent a messenger, with a letter to Day to be ready for the fight the next day; but the messenger, on his way back, pinched with cold, went into a tavern at Springfield to warm himself, and some young men present, suspecting all was not right, so plied him with friendly draughts that they soon put him into a drunken sleep and got from him Day's letter to Shays, saying that he could not fight before the 26th. Of this, therefore, Shays knew nothing. On the morning of the 25th, he moved toward Springfield ' on the Bay Road.' Asaph King, deputy sheriff, mounted a splendid young horse that stood saddled in his barn and started him across the fields to the ' Stony Hill Road.' The snow, knee-deep to his horse, was covered with a crust, and he was obliged in some instances, not only to make

AARON PARSONS AND (2) EXPERIENCE ROBINSON PARSONS.

93

110 | XI. Phoebe Parsons was the daughter of Aaron Parsons and his second wife Experience Robinson.

III. SERGEANT AARON PARSONS, JR.,

102

was born February 14, 1736, at Wilbraham,* Mass., and died February 20, 1799. He married, October 2,

a path for his horse, but to pull down or leap fences. When he came out upon the road, the legs of his horse were streaming with blood. He was far ahead of Shays, and spurring on, reached the arsenal in forty-five minutes from the time he left Wilbraham. Shepard now learned all the particulars of the number and proximity of the force of Shays, which were important to him, and prepared to meet them. The marching was bad, and Shays did not make his appearance on the road till about four o'clock in the afternoon. After some parleying and boasting on the part of Shays, his column moved on toward the loaded cannon of Shepard, who had threatened to fire if he did not halt. The insurgents kept on, not believing that Shepard would dare to fire. It was no time for dallying; yet Shepard, to show all possible forbearance, fired first to the right, then to the left, then over the heads of the column. But still they came on, the harmless roar of the cannon frightening the village more than the insurgents. They are within fifty rods of the battery, and pressing on. It was now time to fire in earnest. The cannon are trained on the centre of the column; the match is whisked in the air; the column comes on; the priming is touched; the smoke belches forth, and the shot fly. Soon the smoke lifts. The column is broken and flying, crying, ' murder.' Three men lie dead, and four are mortally wounded. Shays could not rally his men, and they fled with the utmost precipitation till the scattered column reached Ludlow, where they spent the night. The insurrection was soon after this wholly put down. The insurgents dispersed to their homes, and an amnesty almost general was declared. The sullen feeling in this part of the State survived for a time. Indeed it was at one time considered doubtful whether Massachusetts would cast her lot with the constitution framed by the convention that met in the following May at Philadelphia, presided over by George Washington. The sentiment in Hampshire County was about evenly divided. The vote in the convention was 187 yeas to 168 nays. By special legislation the pecuniary affairs of the State were adjusted so as to relieve to a great extent the sufferings of the people, and soon prosperity filled their purses and garners. The popularity of Shays was very great, however, among some people, and as late as forty years after the Rebellion, ' Hurrah for Shays!' was as common an exclamation in the mouths of many persons, as ' Hurrah for Jackson!' was twenty years later. The great struggle for independence was over; the rebellion consequent on a state of universal bankruptcy was put down, and its causes remedied; the constitution of the State was adopted; the ordinary channels of business began to open to the enterprising; and prosperity, peace, and happiness succeeded the poverty, tumult, and anxiety of war." (Rev. Dr. Rufus P. Stebbins, Historical Address; and M. A. Green, " History of Springfield.")

* " We have never regretted that we were born in Wilbraham. There are various ways in which mental powers are unfolded, directed, educated, and the man becomes fitted for a sphere of successful action in life. The work

1760, Eunice, daughter of Benjamin Warriner. She was born April 3, 1739.

Aaron Parsons, jr., was a soldier of the Revolution.[*]

Ten days later this company was reorganized under Gideon Burt as Captain. Aaron Parsons, jr., became sergeant, and served eight months, being in service at the siege of Boston. (Green: " Official History of Springfield.")

A member of this company wrote the following letter from the seat of war:

Honorid Father, ater my regards to you i take this opertunity to let you no that i am well as i hope that these lines

of education is not done exclusively in the school, the college, or the seminary of learning. There are other influences that perform for us this work. The mountain range, the peak, the crag, the valley, the stream, the spreading landscape and sky, the fireside, and the mother's smile all do for us this work of education. It is with unutterable emotion, therefore, that we return to the spot of earth on which our eyes were first opened, and look from the eminence where, eighty years since, Mr. President, you were first pressed to a mother's bosom, upon the beautiful panorama among the hills, that from the home of your childhood is spread out before us. Those mountain slopes, those valleys, those woodlands and streams, can never be separated either from the thoughts or feelings of those whose cradles were rocked in that amphitheatre among the hills. Nay, those streams to-day, as they roll sparkling in the sunshine, the clouds themselves, as they hang over the landscape, are to us all voice, and they call up memories that refuse to be uttered save with quivering lip and moistened eye.

> " ' Time but the impression stronger makes.
> As streams their channels deeper wear.' "

(Rev. Dr. Russell, Wilbraham Centennial.)

[*] The Boston Alarm of September, 1774, had set over forty thousand soldiers all through New England on the march for the day as promptly as might have been the case in our days of telegraph. But even more marvellous was the speed with which the news of the battle of Lexington the next year got to the Connecticut River. The British soldiers left Boston before daybreak on the 19th of April, 1775, and on the 20th, Captain Elihu Kent, within an hour's notice, was at the head of a Suffolk company of fifty-nine men and a provision wagon, rushing for Springfield, where they took supper, and pressed on at once.

Each Springfield soldier was given one-half pound of powder. There were also given to the soldiers assembled here one hundred and eighty flints.

The Springfield taverns and streets were in a perfect uproar, and during the 20th and 21st soldiers were constantly forwarded. The British troops had left Boston to the tune of Yankee Doodle. In twenty-four hours it was the other army that was playing that tune. Springfield had for months been busy collecting arms and drilling men.

April 20th, Aaron Parsons, jr., with Benjamin, Lemuel, and Joseph Parsons, left Springfield in a company commanded by his cousin, Lieutenant Gideon Burt, which contained Alexander, Samuel, Calvin, Noah, Zadock, and Moses Bliss, besides representatives of the Pynchon, Cooley, Merrick, and other well-known families.

will find you and al my brothers and sisters i have some news to rite in the first place there was a battel between Charlstown and Cambridge and the Kings troops drove our men out of their intrenchment becaus they had no powder and they have burnt Charlstown and have intrenched on Buncors hill and our men have intrenched on winter hill wheir the regulers retreeted to when the first battle was at Concort which was June 16th they fired the same day at Roxbury and threw bums and carkeses in order to set the street on fire but by the goodness of god they did not for our men as soon as they had set it on fire would go out and put it out and they fired no more until last saterday when they fired again and tried to set it on fire but they would go and put it out one of our men took one of the carkeses and brot it up to the general before it went out and they set 2 or 3 houses on fire but they were as ferce as a bloodhown to put them out then the Rodeilanders went down on the neck with 2 or 3 feild peses and fired at them and made their sentrys run to the brestwork and then they fired upon our sentry and killed two of them we are building a fort in Roxbury and diging a trench acrost the neck no more at present so i remaine your obdint son

Jeduthan Sanderson.

Roxbury June 29th, 1775.

THE CHILDREN OF SERGEANT AARON PARSONS, JR., AND EUNICE WARRINER PARSONS.

102

111   I. Sergeant and Elder Aaron Parsons, 3d, was born at Wilbraham, Mass., January 26, 1761, and died at Canaan, New York, February 11, 1815. He married Rachel Preston, September 14, 1785.

112   II. Moses Parsons was born November 1, 1762.

113   III. Adna Parsons was born October 10, 1764.

114   IV. Rufus Parsons was born March 17, 1767, and died October, 1835. He married Annie Parker. Rufus Parsons died from the result of an accident which occurred when he was going to pay a visit to his son Adna. His grandson wrote, "I well remember my grandfather, Rufus, as being a very fine looking man."

115   V. Eunice Parsons was born November 17, 1769, and died April 8, 1829. She married Cyrus Paulk, of Springfield, August 30, 1792.

116 VI. Horace Parsons was born 1776. He married Sarah Paulk.

117 VII. Hosea Parsons was born 1778. He married Sally Upham.

118 VIII. Lucy Parsons was born September 10, 1780, and died in 1854. She married Zardus Olds.

119 IX. Samuel Parsons was born September 19, 1783.

120 X. Patience Parsons was born March 2, 1785.

121 XI. Eli Parsons was born October 23, 1786.

122 XII. Shubael Parsons was born July 8, 1788. His father died in 1799, and in 1802 F. Holton was appointed guardian for " Shubael Parsons, minor."

123 XIII. Sylvester Parsons was born October 29, 1791.

Sylvester is a Woodbridge name, and first appeared in the Parsons family after the marriage of Zenas Parsons to Isabel Woodbridge. Within a few years after the appearance of the name Sylvester in the Joseph-Daniel-Aaron line of Parsons, it is found in the Joseph-Thomas line. Sylvester, son of Thomas Parsons, the proprietor of Parsonfield, Me., led a seafaring life for fourteen years, and then settled in Wilson, N. Y. Shortly after, Aaron Parsons, nephew of the first Sylvester among the Parsons (Joseph-Daniel-Aaron) removed to Wilson, N. Y., where at least one of his children (John Jehiel) was born.

SERGEANT AND DEACON AARON PARSONS, 3D, | 111

was born at Wilbraham, Mass., January 26, 1761, and died at Canaan, Columbia County, N. Y., February 11, 1815. He married, September 14, 1785, Rachel Preston, b. January 23, 1765, d. March 1, 1851, daughter of Asa Preston of Harwinton, Conn.

Asa Preston served in the Revolution in a battalion detached from the Sixth Brigade, Connecticut Militia, for defence of sea-coast of same, to March 1, 1780. He was son of John Preston, Jr., of Windham, Conn., m. Eleanor (dau. of John and Deliverance Town) Stiles of Boxford, Mass.; son of John Preston of Andover, Mass., and Mary Haynes of Haverhill, Mass.; son of Samuel Preston of Ipswich, Mass., son of Roger Preston, b. London, England, 1614, emigrated to Ipswich 1635.

Emily Parsons Holmes wrote in 1888, " My grandfather Parsons was tall and had dark hair. He was a miller by occupation, and a deacon in the Presbyterian church. I have seen many times the big bottle in which he used to keep the communion wine. He served in the Revolutionary army when but a boy. He was one of the outer guard when Andre was hanged. He owned a mill on Whiting's pond in Canaan, and is buried there."

At Garrisons-on-Hudson, young Aaron Parsons was General Rufus Putnam's orderly. This was the foundation of a life-long friendship between the two.

At the close of the War of Independence, General Putnam went to Ohio with Major-General Samuel Holden Parsons, the " intimate friend of Washington."

The name of Aaron Parsons, 3d, is on record in the casualty book in file in the Bureau of Pensions at Washington, as enlisting for six months July 3, 1780, in the Sixth Massachusetts Continental Regiment commanded by Colonel Nixon, and discharged December 4, 1780.

An enlisted soldier, after joining a regiment, was detached on account of his qualifications, to join a regiment of the Artillery Artificers' organizations.

Thus, Aaron Parsons, 3d, became an orderly sergeant in Lieutenant Daniel Fry's command of Army Artificers. His orderly book, in possession of Albert Ross Parsons, ends abruptly on the day of the battle of Rhode Island, when he received a wound in the head, for which he was honorably discharged from further service. The wound never entirely healed, and it occasioned his death in 1815.

In the papers in the office of the City Clerk at Springfield it is recorded that in 1780 Aaron Parsons, 3d, was paid $1,000, and again $200.

(From a communication by Aaron Parsons 3d, to the editors of the Connecticut Evangelical Magazine, conveying the " joyful intelligence of the outpouring of God's Spirit into the hearts of careless and secure sinners " at Canaan, N. Y., in the winter of 1802-3.)

(Conclusion.) . . . "Let us break off from every sinful course and by a faithful obedience to the commands of God lay up for ourselves treasures in heaven. Let us work out our own salvation with fear and trembling, at all times feeling our dependence on the sovereign grace and mercy of God for Divine assistance. Let us be much in prayer at the throne of grace for the outpouring of God's Spirit upon those of the human race who remain careless and secure, that they may be awakened to a consideration of the sinfulness of their ways; that they may realize their ingratitude while they neglect to give God their hearts, and refuse to comply with his requirements; and that they may be brought to humble themselves before God, and take their proper place at the footstool of sovereign grace and mercy. Let us earnestly cry to God for his blessing to rest on all who profess to be the friends of Christ, that they may walk worthy of their high vocation, that they may forsake every appearance of evil, that they may live as lights in the world, and at all times as seeing Him who is invisible, trusting in the mercy of God, and waiting with patience for the coming of our Lord and Saviour Jesus Christ in the clouds of heaven taking vengeance on all that know not God and love not his appearing, when his saints will be rewarded with everlasting life, and be bidden a divine welcome into the immediate presence of God and His Son Jesus Christ, to enjoy eternal felicity and happiness where they will be filled with joy unspeakable and full of glory. But the wicked, and the finally impenitent will be bidden: ' Depart ye workers of iniquity into everlasting punishment prepared for the devil and his angels.'

" Let all awake out of sleep and fly to Christ, the only ark of safety. Seek the Lord while he may be found, call upon him while he is near.

" ' Seize the kind promise while it waits,
And mount to Zion's heavenly gates.'

"Canaan, N. Y., October 15, 1803.

"AARON PARSONS."

THE CHILDREN OF DEACON AND SERGEANT AARON PARSONS, 3D, AND RACHEL PRESTON PARSONS. [111]

124   I. Harriet Parsons was born December 16, 1786, and died November 24, 1870, at Pekin, Niagara County, N.Y. Unmarried. She was named after Harriet Williams Parsons, wife of the Rev. David Parsons of Amherst. Harriet Parsons had a fine mind and proud spirit. Among the noted people of her time whom she numbered among her personal friends, were Fenimore Cooper, President Martin Van Buren, General and United States Secretary of War Porter of Niagara Falls, etc. She was educated at Kinderhook on the Hudson, one of the great schools of the day. As time passed and her friends, associates, and kindred, one by one, entered the silent land, she held herself more and more aloof from people in general; she would never suffer any one to enter the room once occupied by a person deceased, or to examine the effects, letters, keepsakes, etc., left by such an one; and in various ways developed marked idiosyncracies of mind and conduct.

125   II. Captain Jehiel Parsons was born October 6, 1788, and died unmarried June 8, 1825, at Waterloo, N. Y. He was captain of an artillery company and master of the local masonic lodge. On the morning of the visit of General La Fayette to Waterloo, a cannon burst as Captain Parsons was passing, and he was instantly killed (see p. 145, The Death of Captain Jehiel Parsons).

"General La Fayette was escorted from Geneva by a troop of cavalry and was received at the hotel amidst patriotic airs. Among the enthusiastic throng were several old revolutionary soldiers, tottering under the weight of infirm age, who had fought and bled in the same glorious conflict. Two or three of these remaining relics of the struggle for national independence had the high gratification of shaking the hand of the venerable Patriot. A large concourse of respectable citizens assembled at Waterloo to behold the noble, self-sacrificing companion of Washington."

126   III. Calvin Parsons was born October 1, 1790, and died January 13, 1792.

127   IV. Sarah Parsons was born March 29, 1793, and died at Pekin, N. Y., May 4, 1868. She married David Beebe of Sullivan County, N. Y. They went to Niagara County, about the time her mother removed from Canaan to Niagara County.

128   V. Aaron Parsons was born February 3, 1795, and died April 25, 1795.

129   VI. Rachel Parsons was born April 6, 1796, and died April 19th, of the same year.

130   VII. Elder, Sergeant, and Justice Aaron Parsons, 4th, was born June 9, 1797, at Canaan, N. Y., and died August 27, 1866, at Niagara Falls, N. Y. He married, January 20, 1820, Emily Stow of Stockbridge, Mass.

131   VIII. John Parsons was born May 20, 1799, and died unmarried at Auburn, N. Y., May 1, 1825.

132   IX. Eliza Parsons was born December 3, 1801, and died unmarried at Norfolk, Va., July 14, 1828.

133   X. Charlotte Parsons was born February 3, 1806, and died November 3, 1883, at Hart, Michigan. She married John Dayharsh, a descendant of a Hessian family who settled in the Mohawk Valley. Her son, John Parsons Dayharsh, came into possession, after her death, of all the family relics, the family bible, Lafayette's letter to Rachel Preston Parsons, the old tune-book, pitch pipe for starting the hymns, and other mementoes of Deacon Aaron Parsons, 3d.

134   XI. Captain and Elder Charles Parsons was born March 1, 1811, and died unmarried, at Niagara Falls, November 5, 1838. He was named after his great uncle, Captain Charles Parsons, who commanded at Ticonderoga in 1780. He received his Captain's commission from General Scott, at the time when the latter maintained by force of arms the neutrality of the United States on the Niagara River, during the uprising in Canada known as the Patriot War.

In 1837 an insurrection took place in Canada, many of the inhabitants being dissatisfied with governmental methods. It threatened to cause international complications, since many in the United States sympathized with the Canadians. About 700 men, chiefly from New York State, under Mackenzie, one of the leaders of the Canadian revolt, seized and fortified Navy Island, in the Niagara River, within British jurisdiction. They made this a base of operations for raids on the Canadian shore until they were forced to evacuate by a battery on the Canadian side. The steamer Caroline, of which they had made use, was seized by the Canadian militia at a wharf on the American side of the river, and sent, on fire, with ten souls on board, over Niagara Falls. This fiendish deed enraged the American people. Our government sent General Scott with a force of soldiers to prevent infractions of our neutral position. In July, 1842, Great Britain apologized to our government for the violation of territory made in the seizure of the Caroline, and our government accepted the apology and expressed its satisfaction.

OBITUARY.

CAPTAIN CHARLES ALBERT PARSONS. 134

"At Niagara Falls, N. Y., on the 5th instant, in the peace and hope of the Gospel, Mr. Charles Albert Parsons, in the twenty-eighth year of his age, after a lingering illness, which he bore with distinguished Christian patience and resignation. He was for several years an elder in the church and superintendent of the Sabbath school, was devoted and zealous in every department of Christian duty; and was liberal, intelligent, and active in the promotion of every benevolent enterprise. The church with which he was connected, and the society in which he was known, deeply lament his loss, and will long cherish the remembrance of his many virtues."

ELDER, SERGEANT, AND JUSTICE AARON PARSONS, 4TH, 130

born at Canaan, N. Y., learned woollen manufacturing with Millard Fillmore, subsequently President of the United States, in the woollen mills of Isaac Curtis and Co. of Curtisville, near Stockbridge, Mass., in which firm Aaron became a partner.* Subsequently, both Fill-

* Millard Fillmore, the fellow apprentice in Curtis' woollen mills and lifelong friend of Aaron Parsons, 4th, was born in Cayuga County, N. Y., January 7, 1800. He died at Buffalo, March 8, 1874. He served in Congress from 1833 to 1835, and from 1837 to 1843, as a Whig. In 1848 he was elected Vice-President, and on President Taylor's death he succeeded to the presidency. In

more and Aaron Parsons prepared to teach school, from which studies Fillmore subsequently turned to the study of law. Aaron Parsons was married at Stockbridge, Mass., whence he removed to Wilson, N. Y. In the winter of 1826 Aaron taught school in Niagara County. In 1827 he removed to the village of Niagara Falls, where he resided until 1835, engaged in woollen manufacturing. Here he filled the office of justice of the peace. In the fall of 1839 he sold his business and went to Pendleton, where he was elected superintendent of public schools, which office he held for a number of years. Through his efforts the schools were raised to a high standard of excellence.

"General Peter B. Porter, United States Secretary of War, 1828-29, with whom Aaron Parsons was long associated at Niagara, pronounced him a man of very superior mind."

Aaron Parsons was a Democrat, advocating those principles which won for the party its greatest successes, viz., the limitation of the powers of the federal government to those granted by the letter of the constitution, and the increase of the direct influence of the people in the affairs of the government. He was a consistent Christian of the New England Puritan school, mild, yet firm in discipline, but opposed to physical coercion. Family prayer and grace at the table were the rule in his household. Though descended from a line of tall ancestors, he was but of medium height, and while the Parsons were dark-haired men, he inherited from the Prestons sandy hair and fair complexion.

While still at Canaan, he was orderly sergeant in an artillery company. He was a man of courage, and when over sixty years of age, being attacked by four masked burglars in the county clerk's office at Kokomo, Ind.

1850 the Whigs in Congress took the position that the slavery question, which they regarded as settled by the compromise of 1850, should not be opened again. This policy was approved by President Fillmore. Dissension followed in the party in many of the States. In Massachusetts those opposed to the stand thus taken by the leaders were known as Conscience Whigs; those that approved as Cotton Whigs. In New York the supporters of Fillmore's views were called Silver Grays, because they were mostly the older men. They were also called the Snuff-Takers. Those opposing it, headed by W. H. Seward, were called Woolley Heads or Seward Whigs.

(where his son Charles was then county clerk), he defended himself stoutly, so that though his face was bruised so badly as to close his eyes, and he was seriously injured by being violently thrown down, the burglars were foiled in their attempt to get the keys of the safe.

Millard Fillmore sought to draw Aaron Parsons into politics, but upon being offered, when a young man, a nomination to the office of county clerk with the certainty of election, upon condition that he would permit access to the records on Sundays, he refused to give his consent, declined the nomination, and never again permitted his name to be used as a candidate for political preferment.

The following extracts from letters extant, written in his twentieth and twenty-first years, will interest his descendants:

"Lee, Mass., October 21, 1817.

"Dear Sister: I hear nothing from Canaan, the place that was once most dear to me. The place is changed. No more do I visit it. And if I should, it would only bring to mind scenes that are past. No more should I there be greeted by the kind welcome of parents, brothers and sisters. No trace of these remains there, but the ashes of our beloved and ever to be lamented father. For that circumstance I revere the spot.

"In your letter to John you wrote as if you did not find everything as you expected; I was fearful that you anticipated too much. To shun the ills of life we must shun life itself; although some situations are preferable to others. I thank you for your solicitude for our welfare and moral character. Be assured there is a double guard set against the odious vice of intemperance. Who has lived and not seen the pernicious effects of this brutal vice. Man, whose mind is capable of soaring to the heavens, casting himself beneath the brutes that are confined to the earth! Intemperance creeps on insensibly, and those who are caught find the net drawn tight before they are aware. When once pride is lost, and dignity cast down, there is no remedy; their doom is sealed; those men are ruined; ruined forever, for this world and that which is to come."

"Lee, Mass., August 25, 1818.

"Dear Sister: . . . Reading and writing are my principal amusements. I have found by experience that I have not as much time to devote to these purposes as I had before I commenced business for myself. You have often read my thoughts upon the improvement of time. Every day proves to me the absolute necessity of taking each moment and making a good use of it as soon as it comes. The words of an English poet are a lesson to all mankind: 'Our time of life is short. To spend that shortness basely 'twere too long.' To spend our time in the improvement of our minds or in providing for the necessary events of this world, cannot be called 'basely.' But to spend our time in riot or in idleness must be called base in the extreme. How far I act the base part I will not say; I am sensible that my mind is occupied with the fleeting things of this world too much, by far too much for my eternal welfare, and the glory of my Maker. I often think of these things, and as often drive them from my mind. Sometimes I think I have a faint view of my awfully sinful condition, and then I feel as if I would give a world to be free from it if it were in my power. Such impressions are not apt to continue long; the cares of this world soon disperse them. I live under the care of an excellent minister of the Gospel. It is the Rev. Dr. Hyde. I think he feels a particular interest in me. At the first interview I had with him, he took me by the hand as cordially as though we had always been acquainted, and said: 'I know you, and respect you for the sake of your excellent father.' He had previously been informed of my name and parentage. He has ever since expressed a particular regard for me. This happened a year ago. When I informed him I had heard that two of my sisters had made a public profession of religion, he made this reply: 'Then your excellent father's prayers are in part answered.'

"I have now, dear sister, a subject to mention to you that you will little expect from me. During the time that I resided in Stockbridge, I became acquainted with a young lady for whom I have a warm affection. The probability is that I shall at some future period take her hand. She is of respectable family * and in good circumstances; her educa-

---

* The young lady referred to was Emily Stow, his future wife. Her ancestry was as follows:

Emily Stow was the daughter of (1) Elder Zebulon Stow = (2) Hannah Spencer; son of (3) Captain Zebulon Stow = (4) Rosetta Riley; son of (5) Joseph Stow = (6) Sarah Bulkeley; son of (7) Thomas Stow; son of (8) Thomas; son of (9) John. (2) Hannah Spencer was of the Garrard Spencer line from a branch of the "noble house of Spencer," in England, descended from the *Despencer* of William the Conqueror. (4) Rosetta Riley was dau. of (10) Nathaniel Riley = (11) Abigail Montague; dau. of (12) Richard Montague; son of (13) John; son of (14) Richard = (15) Abigail Downing; son of (16)

tion is good, her manners affable, and her disposition pleasant.

"My acquaintance with her has been long. I have deferred mentioning it till now for several reasons.

"Remember me to mother and all the family. I remain, with love and esteem, your brother,

"AARON PARSONS.

"P. S.—The bearer of this is the father of the lady mentioned above."

A letter to Aaron Parsons, 4th, from his brother-in-law, Joseph W. Marsh, affords an interesting picture of a new settler's life in New York State as late as 1820.

"Wilson, April 27, 1820.

"Dear Brother.—We arrived here the end of March, and have taken up our residence in the woods. Our settlement

Peter Montague; son of (17) William; son of (18) Robert; son of (19) William; of the family of Montacute, Earls of Salisbury, descended from Drogo de Montacute, born 1040, went to England with the Conqueror, 1066; from Fergus, king of Isle of Man; and from Orry, king of Denmark. (6) Sarah Bulkeley was dau. of (20) Edward Bulkeley; son of (21) Rev. Gershom Bulkeley = (22) Sarah Chauncey; son of (23) Rev. Peter Bulkeley; son of Rev. Edward, D.D.; descended from Robert, Lord of Bulkeley (temp. King John), and Ormus de Dauenporte, 1086. (15) Abigail Downing was dau. of (24) Rev. Dr. Downing; son of (25) George; son of (26) Sir Jeffrey = (27) Elizabeth Wingfield; dau. of (28) Thomas Wingfield; son of (29) Sir John; son of (30) Sir John; son of (31) Sir Robert = (32) Elizabeth Gousell; dau. of (33) Sir Robert Gousell = (34) Eleanor Fitz-Allen; dau. (35) Sir John Fitz-Allen; son of (36) Richard, Earl of Arundel = (37) Lady Eleanor Plantagenet; son of (38) Edmund, Earl of Arundel = (39) Lady Alice Warren; dau. of (40) John, Earl of Warren and Surrey; grandson of (41) Hamelin Plantagenet, Earl of Warren and Surrey = (42) Isabella de Warren; granddau. (43) William de Warren = (44) Elizabeth Vermandoise; grandson of (45) William the Conqueror = (46) Maud, dau. of (47) Baldwin, Count of Flanders. (22) Sarah Chauncey was dau. of (48) Rev. Charles Chauncey, 2d Pres. Harvard College; descended from (49) Sir William = (50) Joan Bigod; desc. from (51) Chauncey de Chauncey, went from Chauncey in France to England with the Conqueror, 1066; name on Battle Abbey roll. (50) Joan Bigod was desc. from the Bigods, Earls of Norfolk; desc. from William Bigod, "the Conqueror," 1066; desc. from King Charles the Simple; she (50) was also desc. from the de Veres, Earls of Oxford; and from (51) William Marshall, Earl of Pembroke = (52) Isabella de Clare; dau. of (53) Richard de Clare, "Strongbow" = (54) Eva McMorrough, Strongbow's grandfather, the second Earl of Clare, was ancestor of the Plantagenet Kings of England. His wife (54) was dau. of (55) Dermot McMorrough, last king of Leinster, 76th in descent from Milesius of Spain, 99th from Magog, son of Japhet, and 95th in descent from Scota, daughter of Meneptah, and granddau. of Rameses II. of Egypt (the Pharaoh of the Exodus), descendant of the monarchs under whom the Pyramids were built. (See O'Hart's Celtic Pedigrees.) (47) Baldwin was desc. from Beringer, King of Italy, Charles the Bald and Charlemagne. (48) Rev. Charles Chauncey was 6th in descent from (56) Margery Gifford, who was 9th in descent from (57) King William Leo of Scotland, who was 5th from King Duncan

consists of six men, three women, and four children in two houses. Our chief employ has been to fell the stubborn trees which stand thick all around us. The herbage covered the ground very early, and the trees are handsomely green. With the dawn of each morning we are saluted with the drumming of the partridge, and the sweet-tuned notes of innumerable birds. As the day advances we hear the sound of the wood-cock hammering the trees, the axes begin their toil, and the fall of the stately trees causes the woods to ring. The advancing sun cheers the chattering squirrel as he hops from branch to branch, and the timid deer feeds in peace through the day. The return of night is saluted by the owl, and our weary limbs retire to the sweetest rest in peace. The last two days have been spent in burning brush, ploughing gardens, planting a nursery of apple, peach, plum, apricot, and quince trees, and splitting rails. One tree that I worked at was a chestnut measuring four feet ten inches around. I got seventy-one rails from it. Tell your wife that since she has now changed her situation by getting married " [Aaron's wedding had taken place a few weeks prior to the date of this letter] " I remind her, as she did me at my wedding, that she had better settle somewhere near by a schoolhouse for the benefit of her children."

(murdered by Macbeth), who was desc. from King Fergus I., B.C. 330. (56) Margery Gifford was also 6th from Isabel de Albino, who was 4th from (58) Maud de Clare, who was 3d in descent from (59) Judith (niece of William the Conqueror), the granddau. of Robert the Devil (see Meyerbeer's " Roberto "). (58) Maud was 5th from (60) Alfred the Great, who was 23d in descent from Wotan and Freia (see Wagner's " Nibelungs Ring "). (53) Richard de Clare was 5th from (61) Hugh Capet, who was grandson of (62) King Henry the Fowler of Germany (see Wagner's " Lohengrin "), who was 25th from Wotan. (57) King William the Lion was 11th from Prince Rurik of Russia, A.D. 862, also (57) 4th in descent from King Henry I. of France, who was 6th from Basileus the Macedonian, A.D. 867, of the Parthian Royal family descended from Perseus. (30) Sir John Wingfield was 8th from King Edward I., 9th from King Henry III., 10th from King John, 11th from King Henry II., 12th from King Henry I., and 13th from William the Conqueror. He (30) was also 7th from (63) Joan of Acres, who was descended from the Kings of Lombardy, Aquitania and Super Arabia. (Authorities: Anderson's " Royal Genealogies " ; " Chauncey Memorial," etc.)

" Remember that his ancestress was an Egyptian, the daughter of a man of my own class." " How many generations have passed to the tomb since?" " No matter! It brings us into closer relations." (Georg Ebers: " Joshua.")

The Pyramid Mausoleum in Greenwood Cemetery, borough of Brooklyn, New York, reproduces the proportions of the Great Pyramid of Gizeh, and its portal, those of the portals of the temples of Luxor, Thebes and Dendrah. On the right hand is a sphinx, the union of the constellations of Virgo and Leo, with the "Sun of Righteousness" rising with healing in his wings" by the star Denebola in Leo.* This prehistoric Hebrew Egyptian cosmic mystery finds its offshoot in the Christian Virgin and Infant Son, and the Good Shepherd bearing the Lamb (Aries) of the new ecliptical covenant, dating from the pass-over of the vernal equinox from Taurus (Aaron's golden calf) to Aries, *circa* B.C. 2123. On the bronze door is a tablet reproducing an ancient Christian astronomical design in which the cross, bearing the dying lamb (Aries), is erected where the joint of the

equinoctial covenant (Astarte-Easter, "passed over" from Aries to the sign of the Fishes, A.D. 29, as the "candlestick of the sun"* during the Christian dispensation (at the end of which, A.D. 2184, the disciples of the Son will meet Aquarius or "the man bearing a pitcher of water."†)

The mausoleum monumentalizes the identity of his (our Christianity with the prehistoric cosmic wisdom religion which Jesus came *not to destroy, but to fulfill.*

The detached statue on the left of the mausoleum is a memorial to Herbert Spencer Parsons, born **March 16, 1876**, died in the surf at **Long Beach**, L. I., **August 17, 1895**. It represents *Jochebed*, the mother of Moses, as she is about to commit her son to the waves.

The mausoleum was erected A.D. 1900, by Mr. C. H. Van Ness as a gift to his daughter Alice, **in memory** of her son Herbert, **after** a design made by her husband, **Albert Ross Parsons.**

*Compare riddle of Samson (*Hebrew Sun*) Judges xvi, 12-19, (Lion Leo, honey **Melitta**) with shipwreck of Paul (Soul—Sol, Paul—Pol, **Apollyon, destroyer, Rev. ix, 11**; Acts ix, 14); xiii, 9; 1 Cor. iii, 4) Castor and Pollux, Gemini) on the isle of *Melita* (Acts xxvii, 1), whence he sailed in a ship **bearing the sign** of the Gemini—Dioscuri, Acts xxviii, 11; also Jason, *i.e.* "healer" (see Virgil's Prince and Father Jason, *Aen* iii, 168) among the Christians, Acts xvii, 5-7. Leo, the Lion of the Royal Tribe of Judah, Taurus, Aquarius and Aquila appear in Revelation iv, 7

* Revelation i, 12-13; 20; ii, 1, 5
† Luke xvi, 10;
‡ Matthew v, 17.

(From the "Seneca Farmer," June 15, 1825.)

On Wednesday morning last was killed instantly by the bursting of a swivel gun, Capt. Jehiel Parsons, in the 37th year of his age. Under dispensations like the present the best sympathies of our nature are awakened and the heart knows no other solace to offer to the sorrow-stricken relatives than to reiterate the virtues of the deceased. Few men possess more of the virtues which adorn human nature than was possessed by the subject of this notice. His mind was capacious, his feelings liberal and generous to a fault; yet bold, decisive and efficient in all his acts, and his principles and temper partook of the manliness of his disposition and were regulated by it. As a son, he was devoted to a pious and a widowed mother—as a brother he was indulgent and kind—as a neighbor and a citizen he was without display—conciliating and patriotic. His public spirit showed its efficiency on every occasion where personal exposure and exertion were required. This dispensation is rendered more afflicting as the worthy mother had just returned from a long journey occasioned by the death of another son.

General La Fayette had proceeded as far as Syracuse before he was informed of the melancholy occurrence, the committee here not having deemed it prudent to mar his pleasure by the knowledge of a circumstance so peculiarly afflicting. He extremely regretted that he was not made acquainted with the event while here, since notwithstanding the pressure of his engagements he would have stopped and spent the day in mourning with the disconsolate family. He has sent back a deputation to inquire into the minute particulars of the accident.

(From the "Seneca Farmer," June 19, 1825.)

Auburn, June 19, 1825.

General La Fayette—

Dear General: I have the satisfaction of announcing to you that in obedience to the directions with which you honored me, I hastened to visit the family of the deceased Mr. Parsons at Waterloo. His aged mother and surviving sisters were found, as may be supposed, in deep distress at the occurrence of an awful catastrophe which has in an instant deprived them of their protector, and the village of a citizen universally esteemed. I communicated to them as from yourself, sir, the benevolent expressions of your paternal condolence and assured them of the sincere grief with which a knowledge of the accident had affected the heart of *him* in whom all America recognizes a *Father*, and believe me, sir, that in the midst of the solitude of grief, this bereaved family are duly sensible of the value of your condoling friendship; and that the citizens of that place consider their esteem for General La Fayette as enhanced by the remembrance of his excited sympathies in a case of distress so touching and irremediable.

On the joyous morning of your long-anticipated arrival, Capt. Parsons, after an early breakfast, left his widowed mother to repair to his usual place of business. His last words on leaving the house were—"I will arrange my affairs for the day as soon as possible, as I wish to go up to the hotel, and see the General." Ill-fated victim! He had proceeded but a few yards when the fatal accident happened by which he passed immediately out of present being, leaving a family and a town in consternation and sorrow.

The citizens of Waterloo are anxious, sir, that you should not be impressed with an idea that this melancholy disaster took place in the ordinary discharge of a soldier's duties, or at a parade of their military body. The act was strictly individual and arose from the imprudence and rashness of a few persons with whom the deceased had been in no degree connected. . . .

Your obdt. serv't,

G. A. Gamage.

(Extract from reply of the Marquis de La Fayette.)

Washington, August 3d, 1825.

My Dear Sir: I much regret the delay of my answer to your kind letter, June 16th, and also the circumstances which have deferred the condoling tribute of sympathy to Mrs. Parsons. . . . I have understood that arrangements had been made by her son, which would be defeated were they not enabled to pay a sum of money for a tract of land purchased by him. A sum of $1,000 being fully equal to that purpose, I have taken the liberty to send it with my letter to Mrs. Parsons. Receive my best thanks, . . .

La Fayette.

G. A. Gamage, Esq.,
Auburn, N. Y.

THE CHILDREN OF SERGEANT AND ELDER 130
AARON PARSONS, 4TH, AND EMILY STOW
PARSONS.

135   I. Harriet Eliza Parsons, born at Canaan, N. Y.,
February 7, 1821, died at Pendleton, N. Y., July 19,
1844, unmarried.

136   II. Sergeant Frederick Spencer Parsons, born at
Canaan, N. Y., March 30, 1824. Married Eliza, daughter of Richard Welton, of Beech Ridge, Niagara Co.,
N. Y. No issue. After the death of his wife, Mr. Parsons sold his property in Niagara Co., and purchased
seventy acres near East Northport, Long Island.

137   III. Brevet Lieutenant-Colonel and Elder John
Jehiel Parsons was born at Wilson, N. Y., May 21,
1827; died at East Northport, L. I., April 27, 1894.

138   IV. Emily Parsons, born at Niagara Falls, N. Y.,
June 8, 1829. Married Colonel Joseph W. Holmes, of
the Eighth New York Heavy Artillery in the War of
Secession.

139   V. Aaron Parsons, 5th, born at Niagara Falls, N. Y.,
October 20, 1831; died at Wabash, Ind., September 28,
1856, unmarried.

"He was an excellent and estimable young man."—
Buffalo Advertiser.

140   VI. Corporal Zebulon Stow Parsons, born at Niagara
Falls, N. Y., July 31, 1834; killed in the battle of
Monocacy, Md., July 9, 1864, unmarried.

141   VII. Elder Charles Albert Parsons, born at Lock-
port, N. Y., July 11, 1839; died July, 1898, interred at
Peru, Ind., where he long resided, being several times
elected County Clerk of Miami Co. He was a Free
Mason, an Elder in the Presbyterian Church, and for
twenty-three years superintendent of the Sunday-school.
He married Mary Ferris, of Niagara Falls, N. Y. Was
buried with the rites of the Order.

"A final proof of the high esteem in which every one
in the community held Charles A. Parsons was shown by
the attendance at his funeral ceremonies in the Presby-

terian Church, the congregation more than filling the auditorium. The body was viewed by hundreds of people before the ceremonies. The Knights Templar of Logansport and the Peru lodge of Masons took places reserved in the forward part of the church. The Reverend Leon P. Marshall, a former pastor of the church and an especial friend of Mr. Parsons, came from Franklin especially for the service. His words were those of comfort, and of exhortation to all to follow the very high example of Mr. Parsons's life, a precious life that had gone to its reward. Mr. Parsons's private life was noble and helpful to others. His public life was perfect and would stimulate others to follow his good example."—Peru Evening Journal.

BREVET LIEUTENANT-COLONEL AND ELDER JOHN 137
JEHIEL PARSONS was educated by a tutor for a profession, and graduated at De Vaux College, Niagara Falls, N. Y., showing marked talent for classics and mathematics. Deciding upon a business career, he left home at eighteen years of age, and went into business at Buffalo, N. Y. Marrying, at the age of nineteen, he went to Sandusky, O., in 1847, where his eldest child was born. In 1858 he returned to Buffalo, where he was partner in the firm of Parsons and Johnson, manufacturers of printed and blank books, in connection with the printing-house of Thomas and Lathrop, publishers of the "Buffalo Commercial Advertiser." In 1857 he removed to Indianapolis, Ind., where he carried on the same business in connection with the "Daily Sentinel" newspaper. After the war he went to Utica, N. Y., where he resided from 1868 to 1870. He then removed to New York City, where he resided until a few months before his death, when he took up his residence with his brother, Frederick, at East Northport, L. I. In New York City Mr. Parsons organized, and was for several years secretary and treasurer and a stockholder in the New York Sanitary Supply Company, now on a dividend-paying basis. He also devised the novel plans upon which the Columbia Building and Loan Association was organized. On the advice of Shepard Homans, Esq., a prominent actuary and President of the

John J. Parsons

Provident Savings Life Association of New York, the trustees of the Columbia Association voted Mr. Parsons $5,000 of the preferred stock of the said association in exchange for his plans of organization, and he was annually re-elected secretary and treasurer of the corporation, which offices he held at his death.

The family burial-plot and obelisk are at Utica, N. Y., but Mr. Parsons is interred near East Northport. The stone marking his place of rest bears the following inscription:

> "JOHN JEHIEL PARSONS.
>
> Born at Wilson, New York, May 21, 1827,
> Died at East Northport, L. I., April 24, 1894."

"He was a Lieutenant in the Militia, Brevet Lieutenant-Colonel Camp of Instruction for Volunteers, 1861, an Ancient Scottish Rite Mason, 32d degree, and an Elder in the Presbyterian Church.

> "A man of liberal education
> And active, inquiring mind:
> In all the duties of life
> Uncorrupt and honorable:
> Sympathetic and generous,
> Wishing well to all:
> Happy in himself
> And agreeable to his associates,
> He lived for others
> And died rejoicing in the
> Faith of Salvation through
> Jesus Christ."

Mr. Parsons married, February 2, 1846, at Buffalo, N. Y., Sarah Volinda Averill, daughter of Corporal Samuel Averill, Jr., of Gowanda, Cattaraugus Co., N. Y., a soldier of the War of 1812; he was the only son of Samuel Averill, Sr., of Randolph, Plymouth, and West Brookfield, Vt., who was a soldier in the War of the Revolution, a brother of Asa Averill, and son of John[4], line of John[3], William[2], William[1] Averill of Ipswich, Mass.

"The Averills have been public-spirited, decided and energetic in the performance of business and duty."— Cothren's "Woodbury."

The mother of Samuel Averill, Jr., of Gowanda, was Molly Barnes, of Concord, Mass. In her Bible, preserved for three generations in the family, she wrote, in her girlhood, the following lines:

"Molly Barnes is my name,
English is my nation;
Concord is my dwelling-place,
Christ is my salvation."

THE CHILDREN OF BREVET LIEUTENANT-COLONEL JOHN JEHIEL PARSONS AND SARAH AVERILL PARSONS. 137

142 I. Albert Ross Parsons, author of the "Synthetic Method for the Pianoforte"; "Parsifal, the Finding of Christ through Art"; "New Light from the Great Pyramid"; and the present Parsons's Memorial, born at Sandusky, O., September 16, 1847.

143 II. Marie Emilie Parsons, born at Buffalo, N. Y., June 13, 1851.

144 III. Ella Teresa Parsons, born at Buffalo, N. Y., July 18, 1854.

145 IV. Kate Burwell Parsons, born at Buffalo, N. Y., July 15, 1856.

146 V. Frederick Chester Parsons, born at Indianapolis, Ind., November 21, 1859.

147 VI. Harriet Sophronia Parsons, born at Indianapolis, Ind., March 11, 1862; died at Utica, N. Y., March 2, 1869.

148 VII. John Edward Parsons, born at Indianapolis, Ind., March 27, 1865.

149 VIII. Horace Talbot Parsons, born at Indianapolis, Ind., April 9, 1868; died at Utica, N. Y., March 6, 1862.

NOTE.—Detailed information as to Brevet Lieutenant-Colonel John Jehiel Parsons, and his descendants, will be preserved in the custody of the New York Historical Society.

CHILDREN OF CAPTAIN CHARLES PARSONS AND LUCY BALDWIN PARSONS. [105]

150   I. Charles Parsons, b. 1785; had one daughter.

151   II. Ebenezer Parsons, b. 1788; d. young.

152   III. Isaac Parsons, b. 1789; went to Canada.

153   IV. Lucy Parsons, b. 1791; m. John Anderson; had five children.

154   V. Lewis Baldwin Parsons, b. 1793; m. Lucina Hoar.

155   VI. Walter Chamberlain Parsons, b., North Adams, Mass., March 30, 1795; d. June 17, 1859, at Middletown, N. J.; m., March 28, 1829, Mary Moreford; b. December 6, 1800; d. March 23, 1875.

156   VII. Marshall Parsons, b. 1797; d. 1813.

CHILDREN OF WALTER CHAMBERLAIN PARSONS AND MARY MOREFORD PARSONS. [155]

157   I. Lucy Moreford Parsons, b. September 27, 1832; d. in Germany, August 10, 1870; m. Wm. Wurdeman, Civil Engineer, January, 23, 1859.

158   II. Charles Baldwin Parsons, b Monmouth, N. J., July 3, 1835; m., January 20, 1868, Elizabeth M. Bergen, b. October 3, 1848. Enlisted November, 1861, in 1st New York Engineers and served with distinction till close of the Rebellion, July, 1865, on Staff of Major-General Terry as Inspector, on that of Major-General Butler as Engineer, and as Chief Engineer, 25th Army Corps, on Staff of Major-General Weitzel, participating in the battles about Charleston, S. C., and Petersburg, Va. Retired with the rank of Captain and Brevet Major.

LEWIS BALDWIN PARSONS, SEN. [154]

Lewis Baldwin Parsons, b. Williamstown, Mass., April 30, 1793; d. Detroit, Mich., December 21, 1855; m., November 10, 1814, Homer, N. Y., Lucina Hoar; b. October 31, 1790, Brimfield, Mass.; d. October 3, 1873,

Gouverneur, N. Y. He was a successful merchant, a man of uncommon force and energy of character, of rare catholicity in his religious views, as also in the breadth of his charities, and was the founder of Parsons' College, Iowa.

The English ancestry of Lucina Hoar, and the early history of her family in America, may be found in the researches made in both countries by Hon. George F. Hoar, United States Senator from Massachusetts, and published in the New England Historical and Genealogical Register for January, April, and July, 1899.

EXTRACT FROM THE WILL OF LEWIS BALDWIN PARSONS.

" Fourth. Having long been of the opinion that for usefulness, prosperity, and happiness of children, a good moral and intellectual or business education with moderate means was far better than large inherited wealth; I therefore herein dispose of my estate mainly to such benevolent objects and enterprises as I think will conduce to the greatest good, earnestly requesting that all my children after giving to their children a good education with habits of honesty, industry, economy, and liberality, will follow my example in the disposition of the property God may give them."

CHILDREN OF LEWIS BALDWIN PARSONS AND LUCINA HOAR PARSONS. 154

159   I. Octavia Parsons, b., in Scipio, N. Y., October 27, 1815; d. December 25, 1881; m., August, 1838, Wm. Erastus Sterling; b. June 4, 1801; d. March 5, 1861; merchant of Gouverneur, N. Y.

160   II. Philo Parsons, b. Scipio, N. Y., February 7, 1817; d. Winchenden, Mass., January 23, 1896; m., June 27, 1843, Moscow, N. Y., Ann Eliza Barnum; b. September 14, 1822; d., Detroit, Mich., April 25, 1893.

161   III. General Lewis Baldwin Parsons, jr.; b. Genesee Co., N. Y., April 5, 1818.

PHILO PARSONS

162   IV. Lucy Ann Parsons, b. January 11, 1820; d. May 9, 1859; m., at Gouverneur, N. Y., Charles S. Cone, merchant.

163   V. Harriet Matilda Parsons, b. March 22, 1822; d. August 22, 1823.

164   VI. Charles Parsons, b. January 24, 1824; m. Martha A. Pettus; b. March 23, 1830; d. February 13, 1889.

165   VII. Levi Parsons, b. January 24, 1826; d., St. Louis, Mo., April 9, 1850.

166   VIII. Emily Parsons, b. June 11, 1828; d. December 17, 1833.

167   IX. George Parsons, merchant and banker, b. Gouverneur, N. Y., January 2, 1830; m., October 23, 1855, Emily Lycett Barnum, b. April 30, 1830.

168   X. Helen Maria Parsons, b. July 19, 1834; d. August 6, 1863; m., November 16, 1858, George B. Boardman.

PHILO PARSONS.   169

Tribute by Prof. Joseph L. Daniels, of Olivet College, Michigan, Dec. 2, 1897.

Mr. Philo Parsons was born at Scipio, N. Y., February 6, 1817. His early years were spent in Gouverneur, Homer, and Perry, N. Y. At the latter place, he entered into business with his father under the firm name of L. B. Parsons & Son. And he also married there, in 1843, Miss Ann Eliza Barnum. Their long and happy married life was terminated in 1893 by the death of Mrs. Parsons, Mr. Parsons following her three years later, dying at Winchenden, Mass., January 20, 1896. Eight children were born to them, of whom seven survived their parents. In 1844, Mr. Parsons removed to Detroit, Mich., and entered upon the grocery business under the firm of Parsons & James. A few years later he established a private bank. In 1861, when the Government created the national banking system as an aid in carrying on the war, Mr. Parsons was the leader in organizing the First National Bank of Detroit, was its first president, and for many years one of its directors. He did much to promote the commercial prosperity of Detroit. He entered heartily into the project for bringing the Wabash Railroad into the city, was an active member of the Board of Trade, and for a time its president. For many years he represented his own city in the National Board of Trade and was honored repeatedly as one of its vice-presidents. His discussions in these national conventions show a wealth of information, a candor and breadth of view, and a discrimination akin to prophecy. He was an ardent lover of his own city and State, and yet on one occasion explained his vote, apparently against their interests, as "for the greatest good of the greatest number."

Mr. Parsons was active in the municipal affairs of Detroit, and for a time a member of its council. The State, too, more than once conferred upon him distinguished honors and trusts; notably as commissioner to the Yorktown Centennial, and as chairman of the Commission to secure the statue of General Lewis Cass to be placed in the Capitol at Washington. He brought to this work all the enthusiasm of a lifelong friendship and a patriotic pride for the honor of his beloved State. The statue, almost vocal with life, crowned his many months of toil and effort and was one of the great joys of his life. He honored himself in honoring the State.

Yet political offices and honors he did not seek. He even declined to consider them when they merely appealed to his personal ambition. Too much Puritanic and revolutionary blood flowed in his veins to ever regard public offices as anything but a sacred trust, a patriotic service. Mr. Parsons had a lively interest in agriculture, was an active member of the State Agricultural Society of Michigan, and served most acceptably as its president. He was an enthusiast in horticulture and fruit culture, and found relaxation and pleasure in personal work in his own garden, one of the finest in Detroit. He was a royal entertainer, and was never happier than when sharing the hospitality of his elegant home with his friends.

His benevolence was a matter of principle. He took special delight in aiding young men who were preparing for the work of Christian ministry. He was one of the largest and most systematic givers to the cause of missions. He was an enthusiastic believer in education.

While several institutions were looking with eager eyes toward the Ram Library at Heidelberg, Mr. Parsons bought and donated it in its entirety to the Michigan State University. In keeping with his father's spirit, he was especially devoted to the Christian College. He early became interested in Olivet College, Michigan. For thirty-six years he was a member of its board of trustees. He built his name into the history and even the very walls of the college. Parsons Hall and the Parsons Professorship are hon-

Lewis B. Parsons

ored words to-day. Not only his munificent gifts, but his
wise counsels and his lifelong devotion to the work at
Olivet are gratefully remembered. And no less were these
deeds of benevolence a grateful remembrance to Mr. Parsons himself. They were his glory and joy in his later years
of illness. He found a rich reward in the satisfaction of
building himself into institutions of education and religion.
Olivet College grew dearer to him. His home church, the
First Congregational Church of Detroit, grew dearer. His
beloved pastor and his intimate friends at Olivet received
frequent letters full of gratitude and joy for what he had
been permitted to do, and full of trust and hope in prospect
of a blessed immortality. In this spirit, he entered into
rest. His death was literally a sleep. He slept on earth to
awake in Heaven.

BREVET MAJOR GENERAL LEWIS BALDWIN PARSONS. 161

General Parsons, b. Genesee Co., N. Y., April 5, 1818;
Yale College, 1810; Harvard Law School, LL.B., 1844;
Captain of Volunteers, October 31, 1861; Colonel and
Aide-de-Camp to Major-General Halleck, April 4, 1862;
Brigadier-General, May 11, 1865, by autographic order
of President Lincoln, for special services; Brevet Major-
General, April 30, 1866; Democratic candidate for
Lieutenant-Governor of Illinois in 1880 on the ticket
with Judge Lyman Trumbull for Governor. Delegate
to the National Democratic Convention which nom-
inated Grover Cleveland for President in 1884. President Illinois Soldiers' and Sailors' Home, 1893-97; member G. A. R. and Army of the Tennessee, and Companion
of Loyal Legion.

General Parsons's early years were mostly spent at school
or in his father's country store at Gouverneur, St. Lawrence
Co., New York. He entered Yale College in 1836. His father
having suffered severely in the financial revulsions of 1837,
he was obliged to struggle for an education under great
difficulties, yet, by his energy and industry, he graduated
with reputation in his class in 1840. In order to discharge

debts incurred in college, and obtain funds to enable him to pursue his professional education, he taught a classical school in Mississippi for two years, evincing those traits of energy and integrity which not only then met with a just reward, but which have characterized him through his successful life. Entering Harvard Law School, then presided over by Justice Story and Professor Greenleaf, in 1842, he pursued his studies till the spring of 1844, when, turning his steps westward, he landed in St. Louis in March of that year, with funds only sufficient to pay a drayman to take his baggage to a hotel, a good library, for which he owed $600; a determined will, and an honest purpose to succeed. Less than twenty years after, the same man had been the financial manager of the Ohio and Mississippi Railroad— one of the greatest commercial arteries leading to the same city; and had been for years engaged in directing the transportation of great armies, with all their supplies, animals, and munitions, during a long war of the greatest magnitude—controlling, by his single will, under the general order of the Secretary of War, all the vast means and modes of transportation, not only of all the rivers and railroads of the West, but of the entire country—such are the changes of our country and time!

Mr. Parsons, soon after reaching St. Louis, went to Alton and became the partner of Newton D. Strong, an eminent lawyer and a brother of Judge Strong, of the United States Supreme Court. The firm did a large and successful business till Mr. Strong left the State, when Mr. Parsons formed a partnership with Judge Henry W. Billings. In 1853 Mr. Parsons left Alton and became the legal adviser of the great banking house of Page & Bacon, then engaged in constructing the Ohio and Mississippi Railroad, at the same time purchasing the land on which he has since made the large farm on which he now resides. On the suspension of the banking house of Page & Bacon, Messrs. Aspinwall and associates took possession of the railroad, retaining Mr. Parsons as the general western manager. In the various positions of attorney, treasurer, manager, director, and president of this road for nearly a quarter of a century, he discharged his duties so as to secure the perfect confidence of all parties and the public in his integrity, energy, and capacity. In 1860 General Parsons resigned his official position with a view of rest and a European tour; but, perceiving the country was on the brink of a civil war, he resolved to stay at home and serve the nation. Soon after the commencement of the war General George B. McClellan, who, as vice-president of the Ohio and Mississippi Railroad, had known General Parsons and his abilities, offered him a position under him in the East, which was at once accepted, and he proceeded thither.

Early satisfied that the field and the West best suited his taste, Gen. Parsons obtained an order to report to St. Louis, with the view to raising a regiment. On arriving there, General Curtis, commanding the department, placed him on a commission with Captain, now Lieutenant-General, Sheridan, to investigate the affairs connected with General Fremont's administration, which soon led to the celebrated Holt-Davis commission of greater civil powers. In the mean time, General Halleck having taken command, and finding nothing but disorder and confusion in the transportation service—that it was conducted utterly regardless of system or economy—was inefficient and the source of endless complaints by the railroads, who neither knew whose orders to obey nor how to obtain compensation due them, learning of General Parsons's experience and abilities, obtained an order from the Secretary of War placing him on his staff as aide-de-camp, with rank of colonel, and gave him entire charge of the railroad and river transportation. General Parsons accepted the situation with a cheerful confidence, which was amply vindicated by the results, and which soon brought order and harmony out of chaos and confusion. Introducing a few simple, well-defined rules, combining uniformity with responsibility, and efficiency with economy, a revolution was at once effected most satisfactory to the Government officers and the railroads performing service, so that they, as well as all river navigation, became part of a single, central system, acting not only with power and efficiency, but with unsurpassed economy. Such success gained the entire confidence of the Government, and General Parsons's authority soon became complete and co-extensive with the valley west of the Alleghanies, extending from the Gulf of Mexico to the Indian wars, two thousand miles up the Yellowstone, as also the Upper Mississippi. In 1863 the Secretary of War ordered General Parsons to Washington, but revoked the order on his tendering his resignation rather than leave the West. In 1864, however, on an imperative order of the Secretary, he took charge of the Rail and River Transportation of the entire country, and in a brief period perfected a complete organization and introduced rules, regulations, and forms, which were made the permanent basis of action for that important department.

It is a singular fact that, though so successful in all respects, General Parsons twice tendered his resignation in order to raise a regiment for active field service, which was, as it should have been, imperatively declined by the Secretary of War. Happening to be present at the first attack on Vicksburg, he tendered his services and acted as volunteer aid to General Sherman, and subsequently acted in like capacity on General McClernand's staff, at the battle and capture of Arkansas Post, where he was among the first to enter the fortification, and for which he received special notice from the commanding officers. Soon after the surrender of Lee, General Parsons tendered his resignation, his private business imperatively requiring his attention, but was detained by the Secretary of War for many months to aid in important service. The same firmness, energy, and economy have distinguished General Parsons equally in public and private life, and evinced his superior organizing and administrative abilities.

There is upon record abundant evidence from the highest authority—from such men as President Lincoln, Generals Grant and Sherman, Judge David Davis, E. B. Washburne, and others—of most meritorious service, all agreeing that General Parsons's administration saved millions to the Government.

As early as September 13, 1863, that most able and excellent officer, General Robert Allen, then Colonel Parsons's superior, in writing the Secretary of War, asking for Colonel Parsons's promotion, among other things, said: "Having had charge of that most important branch of the service, steamboat and railroad transportation, his duties have been arduous, and highly responsible, and he has discharged them with signal success and ability. His administration of this branch of the department has been eminently satisfactory. No military movement in the West has failed or faltered for lack of transportation or supplies of any kinds. The wants of armies in the field have been anticipated and met with alacrity and dispatch. If industry joined to capacity, and integrity to energy, all possessed and duly exercised in the same person, entitled him to advancement, then I may safely claim promotion for Colonel Parsons."

"It is to General Parsons's matchless combinations that must be attributed much of the efficiency and success that almost invariably marked every military movement in the West. When the climax of General Grant's Western renown was reached in the battles before Chattanooga, and he was transferred to the command of all the armies, with headquarters at Washington, he lost no time in bringing General (then Colonel) Parsons to Washington to direct from that centre the machinery that he had become so completely the master of. In 1864 Secretary Stanton ordered him to Washington, extending his duties to the entire country. May 11, 1865, on the autographic order of President Lincoln, for distinguished services, he was promoted to the rank of brigadier-general, and, on retiring from the service, April 30, 1866, was brevetted major-general of volunteers."

General Parsons's eminent executive ability and success in the rapid movement of large armies for long distances, with their vast supplies and munitions of war, were, among other instances, shown in the movement of General Sherman's army of forty thousand men for the first attack on Vicksburg, as also in the transfer of General Schofield's army from Eastport, Miss., over the Alleghany Mountains, to the Potomac, in midwinter, a distance of fourteen hundred miles, in an average time of eleven days, instead of thirty, allowed by the Secretary of War. This movement was pronounced by the Secretary, as also by English and French authorities, as unequaled in rapidity and success in the annals of war. General Parsons's duties kept him mostly from the field, but when present, during several engagements, he volunteered as aide and received special commendation for services rendered, and was also tendered by Secretary Stanton a position in the Regular Army with rank of Colonel, which he declined.

His record of duty is perhaps best shown by the following extracts of letters from Generals Grant and Sherman:

May 20, 1865, General Grant writes: " The position (chief of rail and river transportation of the armies of the United States) is second in importance to no other connected with the military service, and to have been appointed to it at the beginning of a war of the magnitude and duration of this, and holding it to its close, providing transportation for whole armies, with all that appertains to them, for thousands of miles, adjusting accounts involving millions of money, and doing justice to all, never delaying for a moment any military operations dependent upon you, evidences an honesty of purpose, knowledge of men, and executive ability of the highest order, and of which any man might be justly proud." *

October 29, 1865, General Sherman writes: " I more especially recall the fact that you collected at Memphis, in December, 1862, boats enough to transport forty thousand men, with full equipments and stores, on less than a week's

* General Parsons's Reports, orders and correspondence as found in more than twenty volumes of the " Rebellion Record," will ever be the lasting memorial of his services to his country in the hour of its need.

notice, and subsequently that you supplied an army of one hundred thousand men, operating near Vicksburg, for six months, without men or horses being in want for a single day. I beg to express my admiration of the system and good sense which accomplished results so highly useful to the whole country."

Soon after the war, General Parsons visited Europe and the East, seeking to regain his health, greatly impaired by over four years of incessant labor, he having been absent from duty but twenty-one days while in service.

After two years spent abroad, and several years as president of a bank in St. Louis, General Parsons, in 1874, retired to Flora, Ill., where he now resides, engaged in managing a large landed estate purchased in the early settlement of Illinois.

During the war, while faithfully serving his country, he never wavered in his political faith. Beginning a Douglas war-Democrat, he continued such, though some of his friends firmly believed this long delayed his just promotion. Continuing since the war an earnest but conservative Democrat, he has never been drawn into any temporary political experiments, but has believed that there lay at the foundation of true Democratic principles certain great truths which, in time, would assert supreme power, and in their practical application restore the Government to the simplicity, economy, and honesty of the better days of the republic. General Parsons greatly aided in restoring Democratic majorities in Southern Illinois, not only by his abilities as a public speaker, but by his organizing abilities and great energy of character.

Extract from a letter of General Parsons, November 25, 1897:

"As a Democrat, I voted for Douglas in 1860. After the war began, I gave my utmost efforts to the Government, regardless of politics. Since the war I have been, as I was before, a Jeffersonian Democrat from deep conviction, and that greatly against my personal interest and the solicitation of my personal friends. I have never sought or desired office, but had I become a Republican political honors were doubtless within my reach. Twice I could have gone to Congress as a Democrat, by accepting a nomination, but I had no taste that way."

Extract from report of Captain F. S. Winslow, A. Q. M., to General Parsons, February 13, 1865:

"General—From my peaceful home, looking back on the events of the last four years, and especially fixing my mind's eye on the gigantic movements of armies and supplies, where thousands of miles of distances, and barriers of deserts and mountains were counted as nothing, even I, who had something to do with the detail of this great work, cannot help feeling astonished and asking how was it done? The question will be repeated by our children when they come to read the history of the rebellion; and I hope that you, General, will leave them sufficient records to show how, in the age of steam and electricity, and with these as servants, an energetic mind could move armies with almost the facility with which a family changes its residence, and could supply them with the promptness found in a well-regulated household. * * * To you belongs the credit of having accomplished such great results; to me, the satisfaction of having supported you to the utmost of my ability."—(Compiled from Public Records by the Editor.)

NOTE.— HOW HISTORY ONCE MADE IS AFTERWARDS FALSIFIED.—The general public takes little interest in war beyond reports of battles fought. The clash of arms and a few of the chief actors therein absorb the attention, leaving out of account the strenuous exertions of others whose unremitting and sagacious labors supply the forces and the conditions which make victory possible. Thus, after an interview with Edwin M. Stanton, Secretary of War in the War of Secession, Mr. Henry J. Raymond, then editor of the New York "Times," wrote editorially: "If Secretary Stanton were called on to name the officer who more than any other had distinguished himself in the task of wielding the vast machinery of the Union Armies during all stages of the conflict in response to the plans and requirements of our Generals, he would with little hesitation designate General Lewis B. Parsons of St. Louis. It is to his matchless combinations that must be attributed much of the efficiency and success that almost invariably marked every military movement in the West" [where the first and determining successes of the War were won].

General Parsons's exploit in transferring the army corps of General Schofield from the Tennessee River to the Potomac, in the depths of winter, in less than fourteen days, and that without the loss of a man, an animal, or a gun, Secretary Stanton pronounced an achievement "*without a parallel in the movement of armies,*" and he therefore requested from General Parsons a special report on the exploit, which report is contained in the ninety-ninth volume of the Rebellion Records. The *facts* of the case being thus fully established, it might have been supposed that they would thenceforth remain undisturbed. But

in 1898 there appeared a book written by Mr. Stanton's
Assistant Secretary, Charles A. Dana, whose editorial conduct of the New York "Sun" after the war became
notorious on account of the ceaseless malignity of his
vituperation against General Grant. In this book, entitled
"Recollections of the Civil War," said Dana appropri-
ated to himself the above achievement of General Parsons,
in the following words: "MOVING AN ARMY CORPS 1,400
MILES.—The election was hardly over before the people
of the North began to prepare Thanksgiving boxes for
the army. From Philadelphia I received a message asking for transportation to Sheridan's Army for boxes containing 4,000 turkeys. A couple of months later, in January, 1865, a piece of work not so different from the
'turkey business,' but on a rather larger scale, *fell to me.*
This was the transfer of the Twenty-third Army Corps
from its position on the Tennessee River, to Chesapeake
Bay." His account of how he (Dana) performed this work
(really done by General Parsons) Dana concludes by ap-
propriating, with slight verbal changes, General Parsons's
own summary of results accomplished, from his (the General's) special report to Secretary Stanton! Dana's actual
share in that achievement, consisted in his being directed
by Secretary Stanton to communicate to General Parsons
the fact that said transfer of General Schofield's Army
Corps was desired, and to learn from him (General Parsons) how soon he could promise to effect it. Upon condition that he (Parsons) was given the right to use the
name of the Secretary of War in seizure of cars, boats,
etc., whenever he deemed it essential, General Parsons un-
dertook to transfer said army corps within thirty days.
He actually accomplished it in less than fourteen days, and
that in spite of fog and ice on the rivers and violent snow-
storms in the mountains, amid unusual severities of midwinter.—(Editor.)

CHILDREN OF GENERAL LEWIS BALDWIN PARSONS.

General Parsons married, first, at St. Louis, Mo., September 21, 1847, Sarah Green Edwards; b. September 12, 1820; d. May 28, 1850.

Children:

161   I. Lewis Green Parsons, b. August 3, 1848; Yale University, 1872; d., at Denver, Col., January 29, 1875.

170   II. Sarah Edwards Parsons, b. May 15, 1850; d., at St. Paul, Minn., May 10, 1873.

General Parsons married, second, at St. Louis, Mo., July 5, 1852, Julia Maria Edwards, b. June 8, 1830; d. June 9, 1857.

Children:

171   III. Julia Edwards Parsons, b. September 13, 1854.

172   IV. Charles Levi Parsons, b. March 31, 1856.

After the war and his tour abroad, General Parsons married, third, at New York City, December 28, 1869, Elizabeth Darrah, b. June 25, 1832; d. at Scarborough, Me., September 2, 1887. No children.

From the Encyclopedic History of St. Louis.

COLONEL CHARLES PARSONS,

President of the State Bank of St. Louis.

Colonel Charles Parsons was born at Homer, Cortland Co., N. Y., January 24, 1824. He received an academical education at Gouverneur and Homer, N. Y. After spending several years as a clerk in his father's store, in a bank, and as a partner in a commercial house in Buffalo, N. Y., he removed to Keokuk, Ia., in 1851, where he established and continued for years a successful banking business. On the breaking out of the rebellion, he volunteered, was made captain, and, because of his superior business abilities, was placed in charge of army rail and river transportation at St. Louis, a position which he filled with such eminent success that he was promoted to the rank of lieutenant-colonel. Near the close of the war, he was made cashier of the State

Savings Association, now the State Bank of St. Louis, of which he was elected president in 1870, making his entire term of service in the bank to the present time, thirty-three years. The success of his administration is most conclusively and concisely shown by the fact that for all these years the bank has never failed to make a dividend of at least five per cent. semi-annually, and for the last twenty-three years has made one of eight per cent. semi-annually, and has, in addition, accumulated during these thirty-three years, a surplus of more than $1,100,000.

While amassing a reasonable fortune in his long and active business life, Colonel Parsons has disbursed of his income with liberality and a most catholic spirit, by aiding charitable, religious, and educational institutions, at times in large sums. Colonel Parsons's remarkable success has resulted not more from a natural taste for banking than from his thorough study, accurate knowledge, and comprehensive views of the principles governing commercial and financial affairs, combined with the liberal spirit with which he ever meets and treats private and public interests. The high esteem in which he has been held in financial circles is shown by the fact that for twenty-two years he was annually elected president of the St. Louis Clearing House, was for some years president of the American Bankers' Association, was selected to preside over the World's Congress of Bankers and Financiers at the Chicago Exposition in 1893, and that his name has been often mentioned as a suitable candidate for Secretary of the Treasury, and would, it is believed, have been pressed, but for Colonel Parsons's own opposition thereto. In 1892, when there was much public excitement in regard to city finances, owing to a large defalcation, Colonel Parsons consented at the solicitude of many prominent citizens, regardless of party, to accept temporarily the position of City Treasurer, which office he resigned as soon as full investigation could be made, the books put in proper condition, and a new treasurer elected. Colonel Parsons has been, and still is, president and director in many railroads and other public and charitable institutions, taking an active part and impressing his own personality thereon. There are few men who are more consulted or whose opinions upon public and financial questions are held in as high esteem. Nor is Colonel Parsons merely a business man. Possessing by nature a refined taste, he has during his active life gathered one of the most valuable collections of paintings and other works of art in our country, obtained during repeated visits to Europe and in a trip around the world made in 1894-5, a very interesting account of which last trip was published in a volume for private circulation, showing close and accurate observation of men and affairs.

In politics, Colonel Parsons has been a strong Republican, occupying a prominent position in party councils and contributing liberally for the success thereof. He is also a member of the societies of the Grand Army of the Republic, the Loyal Legion, and the Army of the Tennessee.

Colonel Parsons was married in 1857 to Miss Martha Pettus, a member of one of the old well-known families of St. Louis. She died in 1889, leaving no children.

Extract from a speech by Colonel Parsons at the Caledonian Society dinner, in St. Louis, November 30, 1897.

"Perhaps, as I represent the New England Society this evening, as its former president, you would like to hear something of the Yankees and how they lived sixty and more years ago, when I was a boy; in the changes that have and are taking place nowadays, we are all getting to be different from what we were; even the Japanese are putting on breeches and coats and discarding their queues and kiminos. More's the pity. They will become poor Europeans and lose the originality and unique character, as well as genuine art, they once possessed.

"Well, in my youth, among the Yankees in New England and New York, people were mostly connected with some church, and, generally, business ceased on Saturday night at sundown. Everything ended save works of necessity and mercy. The good orthodox people insisted that the warrant for commencing Sabbath on Saturday night was from the Bible, where it says: 'The evening and the morning were the first day.' Our evenings of Saturdays were spent in learning the Sabbath-school lessons, the catechism, and singing. Ten o'clock Sunday morning was church time, and all who were not ill or too old or too young went to meeting, as it was called. We spoke not of the church as a building, but of the meeting-house. Then came the service; first, the invocation, the Bible reading, the singing, the long prayer, another singing and the sermon, which last was not, perhaps, as long as the Scotch ones; yet it did not lack in that respect. Then Sabbath school of half an hour, after which our lunch, and about one o'clock again another service. The farmers took lunch in summer on the grass around the house; but at other times in the house. It was not customary formerly to have fires in the meeting-house. It was thought best to keep warm by spiritual heat, and the first introduction of stoves was, in many cases, opposed very strongly. In one instance, several ladies fainted the first Sunday after the stoves were put up, but, to their mortification, learned afterward that there were no fires that day in them—a plain case for faith doctors.

The second Sabbath service was like the first, and at its end we went home with the opportunity before us to come again in the evening. Many people had only cold food on the Sabbath. Occasionally some good people had a warm supper, however, and mine were of that sort. When the sun went down, all restraint was thrown off and the solemnity and seriousness that for twenty-four hours had marked every face was succeeded by gayety or great cheerfulness. It was said that even the dogs knew the difference between Saturday and Sunday nights and showed it by jumping and frisking on the latter, instead of lying quietly around as on the former. Sunday was indeed a day of rest for everything, and it was made more so by penal enactments. Indeed, it was said that in Connecticut they whipped the beer for working on Sunday. Travel was not thought proper, except to go to meeting or for the doctor, and as to any amusement, it was not to be tolerated or even thought of. I am told that the same rule existed in Scotland formerly, and it may yet. The great influx of foreign continental population in New England has changed all greatly there.

" In those old days every one worked who was old enough to do so. The farmer rose at 5 a. m. and, after feeding and watering his horses, cows, etc., ate the breakfast that his industrious wife had prepared; he was then ready to go out on his farm to work, or in winter perhaps out in the forest chopping the trees, eating a cold lunch, perhaps of salt pork, uncooked, with bread and cold potatoes. I have seen them doing this, and they said that the fat pork with a little vinegar was excellent; the best sauce was the appetite. I have known these farmers to draw cord wood three or even four miles to town and sell it for 75 cents a cord and take their pay in goods at the store, and sometimes the merchant who bought it would only give dry goods, as the merchants then made greater profits on those than on sugar, tea, etc. There was no eight-hour law then in town or country; people worked early and late as long as they could find anything to do, leaving time for eating, drinking, and sleeping. Crime and criminals were not much known in the country or country villages; no one had time to concoct villainy.

" My father was a merchant, and as soon as his boys were old enough we had our share of work, at first in weeding the garden, bringing in wood, later in cutting wood for the use of the house. I well remember my younger brother and myself, he at eleven and I at thirteen years of age, cutting in spring forty cords of four-foot wood in three parts, splitting it fine, and piling high in the woodshed adjacent to the house, so as to be convenient for the days when great snows should fall and the thermometer get down to twenty and forty degrees below zero, sometimes. Perhaps this training is the reason why I am alive now at the age of seventy-three. As a special encouragement, we got a note drawing seven per cent. interest for such work at twenty-five cents a cord. I remember collecting mine after it had outlawed. Then a little later I learned to get up at 5 o'clock to go to the store, open it, sweep out, and light the fire before breakfast, at 6 or 6.30. After an academic education, I went off one November for a trip to the South, only receiving from my father money to get away, and none to return with. In nine or ten months I returned, bringing home some $50 more than I took away with me, which I handed my father; besides having traveled in three-fourths of the United States and spending some time in Cincinnati, Charleston, Richmond, Philadelphia, and New York, with the ever pleasant memory of ten days in Washington in 1842, when John Tyler was President; Millard Fillmore at the head of the Ways and Means Committee, in which capacity he passed the tariff of 1842. One Saturday, then, I was kindly introduced on the floor of the House by a friend of my father's, and also introduced personally to the President, Secretary of State, Daniel Webster, John C. Calhoun, John Quincy Adams, and Francis Granger. I was telling the above circumstance in my life to a friend, and he said it was not right that I should have given this surplus over what I received to my father; but it was the rule then that a boy's services belonged to his father until he was at his majority, and it was the almost universal custom for boys to work at home until then, and I think it was right. I was only too well pleased to get this leave of absence and to earn the amount of my expenses, returning all I made over that. Why should not a boy pay back by his labor some of the cost of his rearing? In Japan it is deemed a religious duty for a child to take care of the parents at a certain age, and the rich and poor recognize it not as a labor, but pleasure, and expect the retiring from trade of the parent, and all care then to fall on the son. The care of parents was also as customary in old times in Scotland.

If our youths were made to do more physical work in youth, they would be stronger, healthier, and the better for it. Our New England fathers lived well, only the food was plain. All through the country the bread was mainly made of corn and rye meal, mixed, and, while not quite so palatable as wheat, yet without doubt it was more healthy; there was plenty of beef and pork, mutton and chickens, apples and other fruits, and honey, besides nuts in the woods, to say nothing of the turkey and supposed-to-be-unhealthy pies. The New Englander then made no objection to all sorts of fun and sport in reason—the husking bee, spelling school, where all stood up to be spelled down by the most capable; the town and baseball games, skating, and sliding on the ice; in fact, every athletic or proper indoor sport that did not endanger life or limb. I don't believe they would have tolerated the ball games we now have, where there is constant danger to the players. Certainly our Yankee forefathers were not the sad and morose people some conceive them to have been. They had a rough time in settling a new country, when there were no steamers or railroads, when it was a six-days' journey from New York to Boston by land, and life presented its serious side to them. They feared God, and wished to do their duty and get on in the world, and so educate their children that they should do the same. They were not so anxious to get office, either, then as now. One of my early ancestors in Springfield, Mass., petitioned the Town Meeting to be released from all town offices for a year, and on payment of twenty shillings his request was granted. He was not anxious to be in the push, or in any sort of combine. My friends, in many respects we have not improved on these people."

ADDENDA.

CHILDREN OF PHILO PARSONS AND ELIZA BARNUM PARSONS. | 160

173   I. Frances Eliza Parsons, born October 12, 1849. in Moscow, N. Y. ; married, September 26, 1882, to William Fitzhugh Edwards, of Virginia, son of Tryon Edwards, D.D., and Catherine Haltus Hughes, his wife, who died in New York City, October 27, 1897. No children.

174   II. Lewis Baldwin Parsons, born August 7, 1851, in Detroit; married to Harriet M. Streeter, of North Adams, Mass., daughter of Emily J. Spears and Charles Streeter. Three children :

175   1. Anna Helen Parsons, born at North Adams, Mass., September 29, 1874.

176   2. Margaret Elwood Parsons, born at North Adams, Mass., January 4, 1876.

177   3. Josephine McKee Parsons, born at Detroit, Mich., December 26, 1878.

178   III. Edward Levi Parsons, born at Detroit, April 3, 1853. Unmarried.

179   IV. Kate Eugenia Parsons, born at Detroit, June 28, 1854 ; married, February 5, 1880, to Arthur Clifford, son of John Henry Clifford and Sarah Allen, his wife, of New Bedford, Mass. He died February 26, 1881. One child :

180   1. Charles Parsons Clifford, born at New Bedford, Mass., October 23, 1880.

181   V. William Swain Parsons, born June 6, 1856 ; died August 6, 1857.

182   VI. Julia Norton Parsons, born at Detroit, December 31, 1857 ; married, June 11, 1891, to William Edmundstone Boynton, of Winchester, Mass., son of William Boynton and Sarah Morse, his wife. No children.

183   VII. Mary Lucina Parsons, born at Detroit, October 10, 1860 ; married, April 22, 1885, to Frederick Grout Chidsey, of Detroit, son of —— Chidsey and Delia Whalley Grout, his wife. Two children :

184   1. Frederick Parsons, born at Detroit, March 11, 1880.

185   2. Helen Parsons, born at Detroit, July 8, 1887.

186   VIII. Grace Douglas Parsons, born at Detroit, February 13, 1863. Unmarried.

DESCENDANTS OF CAPTAIN JOHN PARSONS AND HIS WIFE SARAH CLARK PARSONS.   25

187   Lieutenant William Parsons, born, 1690 ; died, 1768 ; married, 1714, Mary Ashley, born, 1661. Their son :

188   Lieutenant Samuel Parsons, born, 1733 ; died, 1812 ; married, 1768, Lucy Pomeroy, born, 1739; died, 1782. Their son :

189   Captain Luke Parsons, born, 1774 ; died, 1852 ; married, 1801, Nancy Streeter, born, 1784 ; died, 1853. Their daughter :

190   Lucy Mason Parsons, born, 1803 ; died, 1884 ; married, 1831, Lewis Darling, M.D., born, 1804 ; died, 1882. Their son :

191   Lewis Darling, Jr., M.D., born, 1840 ; married, 1867, Julia L. Day, born, 1843. Their son :

192   Carlos Parsons Darling, born, 1876.

DESCENDANTS OF MOSES PARSONS AND HIS WIFE ABIGAIL BALL PARSONS.

193   Moses Parsons, born Durham, Conn., October 19, 1710; died Windsor, Conn., 1791; married Elizabeth Ventres, born Haddam, Conn., 1710; died Windsor, Conn., May 10, 1790. Their daughter:

194   Abigail Parsons, born Windsor, Conn., April 28, 1747; died Windsor, Conn., November 7, 1817; married, November 19, 1767, her cousin Lieutenant Thomas Hayden, Continental Line, 1775–1783, born Windsor, Conn., June 14, 1745; died Windsor, Conn., November 28, 1817. Their son :

195   Horace H. Hayden, M.D., born Windsor, Conn., October 13, 1769; died Baltimore, Md., January 26, 1844; married February 23, 1805, Maria A. Robinson, born July 22, 1778; died March 28, 1860. Their son :

196   Edwin Parsons Hayden, Lawyer, born Baltimore, Md., August 7, 1811; died May 10, 1850; married September 15, 1832, Elizabeth Hause; born August 23, 1810; died July 3, 1887. Their son :

197   Rev. Horace Edwin Hayden, born Maryland, February 18, 1837; married November 30, 1868, Kate E. Byers. P. E. Clergyman at Wilkes-Barre, Pa. Their son :

198   Horace Edwin Hayden, Jr., born January 6, 1884.

INDEX

I

173

II

III.

MISCELLANEOUS

IV.

INDEX OF PLACES

GARRARD-SPENCER CHART

The noble house of Spencer-Garrard of London, England, and the
Garrard-Spencers of Cambridge, Massachusetts, compared,
with additions, by Albert Ross Parsons, member
N. Y. Historical Society ; N. Y. Genealogical
and Biographical Society, etc.

The chart is based on the following facts : (1) Two opulent
London families, viz., Spencer and Garrard, both represented in
the Haberdashers' Guild. (2) A Spencer-Garrard marriage in
England. (3) Several generations of Garrard Spencers in America,
following Garrard Spencer, named in will of Richard Spencer,
Gent., Haberdasher of London. (4) Michael Spencer (nephew
of said Richard S.), in Cambridge, Mass., said name Michael being
of a London family certified by the Herald's College to be of the
noble house of Spencer.

The chart traces the house of Spencer to the Norman Conquest of England, and that of Garrard (Gerard, Garrett) to Lord
Gerardini of Florence, Italy, prior to said Conquest.   For copy
of Chart (price $2), address

ALBERT ROSS PARSONS, 109 East 14th Street,
New York City, U. S. A.